L.P.M.
The End of the Great War

by

J. Stewart Barney

Double 9
BOOKS

L.P.M.
The End of the Great War

by J. Stewart Barney

ISBN: 978-93-63055-06-3

Published by

DOUBLE 9 BOOKS

2/13-B, Ansari Road
Daryaganj, New Delhi – 110002
info@double9books.com
www.double9books.com
Tel. 011-40042856

ABOUT THE AUTHOR

J. Stewart Barney is a distinguished author known for his compelling storytelling and intricate narratives. His masterpiece, "L.P.M.: The End of the Great War," showcases his exceptional ability to weave historical events with vivid, imaginative scenarios. This book captures a unique perspective on the conclusion of the Great War, blending factual accuracy with creative interpretation. Barney's meticulous research and attention to detail are evident throughout the novel, making it a richly textured and immersive experience for readers. "L.P.M." stands out not only for its historical insights but also for its deep exploration of human emotions and the complexities of war. Through his eloquent prose and masterful character development, Barney has created a work that resonates with both history enthusiasts and literary fiction lovers alike. The novel's compelling narrative and thought-provoking themes ensure that "L.P.M.: The End of the Great War" is a significant contribution to contemporary literature, cementing J. Stewart Barney's reputation as a master storyteller.

CONTENTS

CHAPTER I
THE MAN AND THE HOUR

The Secretary of State, although he sought to maintain an air of official reserve, showed that he was deeply impressed by what he had just heard.

"Well, young man, you are certainly offering to undertake a pretty large contract."

He smiled, and continued in a slightly rhetorical vein—the Secretary was above all things first, last, and always an orator.

"In my many years of public life," he said, "I have often had occasion to admire the dauntless spirit of our young men. But you have forced me to the conclusion that even I, with all my confidence in their power, have failed to realize how inevitably American initiative and independence will demand recognition. It is a quality which our form of government seems especially to foster and develop, and I glory in it as perhaps the chief factor in our national greatness and pre-eminence.

"In what other country, I ask you," he flung out an arm across the great, flat-topped desk of state, "would a mere boy like yourself ever conceive such a scheme, or have the incentive or opportunity to bring it to perfection? And, having conceived and perfected it, in what other country would he find the very heads of his Government so accessible and ready to help him?"

The young man leaned forward. "Then am I to understand, Mr. Secretary, that you are ready to help me?"

"Yes." He faced about and looked at his visitor in a glow of enthusiasm. "Not only will I help you, but I will, so far as is practicable, put behind you the power of this Administration.

"Doubtless the newspapers," his tone took on a tinge of ironic resentment, "when they learn the broad character of the credentials that I shall give you in order that you may meet the crowned heads of Europe, will say that I am again lowering the dignity of my office. But I consider, Mr. Edestone, that I am, in reality, giving more dignity to my office by bringing it closer to and by placing it at the services of, those from whose hands it first received its dignity, the sovereign people. 'The master is greater than the servant'; and to my mind you as a citizen are even more entitled to the aid and co-operation of this Department than are its accredited envoys, our ministers and ambassadors, who, like myself, are but your hired men."

His face lighted up with the memory of the many stirring campaigns through which he had passed and his wonderful voice rang out, responding to his will like a perfect musical instrument under the touch of the artist.

"I tell you, sir," he declared, "I would rather be instrumental in bringing to an end this cruel war which is now deluging the pages of history with the heart's blood of the people, whose voices may now be drowned in the roar of the 42-centimeter guns, but whose spirits will unite in the black stench clouds which rise from the festered fields of Flanders to descend upon the heads of those who by Divine Right have murdered them,—I would rather be instrumental in bringing about this result, than be President of the United States!"

He had risen, as he spoke, and had stepped from behind his desk to give freer play to this burst of eloquence, but he now paused at the entrance of a secretary for whom he had sent, and changing to that quizzical drawl with which he had so often disarmed a hostile audience, added, "And they do say that I am not without ambition in that respect."

He turned then to the waiting secretary, and letting his hand drop on Edestone's shoulder:

"Mr. Williams," he said, "this is Mr. John Fulton Edestone, of New York, whose name is no doubt familiar to you. He is desirous of meeting and discussing quite informally with the potentates of Europe, a little matter which he thinks, and I more or less agree with him, will be of decided interest to them."

He chuckled softly; then continued in a more serious tone: "Mr. Edestone hopes, in short, with our assistance, to bring about not only the end of the European war, but to realize my dream—Universal Peace—and his plan, as he has outlined it to me, meets with my hearty approval.

"I wish you to furnish him with the credentials from this Department necessary to give him *entrée* anywhere abroad and protect him at all times and under all circumstances.

"And, Mr. Williams," he halted the retiring subordinate, "when Mr. Edestone's papers have been drawn, will you kindly bring them to me? I wish to present them in person, and I know of no more appropriate occasion than this afternoon, when I am to receive a delegation of school children from the Southern Baptist Union and the Boy Scouts of the Methodist

Temperance League. I will be glad to have these young Americans, as well as any others who may be calling to pay their respects—not to me but to my office—hear what I have to say on peace, patriotism, and grapes."

With the departure of the secretary he unbent slightly. "Well," he smiled, "you cannot say, as did Ericsson with his monitor and Holland with his submarine and the Wrights with their aëroplane, that you could not get the support of your Government until it was too late. In fact, my dear fellow, when I think of the obstacles so many inventors have to contend with, it strikes me that you have had pretty easy sailing."

"Perhaps," Edestone raised his eyebrows a trifle whimsically, "it has not been so easy as you think, Mr. Secretary."

"Oh, I know, I know!" the other replied. "You still must admit that in comparison with most men you have been singularly fortunate. You have had great wealth, absolute freedom to develop your ideas as you saw fit, and finally the influence to command an immediate hearing for your claims. Do you know that perhaps you are the richest young man in the world today? It is this which, I must confess, at first rather prejudiced me against you."

Edestone laughed good-naturedly. "It is lucky that my photographs were able to speak for me."

"Yes," the Secretary assented. "As you probably have recognized, I am not a scientist, and all your formulae and explanations were about as so much Greek to me, but those photographs of yours were most convincing, and prove to me how simple are the greatest of discoveries. I fancy," he added slyly, "that they will penetrate even the intelligence of a monarch."

"Ah!" He rubbed his hands together. "I can imagine the chagrin and fury of those war lords when they find themselves so unexpectedly called to time, while your device is held over the nations like a policeman's club, with America as its custodian. What a thought! Universal dominion for our country; Universal Peace!"

Some sense of opposition on the part of his companion aroused him, and he levelled a quick and searching glance at the other.

"That is your intention, is it not, Mr. Edestone?" he demanded. "That, upon the completion of your present mission, the Government shall take over this discovery of yours?"

Edestone moved uneasily in his seat. He had naturally anticipated this question, and yet he was unprepared to meet it.

The Secretary frowned and repeated his question. "That is your intention, is it not?"

Hesitating no longer the inventor answered quietly:

"Mr. Secretary, I yield to no man in my devotion to my country, but I am one of those who believe that the highest form of patriotism is to seek the best interest of mankind, and standing on that I tell you frankly that I cannot at this time answer your question. Just now I look no farther than the end of this brutal war. After that is accomplished it will be time enough for me to decide the ultimate disposition of my invention. Its secret is now known to no living soul but myself, and is so simple that it requires no written record to preserve it, and would die with me. It is the result, it is true, of many years of hard work, but the finished product I can and often do carry in my waistcoat pocket.

"Do not misunderstand me," he lifted his hand as the Secretary endeavoured to break in. "I thoroughly realize the responsibility of my position and that my great wealth is a sacred trust. Upon the answer to the question you have just put to me depends the destiny of the world, whether it is answered by myself at this time or by others in the future. Exactly what I will do when the time comes I cannot say, but I will tell you this much, that in reaching a decision I will call to my assistance men like yourself and abide by whatever course the majority of them may dictate."

"But, my dear young fellow, that will not do." The Secretary shook his head. "You are called upon to answer my question right here and now."

He dropped his bland and diplomatic manner as he spoke, and with his jaw thrust forward showed himself the unyielding autocrat, who, in the rough and tumble of politics, had ruled his party with a rod of iron. This man whose wonderful talents and personality had fitted him for his chosen position of champion of the plain people, and whose great motive power, against all odds, that had forced him into the first place in their hearts, was his sincere and honest love of office.

He had now assumed a rather boisterous and bullying tone, showing that perhaps his great love for the rougher elements of society was due to the fact that in the process of evolution he himself was not far removed from the very plain people.

"You have been talking pretty loud about using the 'big stick' over on the other side," he went on sternly, "but that big-stick business you will find is a thing that works two ways. Suppose then I should tell you, 'No answer to my question, no credentials.' What would you have to say?"

"I should say," Edestone's face was set, "simply this, Mr. Secretary, if I must speak in the language of the people in order that you may understand me: 'I should like very much to have your backing in the game, but if you are going to sit on the opposite side of the table, I hold three kings and two emperors in my hand, and I challenge you to a show-down.' I should further say that, credentials or no credentials, I am leaving tomorrow on the *Ivernia*, and that inasmuch as I have a taxi at the door, and a special train held for me at the Union Station, I must bid you good-day, and leave you to your watchful waiting, while I work alone."

He rose from his seat, and with a bow started for the door.

"Hold on there, young fellow, keep your coat on!" the Secretary shouted, throwing his head back and laughing loud enough to be heard over on the Virginia shores. "You remind me of one of those gentle breezes out home, which after it has dropped the cow-shed into the front parlour and changed your Post-Office address, seems always to sort of clear up the atmosphere. When one of them comes along we generally allow it to have its own way. It doesn't matter much whether we do or not, it will take it anyhow. I never play cards, but what you say about having a few kings in your pants' pocket seems to be pretty nearly true. You are made of the real stuff, and if you can do all the things that you say you can do, and I believe you can, nothing will stop you."

"In that case," said Edestone, resuming his seat, "I suppose I may as well wait for my credentials."

And in due time he got them, the presentation being made by the Secretary to the edification of the Baptist School children and the Methodist Soldiers of Temperance and a score of adoring admirers. Then with a hasty farewell to the officials of the State Department, this emissary of peace started on his hurried rush to New York.

His taxi, which he had held since seven o'clock that morning, broke all speed regulations in getting to the station, and the man was well paid for his pains.

Edestone found his Special coupled up and waiting for him. He always travelled in specials, and they always waited for him. In fact, everything waited for him, and he waited for no one. When he engaged a taxi he never discharged it until he went to bed or left the town. It was related of him that on one occasion he had directed the taxi to wait for him at Charing Cross Station, and returning from Paris three days later had allowed his old friend, the cabby, who knew him well, a shilling an hour as a *pourboire*. He claimed that his mind worked smoothly as long as it could run ahead without waits, but that as soon as it had to halt for anything—a cab, a train, or a slower mind to catch up—it got from under his control and it took hours to get it back again.

To him money was only to be spent. He would say: "I spend money because that calls for no mental effort, and saving is not worth the trouble that it requires."

A big husky chap, thirty-four years old, with the constitution of an ox, the mind of a superman, the simplicity of a child: that was John Fulton Edestone. He insisted that his discovery was an accident that might have befallen anyone, and counted as nothing the years of endless experiments and the millions of dollars he had spent in bringing it to perfection. He was a dreamer, and had used his colossal income and at times his principal in putting his dreams into iron and steel.

Upon arriving in New York he was met by his automobile and was rushed away to what he was pleased to call his Little Place in the Country. It was one of his father's old plants which had contributed to the millions which he was now spending.

It was nothing more nor less than a combination machine shop and shipyard, situated on the east bank of the Hudson in the neighbourhood of Spuyten Duyvil.

It was midnight when he arrived. The night force was just leaving as he stepped from his automobile and the morning shift was taking its place. At eight o'clock the next morning this latter would in turn be relieved by a day shift; for night and day, Sundays and holidays, winter and summer, without stopping, his work went on. It got on his nerves, he said, to see anything stop. Speed and efficiency at any cost was his motto, and the result was that he had gathered about him men who were willing to keep running under forced draft, even if it did heat up the bearings.

"Tell Mr. Page to come to me at once," he said, as he entered a little two-story brick structure apart from the other buildings. This had originally been used as an office, but he had changed it into a comfortable home, his "Little Place in the Country."

CHAPTER II
THE ONE-MAN SECRET

With the giving of a few orders relative to his departure in the morning, the brevity of which showed the character of service he demanded, Edestone permitted himself to relax. He dropped into an arm-chair, after lighting a long, black cigar, and pouring out for himself a comfortable drink of Scotch whisky and soda.

For a few minutes he sat looking into the open fire, while blowing ring after ring of smoke straight up into the air. The well-trained servant moved so quietly about the room that his presence was only called to his attention by the frantic efforts of the smoke rings to retain their circular shape as they were caught in the current of air which he created and were sent whirling and twisting to dissolution, although to the last they clung to every object with which they came in contact in their futile struggle to escape destruction.

Edestone loved to watch these little smoke phantoms, their first mad rush to assume their beautiful form and the persistency with which they clung to it until overtaken by another, were brushed aside, or else drifted on in wavering elongated outlines and so gradually disappeared.

They suggested to his fancy the struggling nations of the world, battling with the currents and cross-currents near the storm-scarred old earth, and continually endeavouring to rise above their fellows to some calmer strata, where serene in their original form they could look down with condescension upon their harassed and broken companions below.

The little rings were, however, more interesting to him for another and more practical reason. It was their toroidal movement around a circular axis which moved independently in any direction that first suggested to him the principles of his discovery.

Before him the fire upon the hearth sang and crackled as it tore asunder the elements that had taken untold ages to assemble in their present form, and with the prodigality of nature was joyfully rushing them up the chimney to start them again upon their long and weary journey through the ages.

The bubbles coming into existence in the bottom of his glass, rushing in myriads through the pale yellow liquid to the top and obliteration, set the thin glass to vibrating like the sound of distant bells.

From his workshop came the soft purr of rapidly moving machinery, punctuated now and again by the roar of the heavy railroad trains that thundered past his little flag station.

Had he seen then what the future had in store for him, had he realized that he was in that well-beloved environment for the last time, he would not have hesitated to have gone on along the road that he had marked out for himself. It would simply have made the wrench at parting a little bit more severe.

His musing was interrupted by his man, who had attracted his attention by noiselessly rearranging on the table the objects that were already in perfect order.

"Mr. Page is outside, sir."

It was a call to action. Edestone, without changing his position, said: "Tell him to come in." And then taking two or three deep puffs at his cigar, he blew out into the clear space in front of him a large and perfectly formed ring. Rising he followed it slowly as it drifted across the room, twisting and circling upon itself. Then with a low laugh, which was almost a sigh, after sticking his finger through its shadowy form, with a sweep of his powerful hand he brushed it aside.

"Good-bye, little friend," he said, "we have had many good times together, and whatever you may have in store for me, I promise never to complain. Let us hope that I shall use wisely and well the knowledge which you have given me."

Turning quickly at some slight sound, which told him that he was no longer alone, he threw his shoulders back, and with his head high in the air there came over his clean-shaven face a look of quiet determination, a look before which those who were born to rule were so soon to quail.

Then, with a complete change of manner, upon seeing his old friend and fellow-workman, his face lighted up, and he laughed:

"Well, old 'Specs,' I'm back, you see, and the 'Dove of Peace' is safely caged. He came to hand with scarcely even a struggle." Then as he looked down into the other's worn and haggard eyes which peered up at him through their round, horn-rimmed spectacles, his voice softened and he spoke with a touch of compunction.

"By Jove, old chap, you look all in. I've been driving you boys a bit too hard; but don't you worry. I'm off in the morning, and then you'll have a chance to take it easier. Soon our beautiful *Little Peace Maker*," he winked, "will be tucked safely away in some quiet corner, and you scientific fellows can devote all your attention to your beloved bridge, while I bid up The Hague Conference for a no-trump hand.

"But to business now. How did the films for the moving pictures come out?"

"Splendidly."

"Good. I'll have you run them over for me presently. I don't want to show too much when I give my performances for Royalty, you understand; just enough to scare them to death. And how about the wireless? Did you test that out, and tune it to my instruments, as I asked you?"

With a satisfactory answer to this also, he ranged off rapidly into a dozen other inquiries.

"Does Lee understand exactly where he is to go, and what he is to do, if by any chance he is discovered there? He does, eh? Well, I don't think he need anticipate the slightest trouble in that regard; but we've got to be prepared for every emergency.

"Now, 'Specs,' I want you to get off tomorrow night. Leave enough men about the plant, and have sufficient work going on, so that your absence may not excite comment. Go by way of Canada, and as soon as you are safely out of here, take your time and run no unnecessary risks. As soon as you are settled, communicate with me, once only every day at exactly twelve o'clock Greenwich time, until I answer you. I shall then not communicate with you again until this peace game is up and we are forced to show our hands."

He paused a moment as if to make sure that he had overlooked nothing; then resumed his instructions.

"Captain Lee's men all understand, I believe, that we are playing for a big stake, and that the work we have on hand is no child's play; but it will do no harm to impress it on them again. I sincerely hope that no rough work will be required; but they may as well realize that I intend to have absolute obedience, and shall not hesitate at the most extreme measures to obtain it. They must be drilled until every man is faultlessly perfect in the part he is to play. We may all be pronounced outlaws at any time with a price upon our heads, and therefore, before leaving here, I wish that none be allowed to join the enterprise except those who willingly volunteer for the sake of the cause. The men who are unwilling to volunteer, and yet know too much, must be taken and held *incommunicado* in some perfectly safe place until such time as I notify you.

"I think that is all," he reflected. Then, while the other man watched him curiously, he stepped to the safe, and opening it brought back a small, hardwood box about six inches square.

"I have never explained to you, Page," he said, "the exact construction of the instrument that is contained in this box. As you know, there is but one other instrument like this in the world, and that you know is in a safe place. My reason for not taking anybody into my confidence was not from any lack of faith in you or my other trusted associates, but simply in order to be absolutely sure at all times and under all circumstances that I was the only one in possession of this secret."

And turning to the fireplace he threw the box with its contents directly on to the burning logs.

Page gave a slight gasp as he saw the wooden receptacle catch, and half stepped forward as if to rescue it, but Edestone quickly raised an interposing hand. Then he turned to his companion with a smile.

"That was my first very clumsy model. The actual mechanical construction of this instrument is so simple," he said, "that I can at any time construct one which will answer all purposes that I may require of it until I see you. I intend to amuse myself on the *Ivernia* during the crossing constructing a new smaller and more compact instrument, combining with it one of the receivers which you have attuned to your wireless. See that these as well as the following," handing "Specs" a list of electrical supplies, "are put in Black's steamer trunk. And now, let's have a look at those films."

He followed this with a tour of inspection of the entire establishment, although the latter was largely perfunctory in character, since he knew that for days everything had been in readiness for his orders, waiting only for his return from Washington; then returning to his quarters, he tumbled into bed to catch a few hours of sleep before again whirling off at a sixty-mile-an-hour gait to board his steamer at the dock.

His plans were completed. His men, down to the lowest helper, were fellows of tested experience and education, many of them college graduates, while his "commissioned officers," as he called them, numbering sixty, were all experts in their respective lines. They had been drawn from all ranks of life, from the college laboratory, the automobile factory, and the war college. There were among them bank clerks, former commanders of battle-ships, doctors, lawyers, soldiers, and sailors. In fact, his little world was a perfectly equipped and smoothly running community with all the departments of a miniature government, save only a diplomatic service, and that he combined with his own prerogatives as Executive and Commander-in-Chief.

One thing he did not have in all his company, so far as he knew,—and that was a weakling. So thoroughly had he sifted them out, and applied to each of them the acid test, that he was sure he could rely on them, as he liked to say, "to the last ditch."

For the rest, although he had taken only a few of them into his confidence as to his real purposes and intentions, he had assured each recruit that he would be required to do nothing that was contrary to his duty to his fellow-man, his country, or his God.

And tomorrow the wheels would be set in motion. The undertaking to which he had dedicated his life and colossal fortune would be launched.

It was characteristic of Edestone that no sooner had he laid his head upon the pillow than his eyes closed, and he slept as peacefully as a tired child.

CHAPTER III
CROSSING WITH ROYALTY

After a perfectly uneventful voyage, the *Ivernia*, with Edestone and his three men aboard, swung slowly to her dock. As the big vessel had approached the coast the few cabin passengers were at first a little nervous, but the contempt in which the officers held, or pretended to hold, the submarine menace made itself soon felt throughout the ship, and but for the thinness of their ranks all went as usual. It is true that the little group of army contract-seekers and returning refugees seemed to enjoy constituting themselves into special look-outs, and regarded it as their particular duty, as long as it did not interfere with their game of bridge, or might cause them to lose a particularly comfortable and sheltered corner of the deck, to notify the stewards if they happened to see anything which to them looked like a periscope or floating mine.

Throughout the voyage Edestone kept very much to himself and in his quarters occupied himself constructing a new instrument, and to the hard-rubber case that had been provided for it he attached a wireless receiver. In some of this work he was assisted by Stanton and Black, two electricians he had brought with him, who, with James, his valet, made up his party.

He had little time and less inclination to observe his neighbours, who occupied the corresponding suite just across the passageway; but his man James, who had been formally introduced to their servants, insisted upon telling him all about them. They were, James said, the Duchess of Windthorst and her daughter, the Princess Wilhelmina, who were returning from Canada, where they had been visiting the Duke of Connaught at Toronto.

But, if Edestone was preoccupied, the Princess, on the contrary, being a girl of nineteen, with absolutely nothing on her mind, had not failed to note the handsome young man across the passage. Unconsciously answering to the irresistible call of youth, which is as loud to the princess as to the peasant, she had watched him with a great deal of interest, and had been fascinated by his faultless boots and the fact that he failed to notice her at all.

Yet Edestone, it may be remarked, was not the only person on board favoured with the royal regard. The Duchess, with the propensity of her kind on visiting the States, had selected for her rare promenades on deck a Broadway sport of the most absurd and exaggerated type, known as "Diamond King John" Bradley.

This vagary is explained by the fact that the social chasm separating them from all Americans is, to their limited vision, so infinitely great that it is impossible for them to see and to understand the niceties that the Americans draw between the butcher of New York and the dry-goods merchant of Denver; and since it is impossible to see nothing from infinity, they content themselves by selecting those who are, in their opinion, typical, in order that in the short time they can give to this study they may learn all of the characteristics of this most extraordinary race, who on account of the similarity of language have presumed to claim a relationship with them. They will not accept as true what much of the world believes: that Old England is in her decadence, and that her only hope is in those sons who have left her and who, away from the debilitating influence of the poisonous vapours arising from the ruins of her glory, are developing the ancient spirit of their ancestors and are returning to her assistance in her time of need.

As to the Princess, Edestone, although he noted that she was extremely attractive in face and figure, did not give her a second thought. He was amused at the attitude of the Duchess and her class, and was willing to accept it, but it did not arouse any desire on his part to follow the lead of the gentleman from Broadway and seek their acquaintance. As a matter of fact, he had always found the young women of the upper classes of England either extremely stupid or perfectly willing to appear so to an American of his class.

Still, as it happened, he did meet the Princess. One night after dinner he found her struggling with the door into the passage which led to their adjoining apartments. She was, or pretended to be, helpless in the wind that was blowing her down the deck as she clung to the rail, and, quietly taking her by the arm, he pulled her back to the door, where he held her until she was safely inside. This was all done in a perfectly matter-of-fact manner, and she might as well have been a steamer rug that was in danger of being blown overboard. Then before she had time to thank him, the door was blown shut, and he had resumed his solitary walk along the deck.

The next time that the Princess saw him, although she felt sure that he must have known that she had looked in his direction, there was no indication of any desire on his part to continue the acquaintance. He had apparently entirely forgotten the episode or her existence, and the pride of a beautiful young girl was hurt, and the dignity of royalty offended—but the first was all that really mattered.

And so the voyage ended. The passengers all seemed perfectly willing to go ashore, notwithstanding their assumption of indifference to the German blockade. Edestone, as usual, was met by the fastest form of locomotion, and before the trunks and bags had begun to toboggan down to the dock, he was whirling up to London in the powerful motor car belonging to his friend, the Marquis of Lindenberry. Edestone had notified him by wireless to meet the steamer, and they were now being driven directly to the Marquis's house in Grosvenor Square. Stanton and Black were left behind with James, who condescended with his superior knowledge to assist them in getting the luggage through the custom-house.

"Well what in the name of common sense has brought you over to England at such a time as this?" demanded Lindenberry, after the automobile had swept clear of the town and with a gentle purr had settled down to its work. He leaned over as he spoke, to satisfy himself that the chauffeur, having finished adjusting his glasses with one hand while running at top speed, finally had both hands on the wheel, and then turned expectantly to his companion.

"Oh, I see," Lindenberry nodded when he found that he got no satisfactory answer to this or the other inquiries he put; "you evidently do not propose to take me into your confidence. Still, I would not be so deucedly mysterious, if I were you. I call it beastly rude, you know. Here I have come all the way from Aldershot, and am using the greater part of my valuable leave in response to your crazy wire. Tell me, is it a contract to deliver a dozen dreadnoughts at the gates of the Tower of London before Easter Sunday?" and his eyes twinkled, "or have some of your young Americans enlisted and the fond parents sent you over to rescue them?"

Edestone smiled. "Well, the first thing I want, Lindenberry, is a little chat with Lord Rockstone."

"Oh, is that all?" with a satiric inflection. "Well, why in the name of common sense didn't you say so at first? I do not know, however, that I can positively get you an appointment today. You must not mind if His Lordship keeps you waiting for a few minutes if he happens to be talking with the Czar of Russia on the long-distance telephone. You know, we over here are still great sticklers on form. We are trying hard to be progressive, but we still consider it quite rude to tell a King to hold the wire while we talk to someone else who has not taken the trouble that he has to make an appointment. You must remember that he has perhaps dropped several shillings into the slot, and would naturally be annoyed if told by the girl that time was up and to drop another shilling.

"Or Lord Rockstone may perhaps be just in the midst of one of his usual twenty-four-hour interviews with an American newspaper representative," he continued his chaffing. "Now if he does not invite Graves and Underhill and Apsworth to have tea with you, you might drop in at Boodles' on your way back from the city, and we will just pop on to Buckingham Palace and deliver to Queen Mary the ultimatum from the suffragette ladies of the Sioux Indians."

Edestone laughed so heartily that the footman nearly turned to see if something had happened. "And they say that you Englishmen have no sense of humour. The trouble with you though, old top, is that your joke is so deucedly good that you don't see the point yourself."

They were just passing through one of Rockstone's military camps, where England's recruited millions were being trained, and cutting short his badinage Edestone gazed at the scene with interest.

"It does seem a pity that all these fine young fellows should be sacrificed in order to settle a question which I could settle in a very short time," he said, becoming more serious.

"Settle it in a very short time?" repeated Lindenberry. "I would like to know how you propose to do it. I know you are full of splendid ideas, and invent all kinds of electrical contrivances to do things that one can do perfectly well with one's own hands. I suppose you would take a large magnet and with it pull all of the German warships out of the Kiel Canal, and hold them while you went on board and explained to Bernhardi and von Bülow the horrors of war, and if they did not listen to you, you would, like the Pied Piper of Hamelin lead them off with all the other disagreeable odds and ends, submarines and Zeppelins, to an island, way, way out in the ocean, where they would have to stay until they promised to be good little boys?"

"Well, wouldn't that be better than killing a lot of these fine young fellows you have here?" demanded Edestone, although he smiled at his friend's fantastic idea.

"You Americans are developing into a nation of foolish old women," taunted Lindenberry, "and the sooner that you get into a muss like this one we're in, the sooner you will get back that fighting spirit which has made you what you are. You are fast losing the respect of the other nations by your present methods, always looking after your own pocket-books while the rest of the world is bleeding to death."

Edestone was thoughtful, and appeared to have no answer for this, and Lindenberry reverted to his request.

"If you really want to have an interview with Lord Rockstone, Jack, I think I can possibly arrange it. I will telephone to Colonel Wyatt, who is on his staff, and find out what he can do for you."

And so they chatted until coming to Grosvenor Square where they got out of the automobile in front of an unpretentious red brick house with an English basement entrance, trimmed with white marble and spotlessly clean.

Lindenberry at once telephoned to Colonel Wyatt, who said that Lord Rockstone was in and that if Edestone would come around at once he would see to it that his letters were presented. As to an appointment, he could promise nothing, but he did say to Lindenberry, not to be repeated, that the Department was not at that time very favourably disposed toward Americans.

With his usual promptness, Edestone jumped into his automobile and started for Downing Street, not stopping even to wash his face and hands nor to brush the dust from his clothes.

At the door he was met by an officer in khaki, was told that Colonel Wyatt was expecting him, and was asked if he would be so kind as to come up to the Colonel's office. There he was told that his credentials and letters could be presented that afternoon, but there was practically no chance of an interview, as Lord Rockstone was leaving the War Offices in a few minutes.

Word was finally brought in that Lord Rockstone would see Mr. Edestone and receive his letters, but regretted that he would be unable to give him an appointment, as he was leaving for the Continent in a few days and affairs of state required his entire time—which translated into plain English meant: "Come in, but get out as soon as you can."

Shown into a large room, he saw seated at a big desk the man who is said to have said that he did not know when the war would end, but he did know when it would begin, and fixed that date at about eight months after the actual declaration—after millions of pounds had been expended and hundreds of thousands of English dead.

Cold, powerful, relentless, and determined, Edestone knew that it was useless to appeal to a sense of humanity in this man who, sitting at his desk early and late, directed the great machine that slowly but surely was drawing to itself the youth and vigour of all England, there to feed and fatten, flatter and amuse these poor boys from the country, and with music and noise destroy their sensibilities before sending them across the Channel to live for their few remaining days in holes in the ground that no self-respecting beast would with his own consent occupy.

To appeal to a sense of duty so strong in him as applied to England, was one thing; but to convince him that Edestone as an American had a sense of duty to the nations of Europe was something quite different. This man of steel had no imagination, he was convinced, and to ask him to follow him in his flights would be as useless as to request him to whistle Yankee Doodle.

He had a chance to decide all this while Rockstone, who had risen and received him with courtesy, was reading the letters he presented. The great soldier's face never changed once as he read them all with care.

"Your credentials are satisfactory," he finally said, "but I do not quite understand what it is you wish. Your letters say that you do not want to sell anything, which is most extraordinary; I thought you Americans always wanted to sell something." And his face assumed the expression of a man who, having no sense of humour, thought that he had perhaps made a joke.

"If you have drawings and photographs of a new instrument of war," he caught himself up abruptly, "I should greatly prefer that you submit these to the Ordnance Department; but since your Secretary of State has been so insistent, I will look at them tomorrow. I will give you an appointment from 9 to 9:15."

And he rose and bowed.

CHAPTER IV
THE FIRST REBUFF

At exactly a quarter past nine the following morning, Lord Rockstone with military precision rose from his desk.

"I fear that my time is up, Mr. Edestone," he said, glancing at his watch. "I have enjoyed this opportunity of meeting you and listening to your presentation of your theory. Your drawings are most interesting; your photographs convincing, if—" he paused, his lip curling slightly under his long tawny moustache,—"if one did not know of the remarkable optical illusions capable of being produced in photography. Our friends, the Germans, have become particularly expert in the art of double exposure."

Then, as if he thought he might have said too much, he added less crisply:

"Please do not understand that I doubt either your sincerity, or that of the Government at Washington in this matter; you may have both perhaps been deceived. I hope that your stay in England may be pleasant, and I regret that this war will prevent you from receiving the attention to which your letters and your accomplishments would entitle you."

With an expression on his face that said plainer than words: "This is the last minute of my most valuable time that I intend to give to this nonsense," he bowed formally, and reseating himself at his desk, took up papers.

Then without looking up, "Good morning, Mr. Edestone."

The American did not allow himself to show the slightest trace of annoyance at the brusque dismissal.

"You will at least permit me to thank you for your kind intentions, sir," he said; and standing perfectly still until he had forced Lord Rockstone to look up, he added with a smile, "We may meet again, perhaps."

There was something about his perfect ease of manner as he stood waiting which showed that although he would not condescend to notice it, he was both conscious of the War Minister's unpardonable rudeness and intended to make him acknowledge it.

Rockstone hesitated a moment; then with a belated show of courtesy came from behind his desk, and stiffly extended his hand.

"You Americans are the most extraordinary people," he said; "I must admit, I never quite understand you."

"Then you must grant us a slight advantage," rejoined Edestone evenly; "because we believe we do understand you Englishmen. If there had been the same clear understanding on your side in the present instance it would have been more to your interest, I am satisfied; for then instead of merely disturbing you I should have aroused you."

"It is not a question of arousing me as you call it. You are dealing with the Government of the Empire, and, as you know, England moves slowly. The suggestion that I invite His Majesty to see a lot of moving pictures of an impossible machine, if you will pardon me, is preposterous. If you really wish to sell something to the War Department, although I understand you to state that you do not, nothing is simpler. Ship one of your machines to England, give a demonstration, and whereas I cannot speak with authority, I am confident that England will pay all that any other Government will pay. As to our friends, the enemy, our ships will attend to it that nothing goes to them that can be used against us." His jaws snapped, and his cold greenish-grey eyes flashed, as he gave another curt bow of dismissal.

Edestone had no alternative but to leave; but as he turned to rejoin Colonel Wyatt, who had stood stiffly at attention throughout the entire interview, he could not resist one parting shot.

"Do not forget, Lord Rockstone," he said, "that England six months ago spoke lightly of submarines."

The War Minister pretended not to hear; but no sooner had the door closed upon his offensive visitor than he caught up the telephone. "Get me the Admiralty, and present my compliments to Mr. Underhill," he directed sharply. "Tell him I would like to speak to him at once."

He turned back to a tray of letters left upon his desk to sign, but halted, his pen held arrested in air.

"Suppose," he muttered, "the fellow should actually have—? But, pshaw! It's simply a mammoth Yankee bluff. That Foreign Department at Washington is just silly enough to believe that it can frighten us with its manufactured photographs. They are so anxious over there to stop the war, that they would resort to any expedient—anything but fight."

The telephone tinkled.

"Ah! Are you there Underhill? Yes, this is Rockstone. I called you up to warn you against a madman who is now on his way to see you. You can't well refuse to give him an audience, for he has such strong letters from the American Government that one might imagine he was a special envoy sent to offer armed intervention and to end the war. But in my opinion he is merely a crank or an impostor, who has succeeded in obtaining the support and endorsement of their State Department.

"What is that? Oh yes; he's an American. His name? How should I remember! I wasn't interested either in him, or what he had to say. He pretends to have discovered some new agency or force, don't you know, and tries to prove by a lot of double-exposed photographs that he has broken down the fundamental laws of physics, neutralizing the force of gravity, or annihilating space by the polarization of light, or some such rot.

"Do not kick him out. He has letters not only from his Government, but from some of its most prominent men whom it would be unwise to offend at this time. Just listen to his twaddle about universal peace and that sort of thing, and then pass him on to Graves with a quiet warning such as I have given you."

Meanwhile Edestone, having taken leave of Colonel Wyatt, was making his way out of the building, when he found himself accosted in the dimly lighted corridor by a man in civilian clothes whom he recognized as a New York acquaintance of several years' standing.

"Well, look who's here!" he greeted Edestone lustily as he extended his hand. "What brings you into the very den of the lion? Is it that, like myself, you are helping dear old England get arms and ammunition with which to lick the barbarians on the Rhine?"

Glancing around cautiously he lowered his voice. "Make her pay well for them, my boy; she would not hesitate to turn them on us, if we got in her way."

Edestone laughingly disclaimed any interest in army contracts, but at the same time avoided divulging the actual mission upon which he was engaged.

There was something in his companion's manner that put him rather on his guard; he remembered smoking after dinner not more than three or four months before in the house of one of the most prominent German bankers in New York, and listening to this man, who had expressed himself in a way that might have suggested somewhat pro-German sympathies. Edestone had at the time attributed this to a consideration for their host and to the fact that the German Ambassador was present; but he recalled that, although the speaker was most violent in his protestations of neutrality, someone had suggested at the time that he was of a German family, his father having been born in Hesse-Darmstadt. He was a man of wealth, with establishments in New York and Newport, at both of which places Edestone had been entertained. His loud and hearty manner stamped him as a typical American, but his large frame, handsome face, and military bearing showed his Teutonic origin.

"You surprise me Rebener." Edestone's eyes twinkled slightly at these recollections. "I should have supposed, if you had anything of the kind to sell, that it would be to your friend, Count Bernstoff. However," he laid his hand on the other's arm, "it's an agreeable surprise to run across a fellow-countryman, no matter what the cause. Are you going my way?"

"No," Rebener told him, he had an appointment on hand with one of the bureau chiefs in the Ordnance Department.

"Well then suppose you dine with me tonight," suggested Edestone. "I am stopping at Claridge's and shall be awfully glad if you can come. I am entirely alone in London, you see; my cronies, I find, are all dead or at the front."

"Delighted, my boy. But listen! Don't have any of your English swells. Let's make this a quiet little American dinner just to ourselves, and forget for once this ghastly war."

"At eight o'clock, then," Edestone nodded.

"And a strict neutrality dinner, remember. That is the only safe kind for us Americans to eat in London."

"All right, Rebener, as neutral as you please. *A bientôt.*" And with a wave of the hand he passed on down the corridor and out of the building. His appointment with Underhill, Chief of the Admiralty, was not until 11:30, so he put in the time by sauntering rather slowly along the Thames Embankment.

He regretted now that, in talking with Lord Rockstone, he had not made a little more show of force, for had he assumed a more dictatorial manner he would have at least aroused the fighting spirit in his stern antagonist, who might then have taken some interest in crushing him under his heel; whereas now he saw plainly that Rockstone considered him beneath his notice, and thereby much valuable time had been lost. Yet he did not wish to make any show of force until he knew positively that his men were all at their stations, and that the *Little Peace Maker* was near at hand. He must be in a position to use force before playing his last card, and he had not as yet heard from "Specs." Although he knew that their instruments were perfectly attuned, he had not, up to twelve o'clock of the day before, received a single vibration.

At this point he was interrupted by encountering another American who also insisted upon stopping and shaking hands. This was a young architect from New York, who had from time to time done work for his father's estate and who had also made some alterations at the Little Place in the Country for Edestone himself. He was a tall, lank young man of about twenty-seven, with little rat-like eyes, placed so close to his hawk-like nose that one felt Nature would have been kinder to him had she given him only one eye and frankly placed it in the middle of his receding forehead. His small blonde moustache did not cover his rabbit mouth, which was so filled with teeth that he could with difficulty close his lips.

"What has brought you to London, Schmidt? Aren't you afraid that these Englishmen will capture you and shoot you as a spy?"

"Sh! Not quite so loud please, Mr. Edestone; these English are such fools. They think that because a man has a German name he must be a fighting German, when you know that I am a perfectly good naturalized American citizen. My passport is made out in the name of Schmidt, and that's my name all right, but I call myself Smith over here to keep from rubbing these fellows the wrong way."

"Well, Mr. 'Smith,' you have not told me what you are doing in London."

"I have been sent over by a New York architectural paper to make a report upon the condition of the cathedral at Rheims. I stopped over in London to get my papers viséd by the Royal Institute of Architects." Then, lowering his voice, and keeping his eyes on a policeman who was apparently watching them with interest: "I am sorry to see you here, Mr. Edestone. This is no place for us Americans, and my advice to you is to get out of here as soon as you can, and don't come back again until the war is over."

Edestone felt that he would have said more but they were interrupted by the policeman who said: "Excuse me, gentlemen, but these be war times, and me ordhers are to keep the Imbankment moving."

CHAPTER V
ECHOES FROM THE WILHELMSTRASSE

After leaving the War Offices, Rebener went directly to the nearest public telephone.

"Hello, Karlbeck," he called, after satisfying himself by mumbling a jumble of unintelligible words and numbers that he had the man he wanted on the wire. "Is Smith there? What? Thames Embankment? What did you say is the number of that officer? Oh, my old butler, Pat! That's all right. Now listen; if I should miss Smith and he comes in, tell him to call me at my hotel at once. I have made an engagement for dinner with our man for eight o'clock tonight, but you and H. R. H. need not be at my rooms until half-past eight. You understand, eh? Good-bye."

He strolled out, following Edestone's course with the air of a man wishing to enjoy this beautiful spring morning, and approaching the officer who had interrupted the interview between Edestone and Smith, he said, with a little twinkle in his eye: "Will you tell me which of these bridges is called the London Bridge?"

The blue-coated Pat, with Hibernian readiness, caught the humour of the situation. "Shure, I would gladly, but 'tis a strhanger I am here mesilf," he grinned as he smothered the entire lower part of his face with his huge paw of a hand, and significantly closed one eye.

"Pat, your fondness for joking will get you into trouble yet. Did Smith turn Edestone over to you?"

"He did, and I mesilf took him up to the Admiralty where he is now. 4782, I think they called him, takes him up from there, and will keep him until he hears from either you or Smith."

"Where has Smith gone?"

"Shure he's up at Claridge's, bein' shaved by Count von Hottenroth."

"Now, now, Pat, if you don't stop that joking of yours I'll certainly report you to the Wilhelmstrasse."

"And they said I was to be the first King of dear old Ireland!" as with a broad grin on his face he raised his hand as if drinking. "Der Tag!" he cried, thereby causing several passers-by to laugh at the idea of a London bobby giving the sacred German toast.

Rebener, leaving him, went directly to his rooms at The Britz where he was received with the greatest consideration by everybody about the place. He was shown to the royal suite by the proprietor himself, who after he had carefully closed the door upon them stood as if waiting for orders.

"Call Claridge's on the 'phone, and tell Smith who is being shaved," he smiled at the recollection of Pat's jest, "to meet me here at once. I do not want him seen in the hotel, so tell him to come in by the servants' entrance, and you bring him up on the service elevator and in here through my pantry and dining-room."

The proprietor retired to attend to this, but was soon back, and Rebener continued his instructions.

"Luckily Edestone invited me to dine with him tonight before I had a chance to invite him," he said, "but I will persuade him to come here and dine with me."

"So, Mr. Bombiadi," he turned to the proprietor, "I shall want dinner here for four at 8:30. See to it yourself, will you, that my guests are brought through my private entrance, and one especially—you know who—who will be incognito, must not be recognized. Not that there could be any objection to these men dining with me here—a common rich American, who loves to spend his money on princes and things—but by tonight this man Edestone will be watched by at least twenty men from Scotland Yard, and they suspect anyone of being a German spy, be he prince or pauper."

Their conversation was interrupted at this point by the arrival of Smith, who came in very much excited. Sniffling and rubbing his nose with the back of his forefinger, like a nervous cocaine fiend, he broke out agitatedly:

"Mr. Rebener, I'm getting sick of this job. When I undertook to find out for you what was going on at the Little Place in the Country, I was working for Germany as against the world, and anything that I can do for her I am glad and proud to do, but that Hottenroth talks like a damn fool. Excuse me, Mr. Rebener, but he don't want to stop at anything. He says that if he pulls off this thing the Emperor, when he gets to London, will make him Duke of Westminster, or something, and six months from now he will appoint me Governor-General of North America. I tell you, Mr. Rebener, that fellow is plumb nutty."

"Pardon me, Mr. Rebener," interposed the proprietor, "it is true that Hottenroth is excitable, but he is faithful to the Fatherland and an humble servant to His Imperial Majesty. He has been in charge of a fixed post in London for fifteen years. He was one of the very first to be sent here, and he was in Paris before that. He would die willingly for the Fatherland, as would I, and if this Schmidt, I mean Smith, thinks there is any sin too great to be committed for the Fatherland, he is not worthy of a place among us, and the sooner we get rid of him the better." And he looked at the unfortunate Smith in a way that showed he was willing to do this at any moment.

But Rebener, who had lived all his life in America, and like Smith did not thoroughly agree with the philosophy of German militarism—before which everything must bow—hurriedly raised his hand.

"Come, come, you are both getting unnecessarily excited. Don't let us try to cross our bridges until we get to them. What did von Hottenroth have to report?"

"It was not very satisfactory, to tell you the truth, Mr. Rebener," said Smith; "they searched through all of his things and they found nothing but a drawing of a Zeppelin of our 29-M type, with some slight changes, which Hottenroth said don't amount to anything, and some photographs of Mr. Edestone himself, doing some juggling tricks with heavy dumb-bells and weights, but we learned afterwards from the porter that an expressman had left two large and heavy trunks marked, 'A. M. Black and P. S. Stanton,' at No. 4141 Grosvenor Square East."

"Well what is the report," demanded Bombiadi, "on No. 4141 Grosvenor Square?"

Smith read from a memorandum book: "Lord Lindenberry, who is a widower, lives there with his mother, the Dowager. The old lady is now up at their country place, in Yorkshire, and the Marquis went on to Aldershot last night after having dined with Edestone at Brooks's and dropping him at Claridge's at 12:15 A.M. The house is only partially opened; there are only a few of the old servants there."

"And do you think these trunks contain the instrument which you reported to us from America was always kept in the safe at the Little Place in the Country?" snapped the hotel proprietor.

"I don't know," whined Smith. "Mr. Edestone probably has it with him."

"Well, we must get hold of it before he shows it to Underhill," frowned the proprietor, "that is, if it has not been shown already, and in that case we must get hold of Edestone himself."

"Now that is exactly what is troubling me," Smith's voice rose hysterically. "I'm not going to stand for any of that rough stuff, Mr. Rebener. Mr. Edestone and his father have both been mighty good to me, and if anything happens to him I'll blow on the whole lot of you."

"So?" The proprietor's pale fat face was convulsed with a look of hatred and contempt. "Then we are to understand, Smith, that if we find it necessary to do away with Edestone you wish to go first? You dirty little half-breed," he growled in an undertone. "Your mother must have been an English woman."

"Here, here, you two fools!" Rebener broke in with sharp authority, "there is no question of 'doing away' with Edestone, as you call it. What we're after is the invention and not the man himself, and we'll not get it by 'doing away' with him. I am, like Smith here, opposed to murder, even for the Fatherland."

"But it is not murder, Mr. Rebener," interrupted the proprietor, "if thereby we are instrumental in saving thousands of the sons of the Fatherland."

"That would not only not save the sons of the Fatherland, but would put an end to our usefulness, both here in London and in America, especially if Edestone has already turned the whole thing over to England. The very first thing for us to do is to find out how the matter stands. If the Ministry knows nothing, we must work to get him to Berlin, and then even you fire-eaters may safely trust it to the Wilhelmstrasse. If it should happen, however, that the British Government has the invention, His Royal Highness tonight will try to get enough out of Edestone to enlighten Berlin, and in that way we shall at least get an even break. That is, always provided that Edestone has not a lot of the completed articles, whatever they may be, at the Little Place in the Country. That would put us in bad again, and it will be up to Count Bernstoff to attend to it from the New York end."

"Of course, Mr. Rebener," said the proprietor, "we can do nothing until we hear from His Royal Highness, but I am satisfied that he will say Edestone must not be allowed to go to Downing Street tomorrow to continue his negotiations, unless in some way we can get hold of this secret tonight."

"Well, I'll be damned if I'll—!" started Rebener angrily, when he was interrupted by the proprietor, who holding his finger to his lip, said:

"Please, Mr. Rebener, please! Always remember that the service on which we are engaged has no soul and a very long arm." Then dropping into the persuasive and servile tone of the *maître d'hôtel*: "I propose, Mr. Rebener, that you allow me to send you up a nice little lunch, some melon, say, a *salmon mayonnaise* or a *filet du sole au vin blanc* and a *noisette d'agneau* and a nice little sweet, and you must try a bottle of our Steinberger Auslese '84.

"And Smith," he turned to the humbler agent, "you had better get in touch with 4782, who is reporting to His Royal Highness every hour. His last message was that Edestone is still with Underhill, so you get down to the Admiralty and report to me here as often as you can. Edestone will probably lunch quietly alone somewhere, as I know that all of his friends are at the front, but don't lose him until you turn him over to Mr. Rebener tonight at 8 o'clock." His eyes narrowed as they followed the skulking figure of the architect out of the room.

"That fellow needs watching," he muttered to Rebener. "He has lost his nerve. He is not a true German anyhow. But if he makes a false step, 4782 knows what to do and you can depend upon him to do it. We do not know who he is, but he is a gentleman, if not a nobleman, and he will kill or die for his Emperor."

Smith, in the meantime, had gone down the service stairs and out at the rear of the hotel. He was thoughtful, and when he was settled in his taxi, after having directed the chauffeur where to drive, he said to himself:

"They are going to kill him tonight unless they get that machine, or else can fix it so that Rockstone doesn't get it tomorrow, that is if Underhill hasn't got it already. I wish I'd never started this business; I never thought it would go so far, and what do I get out of it? A German decoration which I can't wear in America, and God knows I don't want to live in Germany, and seventeen dollars a week. I'm not going to stand for it, and that's settled."

Arriving in front of a little restaurant he entered and sat down at a table near a window looking out on Whitehall Place. The proprietor, who was another German, came over to him, and while ostensibly arranging the cloth spoke to him in an undertone in his own language.

"Edestone is still with Underhill," he said. "The taxi driver on the stand opposite, the one who looks as if he were asleep, is 4782. In that way he keeps the head of the line, you see, and when Edestone comes out, if he doesn't take that cab, 4782 can follow him until he alights again, and then he is to telephone His Royal Highness. So you sit here and have lunch, where you can see what is going on."

Then, turning to a group of his regular customers at another table, the jovial host in a loud voice and in perfect English took a violent pro-Ally part in the war discussion that was going on.

CHAPTER VI
A RUSTY OLD CANNON-BALL

Edestone had met the Honorable Herbert Underhill before, both in America and in the country houses of England. The two were about the same age, and as Underhill's mother was an American, Edestone had hoped that he would not have quite so much trouble in getting him to look at the matter from an American point of view.

Underhill, however, was just on that account a little bit more formal with the cousins from across the sea than were most of the men of high position in Europe. He was undoubtedly taken aback and thrown off his guard when he found that Edestone was the dangerous American lunatic of whom he had been warned. In the first place, he knew that there was not the slightest chance of his being an impostor, and he also knew exactly how much of a lunatic he was. He knew, in fact, that he was a hard-riding, clear-thinking, high-minded Anglo-Saxon of the very best type to be found A Rusty Old Cannon-Ball anywhere, and he smiled as he thought of Rockstone's advice not to kick him out of the Admiralty.

With considerable show of cordiality, he invited his visitor into a small room adjoining his large office, and sat him down at the opposite side of a wide table.

"Lord Rockstone told me you were coming, but did not mention your name. He is quite a chap, that Rockstone. Not what you Americans would call a very chatty party, however. Now what can I do for you? Lord Rockstone tells me that you have some new invention, or something of the sort, that will help us to finish up this little scrimmage without the loss of a single Tommy. Well, that is exactly what we are looking for, and you American chaps are clever at thinking out new ideas. He tells me, however, that you do not wish to sell it. Now I can understand better than he why that part would be of no especial interest to you; but can't we deal with a Syndicate, or a Board of Underwriters, a Holding Company, or some of those wonderful business combinations that you Americans devise in order to do business without going to jail? Is the poor starving inventor some billionaire like yourself, who works only for honour and glory? In that case we might get an Iron Cross for him. In fact, we might get one blessed by the Emperor himself, by Jove!"

Edestone laughed. "Well, Mr. Underhill, you cannot deny inheriting a certain amount of American wit. I have so often heard the older members of the Union Club tell stories of Billy Travers's witty sayings. He must have gone the pace that kills. One of the old servants used to tell that whenever Travers and Larry Jerome and that set came in for supper, they expected the waiters to drink every fifth bottle; it made things more cheerful-like — but *revenons à nos moutons*. Lord Rockstone is right, I do not want to sell my discovery, for mine it is. I am the penniless inventor. I only want an opportunity of showing it to the heads of the Powers that are now at war, and of demonstrating to them the stupendous and overwhelming force that is now practically in the hands of the greatest of the neutral governments, and thus try, if possible, to convince them of the uselessness of continuing this loss of life and treasure.

"If I could demonstrate to you, Mr. Underhill, that I could, sitting here in your office, give an order that would set London on fire and send every ship in the English navy to the bottom in the course of a few weeks, would you not advocate opening negotiations for peace? And were I to show the Emperor of Germany that his great army could be destroyed in even less time, would he not be more receptive than we now understand him to be?"

"Why, Mr. Edestone, I most certainly should," the First Lord of the Admiralty granted with a smile, "and I think that perhaps the German Emperor would be amenable under the circumstances, but as they say in your great country, 'I am from Missouri, you must show me.'"

He changed his position and glanced at Edestone as if he were beginning to think that possibly Rockstone might be right in his estimate after all.

"Very well, Mr. Underhill; it is now five minutes to noon, and I think that I will be able to show you in exactly five minutes."

He took from his pocket a leather case, such as a woodsman might use to carry a large pocket compass, and removing the cover set out upon the table an instrument that was entirely enclosed in vulcanized rubber. On the top, under glass, was a dial, with a little needle which vibrated violently, but came to a standstill soon after being placed on the table. Two small platinum wires, about twelve inches long and carefully insulated, issued from opposite sides of the hard rubber casing.

Underhill's face at first bore only an expression of mild amusement, but as Edestone evidenced such a deadly earnestness, he showed more interest and said with a rather nervous laugh: "Look here, old chap, don't blow the entire English navy out of the water while you're closeted here with me. I must have some witness to prove that I didn't do it or I might have to explain to the House of Commons."

Edestone, a hard and drawn look about his mouth, paid no heed, but taking his watch out of his pocket fixed his eye on the little needle of the instrument and waited as the last few seconds of the hour ticked off. As the second hand made its last round, and the minute hand swung into position exactly at twelve, he leaned over the table as if trying by mental suggestion to make the instrument respond to his will. But it remained perfectly quiescent, and with a half sigh and a tightening of the lines about his mouth, he closed his watch. Could it be possible, he thought, that "Specs" had forgotten his instructions always to use Greenwich time?

He was about to replace the instrument in its case, when he was startled by a clock on the mantel, which began to strike the hour of twelve. Involuntarily he counted the strokes as they chimed slowly, and as the vibrations of the last stroke faded away the little needle swung an entire circuit of the dial, returning to its original position. This was repeated three times.

Underhill, although still interested in what was going on, seemed a bit relieved when nothing more startling happened.

"Oh, I say, you know, you gave me quite a start," he jested. "I thought that you were going to set London on fire, and you simply seem to be taking your blood-pressure."

Edestone still paid not the slightest attention to him, but after glancing about the room walked over to the mantelpiece where he picked up an old twelve-inch cannon-ball, which with considerable difficulty he brought back and placed on the table by the side of his instrument. His eyes once more roved about the room as if he were seeking something, and stepping deliberately to a passe-partout photograph of King George V., he ripped off the binding with his pocket-knife and tore from it the glass.

"Oh, I say, now, Mr. Edestone, those cow-boy methods don't go here in London, and if you cannot behave a bit more like a gentleman, I'll have you shown to the street."

"We have more important matters on our hands just now, Mr. Underhill, than whether or not I am a gentleman," snapped the American, his face set and serious as he with nervous fingers laid the glass on the table.

Rolling the cannon-ball to him, he lifted it very gently on to the glass plate, and then taking a key from his pocket he appeared to wind up on the inside of the instrument some mechanism which gave off a buzzing sound. Next he drew on a pair of rubber gloves with vulcanized rubber finger tips, and moistening with his lips the ends of the two platinum wires, pressed them to either side of the ball, first the one and then the other. A spark was given off when the second contact was made, and the room was filled with a pungent odour as of overheated metal which caused both men to cough violently.

Following this, with great care, and using only the tips of his fingers, he lifted the glass plate with the ball on it. When he had raised it his arm's length above the table, like a plum pudding on a platter, he took the glass away, leaving the ball hanging unsupported in the air.

He sat down and smiled across the table into the astonished, almost incredulous, face of his companion.

"And now, Mr. Underhill, I hope you will pardon my rudeness," he apologized lightly; "but I get so interested in these little tricks of mine that sometimes I forget myself. If you will permit me, I shall, when I go to Paris, order from Cartiers's a more befitting frame for His Majesty, and shall beg you to accept it from me as a little souvenir of our meeting today."

Underhill made no reply. His whole attention was riveted on that amazing ball, and Edestone, a trifle mischievously, added: "If you have a perfectly good heart, and think you can stand a bit of a shock, touch that ball lightly with your finger."

"My heart's all right, and I am prepared for anything," Underhill surrendered, as he reached up and touched the innocent looking rusty old cannon-ball, whose only peculiarity seemed to be its willingness to remain where it was without any visible means of support.

The room was suddenly filled with a greenish light, as if someone had just taken a flash-light photograph. Underhill was thrown violently back into his chair, and the ball crashed down on the table, splitting it from end to end.

Without moving a muscle of his face, and taking no notice of the gestures of pain made by Underhill as he sat rubbing his arm and shoulder, Edestone resumed:

"Mr. Underhill, I will not take any more of your valuable time to show you my drawings and photographs, but I beg you to say to Sir Egbert Graves that you do not think with Lord Rockstone that the American Secretary of State has been deceived, and that you hope he will, when he sees me tomorrow, try to forget for a while that he is an Englishman and be a little bit human. You know, Underhill, confidence and pigheadedness are not even connected by marriage; much less are they blood relations. By Jove," he grinned, "you can tell him I'll stick him up against the ceiling if he insists upon handling me with the ice tongs and leave him there until you take him down; that is, if you care to take another little shock."

Underhill, although he might have thought at another time that it was his duty to resent such light and frivolous reference to the heads of His Majesty's Government, was now, however, occupied with more serious reflections, and overlooked the offence.

"I am sure," he said, rousing himself, "that if Sir Egbert is convinced that you are working for the sake of humanity he will be most happy to make use of your talents."

"That is exactly what I want him to do," returned Edestone, "but not in the way in which you mean. I wish to be given authority to open negotiations for peace with the Emperor of Germany. Now, Mr. Underhill, do we understand one another?"

He rose to leave with this, but Underhill, stepping quickly forward, laid a hand upon his arm.

"You don't suppose for a moment, Mr. Edestone, that we will allow you to leave England and go to Germany to sell them your invention and have it used against us?"

"You have my word, Mr. Underhill, and that of the American Secretary of State, that it is not my intention to sell to any government. With that assurance, unless your Ministry wishes to risk the chances of war with the United States, I think it will allow me to leave England and go anywhere I please. Good-morning, Mr. Underhill. I am sorry to have taken up so much of your valuable time, even more sorry to have broken His Majesty's beautiful old oak table."

CHAPTER VII
DIPLOMACY WINS

Underhill, left alone, sat for some moments looking from the broken table to the cannonball and then back again. Finally he picked up a fragment of glass, for the Royal face protector had likewise been broken, when the good old English oak had met its defeat at the hands of this Hun of the world of science, and with it, very gingerly, he tapped the iron ball—this rusty old barbarian which had set at naught the force of gravity, had violated all the established laws of nature, and had like the Germans in Belgium smashed through.

Finding that nothing happened, he hesitated for a moment, and, then, bracing himself against the shock, he touched his finger gently to this rude old paradox. There was no shock, and, reassured, he leaned across the table and tried with both hands to lift the cannon-ball.

"That part is genuine there is no doubt," he granted. "That old cannon-ball must have been here since—?" He gave a start as his eyes caught the inscription pasted upon it, which was:

"A freak cannon-ball, made at the Forge
and Manor of Greenwood, Virginia, 1778.
Presented in 1889 to Lord Roberts by
General George Bolling Anderson, Governor
of the State of Virginia."

"How extraordinary!" he exclaimed. "These Americans are popping up at every turn."

He passed out into the large outer office, and, glancing at his watch, summoned an undersecretary.

"It is now just a quarter after twelve," he said, "and the Cabinet lunches at Buckingham Palace at two. Present my compliments to Lord Rockstone and Sir Egbert Graves, and say that I should like to see them both here for a few minutes on a matter of the greatest importance, and that much as I regret to trouble them it is absolutely necessary that this meeting be held in my office and before they go on to the Palace."

To another attendant who, moved by curiosity, was going in the direction of the smaller room, he said: "Place a sentry at that door when I leave. No one is to be allowed to enter that room until I give further orders."

A telephone orderly came in a few minutes later to say that his message had found Lord Rockstone and Sir Egbert Graves together, and that they both would be with him within the half-hour.

Underhill was now fully convinced that Edestone possessed some wonderful invention or discovery which the United States intended to use as a final argument for peace, and, with the aid of this discovery, render untenable any position in opposition to its will taken by England or any of the other Powers. Had he dreamed that the United States was as ignorant as to the nature of this invention as he himself was, the history of the world might have been changed.

When Graves and Rockstone arrived, he greeted them with serious face and at once drew them into private conference.

"Gentlemen," he said, "I am sorry to have to trouble you to come to me, but I am confident that you will forgive me when you understand my reasons for insisting upon a meeting here." Keeping both men still standing he continued: "I have a strange story to tell, so strange in fact, that you gentlemen would be justified in doubting not only my word but my sanity, had I nothing to show you in corroboration."

Both men stood like graven images; one like a soldier at attention; the other, his hat and cane in his right hand and the tips of his two first fingers resting lightly on the table behind which Underhill was standing, his thin, clean-shaven, mask-like face as expressionless as if it belonged to a head that had been stuck on the end of a pike and shoved out across the table for Underhill to look at, instead of to one well placed on his broad athletic shoulders. They both knew that Underhill was young and had inherited from his beautiful American mother a nervous and temperamental disposition. They also knew that this was tempered by the crafty cleverness of the blood of the hero of Blenheim. They had come prepared for one of his excitable outbursts, although they knew he would not have been so insistent had there not been good cause.

"Will you be so kind as to walk into this room with me?" He pointed toward the door of the small room.

Still with that show of utter imperturbability the two complied, continuing to gaze stolidly as their associate, closing the door behind them, called their attention to the cannon-ball and broken table.

"Exhibits A and B"; he waved his hand toward the two objects. "I wanted you to see these in order to convince you that I have neither been dreaming, nor am I the victim of an aberration."

Then with great care and endeavouring to maintain a semblance of self-possession, he described his recent experience, omitting no single detail that he could recall. He showed them exactly where and how he had been sitting, and followed every movement made by Edestone, even to the ripping of the glass from the portrait of the King, until finally, as if overcome by the strain that he had put upon himself to appear perfectly calm, he ended with a nervous little laugh.

"Will you look at the inscription on that blooming old cannon-ball? It really seems quite spooky."

Graves moved forward and thoughtfully examined the split table and the rusty old relic of Valley Forge, but Rockstone did not offer to stir. With what was almost a sneer on his face he met the challenging glance of his younger confrère.

"I would not have believed, Underhill," he said impatiently, "that you with your experience with the fakirs of India could have been taken in by so old a trick." He half-closed his eyes as if to indicate that for him at least the incident was closed.

Underhill frowned. "You are wrong, Rockstone," he exclaimed impulsively. "This man is no faker, nor am I so easily imposed upon as you seem to think. I tell you that we are called upon to deal with a new agency that can neither be disputed nor sneered away, and unless we can contrive some way to oppose it, the United States will step in and force a peace upon us—a peace that will leave Europe exactly where it was before the war—and keep it so, while she herself can go ahead unchecked and take possession of the whole Western Hemisphere. Don't you see the scheme?"

"Where is this extraordinary individual?" inquired the Foreign Minister, completing his inspection of the table. "What has become of him?" His thin voice was as evenly modulated as if he were asking where he had put his other glove.

"Oh, probably at Boodle's or Brookes's lunching with some of his friends," Underhill answered indifferently. "He left here only a short time ago. And you need not be afraid, Sir Egbert," with a significant glance. "A very careful eye is being kept upon his movements. We can get him at any moment if we want him."

Graves nodded, and then went on meditatively.

"It is of course entirely irregular," he said, "but from what both of you gentlemen tell me as to the nature of his credentials, there can be little doubt that the man is here with the approval of his Government, if not as an authorized representative. The sole question, therefore, is whether or not he does possess such an invention or discovery as he claims— —"

"But can you doubt that?" demanded Underhill hotly.

"And whether," proceeded Sir Egbert without change of tone, "granting that the contrivance is of value, the United States will permit its purchase for use in the present war.

"On the first proposition, I can only say that if he has this invention, as my young friend of the Navy stands so firmly convinced, it is tantamount to admitting that the United States has a new and terrible instrument of war, in which case it would be most unwise to offend her. If he has not, there certainly can be no objection to allowing him the opportunity of offering to our enemies something that is of no value. Therefore, that seems to settle the question as to the advisability of detaining him, as has been suggested. I should strongly favour letting him go when and where he pleases.

"Assuming that he has in his possession facts or mechanisms that would give to one nation such stupendous advantages over the others as he claims, we must not forget that the United States has had these facts and mechanisms for some time. Therefore, it would be ill-advised to detain him forcibly, for the United States' answer to this would be a declaration of war in which the superiority of her position would be overwhelming.

"I'm inclined to believe that the reason he does not wish to sell his discovery is because he has not obtained permission from his Government to do so. They intend to dispose of it to the country with whom they can make the most favourable bargain. I think indeed that under all circumstances the best policy for this Government is to treat this man with the greatest possible consideration. If he has the power to do us harm, we must put him in such a position that he will not wish to do it; and if he has not, our treatment of him will have a tendency to draw the United States nearer to us than she is at present. We must, at least, pretend to take the American Secretary of State at his word. Whereas I do not think that there is any doubt that America is influenced entirely by selfish motives, she is now our friend, and as long as this war goes on it is to the interest of Great Britain to keep her so."

"A very good idea, Sir Egbert," agreed Underhill. "That is absolutely the only way to deal with this man. He says that he is almost a pure Anglo-Saxon, you know, and he is as proud of it as if he were an Englishman. He is the ninth in direct line from the original old chap, or rather young chap, who went from England to Virginia in 1642. Think of it! Say what you may, blood is thicker than water. That fellow is at heart an Englishman; he has been away from home nearly three hundred years."

Graves gave a little bow of comprehension. "When Mr. Edestone calls on me tomorrow," he said, "I shall not even touch on the question of the purchasing of this alleged invention, but shall offer to facilitate in every way his mission as peacemaker. I shall take him at his word that he does not intend to sell to any one, and try to persuade him that, if he is bent on coercing any people, the English are not the ones that require this, as they are in perfect accord with him, and that he would accomplish his purpose much more quickly if he would bring force to bear upon the German Emperor."

"But, Sir Egbert," broke in Underhill excitedly, "he says that he wants us to authorize him to open peace negotiations with the Kaiser, and I think he rather intimated that if we should refuse he would use force, which of course means the United States."

"Well upon my word!" Rockstone's eyes flashed, and an indignant expression took the place of the rather bored look with which he had been listening. "That is pretty strong language to use to His Imperial Majesty's Government, and for my part I think that this young gentleman and his little trick box should be shipped back home with a very polite but emphatic note to the effect that when England wishes the good offices of the United States in bringing this war to a close, she will call for them. As to the young man himself, I should say to him that if he were caught trying to get into Germany he would be looked upon as a spy endeavouring to render assistance to the enemy, and would be treated accordingly."

"But wait a moment, Rockstone," said Sir Egbert. "You are forgetting that this Mr. Edestone is in some measure at least the representative of his country. We cannot afford to offend the United States of America, even though his manners are bad."

"To the contrary," muttered Underhill, "his manners are surprisingly good."

Sir Egbert slightly inclined his head in acknowledgment of the correction. "There is the point too," he went on, "as to whether or not he is an impostor. If he is, why should we allow the American comic papers to put us in the same category with their own Secretary of State, at whom they have been poking fun for years, when they discover that this exceedingly clever young man has taken us in also?

"No, no, to me the matter seems very simple. Uncle Sam has got something he wants to sell. Good or bad it makes no difference; he wants to sell, and sell it he will to the highest bidder. Why refuse to consider his offer on the one hand, or why appear to be too anxious to close with him on the other? Let him offer it to the enemy; he will certainly come back for our bid before closing with them."

"Do you know, Sir Egbert," Lord Rockstone somewhat reluctantly allowed himself to be won over, "since you put it that way I think that perhaps you are right. Diplomacy is probably the strongest weapon with which to deal with this young man. He did not impress me as one to be easily bluffed by show of force."

"Nor should I be bluffed, even by you, Rockstone," said Underhill somewhat ruefully, rubbing his arm, "if I had the power that this chap has locked up in that little rubber box and stored away in that long head of his."

"Well, let us make a decision: does His Majesty go to Washington or shall the Chautauqua lecturer extend his professional tours to include London?" Graves gave his sly secretive laugh. Then as if ashamed of his momentary levity, and changing his entire manner, he said: "Well, gentlemen, what do you propose?"

"I rather think we are unanimous," said Underhill, "in considering that Mr. Edestone should be given a fair hearing. The final answer to his proposition can be given, of course, only after it has been discussed in full cabinet."

"That would perhaps be the best way to leave the matter," approved Rockstone.

"We are agreed then, it seems," said Graves, and they left together for Buckingham Palace.

CHAPTER VIII
THE SPY-DRIVEN TAXI. —

On coming out of the Admiralty, Edestone, a trifle preoccupied, was about to take the taxi with the rather sleepy driver which stood at the head of the line. But the thought came to him, where shall I go? As he had told Rebener, none of his pals were in town and he had absolutely nothing to do until dinner at eight o'clock. Why not take lunch at some quiet little place in the neighbourhood?

"I say, cabby, is there any sort of a decent restaurant around here where one can get a very nice little lunch?"

"Yes, sir, thank you, sir"; the chauffeur rather abruptly came into full possession of his faculties. "There is a very neat little place right across the road, sir, thank you, sir," and he pointed in the direction of the window at which Schmidt was sitting.

"Ah, thank you, cabby," said Edestone in his usual kind manner with people of that class. He was rather struck by the handsome face of the man, although it was covered over with grease and grime. "Here is a shilling. Don't you think I might be able to walk that far this beautiful day?"

"Yes, sir, thank you, sir." The man showed no appreciation of the humour. "Would you be wanting a cab later on, sir? If so I'll just hang about, sir. Times is hard in these war times, sir."

"Certainly, wait by all means," said Edestone with a jolly laugh. "Set your clock. Now open your door and drive me to that restaurant over there, and then wait for me till I have had my lunch. By the time that I get through with you I think you will find that you have done a good day's work."

"I am sure of it, sir." The chauffeur hid a surreptitious chuckle with his very dirty hand.

On entering the restaurant the first person Edestone saw was Schmidt, and he gave a little nod of recognition.

"Well, Mr. Schmidt, we seem to be meeting quite often this morning. I hope that I am to infer from your presence that I will be able to get some of your delightfully greasy German dishes."

But at this point he was interrupted by the proprietor, who came bustling up, trying to force him to take a seat at a table in another part of the room.

"German dishes?" stammered the restaurant keeper. "Not at all. That was when the place was run by Munchinger, but he went back to Germany last July, and this place is run by me, and I am a Swiss. Still, sir, if you are fond of the German dishes I think I might be able to accommodate you, sir."

"Well, suppose I leave that entirely to you. I can't by any chance get a large stein of Münchener beer?"

"No, sir, I am sorry. I can get you some French beer though, which we think is much better. You know that Admiral Fisher has got those Dutchmen bottled up so tight that they tell me the beer won't froth any more in Germany." And he burst into a roar of laughter in which he was joined by a chorus of adoring customers sitting about at the different tables.

Edestone sat down while the proprietor in person took his order to the kitchen. In a very short time, the man returned and put down before him a *gemüse suppe*, following this with *schweine fleisch, sauerkraut*, and *gherkins*—a luncheon which might have been cooked in a German's own kitchen—and set before him a glass of beer which Edestone would have sworn had not been brewed outside of the city of Munich.

The proprietor bustled about, laughing and cracking clumsy jokes with everyone who would listen to him, and his jokes seemed to Edestone to be almost as German as his beer. In this way he finally worked over to where Smith was sitting, and as he pretended to arrange something on the table whispered sharply: "Go to the lavatory."

Smith, unable to eat, sat toying with his food. He gulped his beer as if it choked him. He turned around several times to look at Edestone, but the latter after his perfunctory greeting took no further notice of him. At last, paying his check, the man walked to the rear of the restaurant and into a small, dark, badly ventilated room under the stairs. The place was so dimly lighted that he could scarcely see in front of him a wash basin, but as he was wondering what he was expected to do next he heard a voice that seemed to come from a little partially opened window that looked out into a dark ventilating shaft to the left of the basin. "Pretend to wash your hands," the voice whispered cautiously. Smith did as he was directed and found that he thus brought his left ear close to the window opening.

"Now listen," said the voice, speaking rapidly in German. "God is with the Fatherland today! 4782 has been engaged to wait. Hottenroth has telephoned that our man undoubtedly has his instrument with him. The order is for you and 4782 to get it from him this afternoon at any cost. 4782 knows what he is to do." And the window closed softly.

Smith broke out into a cold perspiration. He knew that he was looking death straight in the face, and in a twinkling his mind carried him back over his entire life. He clutched at his throat as he realized his horrible situation. His present position in the grip of this relentless but invisible master had come about so gradually that he had not realized how firmly he was caught until now it was too late. Not being borne up by the hysterical exaltation of the true-born Prussian, he resented that he should be the one selected to do this ghastly thing.

He staggered back into the restaurant where the proprietor, laying a hand upon his arm, and laughing loudly and winking as if he were telling a risqué story, muttered some further directions into his ear.

"He is preparing to go now. Join him and don't leave him until—" he broke off and rushed over to Edestone who had risen from the table and was taking his hat and cane from the waiter.

"I hope, sir, you found everything perfectly satisfactory?" he bowed.

"Very nice indeed," said Edestone, handing him a half-crown. "I am glad to have discovered your place and I shall come again."

At the door he encountered Smith, who was lingering about as if waiting for him.

"Oh, Mr. Edestone," he forced himself to say, swallowing and fumbling with his mouth. "I remember when I was fixing up your Little Place in the Country for you that you took a great deal of interest in old English prints. Well, I have just found an old print shop over in the Whitechapel district with some of the most wonderful old prints, and if you have the time to spare I would like to take you over and have the old man show them to you."

"I should like to very much," said Edestone. "I have just been wondering what I should do with myself this afternoon."

"The Kaiser and God will bless you for this," the restaurant keeper whispered into Smith's ear, after he had bowed Edestone out to the sidewalk.

"Mr. Smith, will you please give the address to the driver," said Edestone as he stepped into the taxi. Smith leaned over and gave some mumbled instructions to the chauffeur, who had remained upon his box; then he took his place at the side of his friend and patron.

But no sooner had the motor started than he turned to Edestone. "Mr. Edestone," —his voice trembled so violently that he could scarcely speak,— "please do not move or seem surprised at what I am going to say."

Edestone drew back slightly and looked at him. He thought at first that the man had suddenly lost his reason. Smith was perfectly livid and his little eyes were starting from his head. His mouth was open and he seemed to be vainly trying to draw his blue lips over his great dry yellow teeth on which they seemed to catch, giving him the appearance of a snarling dog as he cringed in the corner of the cab. One hand was pulling at his collar while with the other he clutched at the seat in a vain effort to restrain the tremors which were shaking him from head to foot. "Don't speak. I must talk and talk fast," he said.

Edestone leaned forward as if to halt the car, but the fellow caught him by the knee in a grip almost of desperation.

"For God's sake don't do that!" he pleaded. "He will kill both of us. Oh, don't you understand? He is a German spy. I am German, Rebener is German, we are all Germans—all spies. We have been watching you for the past six months. This man is now driving you to a place where they will certainly kill you unless you turn over that instrument which you have in your pocket."

At this Edestone started. Although he could scarcely control himself and felt like strangling the chicken-hearted wretch, he recovered himself in time to say with a look of disgust, "You poor miserable creature."

"I know, Mr. Edestone, but please keep quiet. I may save you if you will do as I say. I don't know about myself. I am a dead man for certain, though, if you let him once suspect," and he motioned in the direction of the chauffeur. Then continuing he gasped out: "Stop the taxi anywhere along here: get out and go into some shop. When you come out again say to me that you have decided you will look at the prints some other day, and that you will walk to the hotel. Discharge and pay him. I will re-engage him and as soon as we get out of sight you take another taxi and drive straight to your hotel. But you must be careful; he knows that you have the instrument with you. They are desperate enough to do anything. Your life is in danger."

Edestone, thoroughly enjoying the excitement of the situation, had absolutely no fear either for himself or for the instrument, since as a matter of fact he knew that he could destroy that at any moment. He felt sorry for Smith, however. He pitied him for his weakness but realized that he was risking his life to save him, so he did as he was urged.

While he was in the shop 4782 got off the box, and, looking into the cab, said sternly to Smith in German: "If you are playing me any of your American tricks, you half-breed, you will never see the sun set again."

Also, when Edestone returned and discharged him with a very handsome tip, he did not seem especially gratified, and when poor Smith in a trembling voice re-engaged the taxi, the driver almost lost control of himself. Had he done so, Edestone, who was watching him closely, would have been delighted, since he would have liked nothing better than to have forced the fellow to show his hand then and there. He was again struck with the chauffeur's appearance as he stood talking to Smith for he had the air of a gentleman and even through his dirt looked above his position. Leaving them there, the American strolled along, and, after a block or two, hailed another cab and ordered it to drive to Claridge's. He really did not think to look about him, but had he done so he might have discovered that he was being followed by the first taxi with its woebegone passenger and its handsome chauffeur.

Arriving at the hotel he was interested to see standing in front of the door a carriage with men in the royal livery, and he was met at the entrance by the proprietor himself in a frightful state of excitement.

"Mr. Edestone, one of the King's equerries is waiting in the reception room to see you. I have been calling you up at every club and hotel in London."

Edestone went into the reception room where he was met by an officer in the uniform of the Royal Horse Guards, who after going through the formality of introducing himself delivered his message:

"His Majesty, the King, instructs me to say that he will receive you and inspect your drawings, photographs, etc., at Buckingham Palace this afternoon at half-past four o'clock."

CHAPTER IX
BUCKINGHAM PALACE

To nearly every man, especially if he happened to be an Englishman, the fact that he had received a Royal Command would have been sufficient to make him, if not nervous, at least thoughtful. Edestone was, however, so incensed at Rebener and so disgusted with Schmidt and so angry with the entire German Secret Service, that it came to him as a relief, like an invitation, from a gentleman older and more distinguished than himself, to dine, or to see some recently acquired painting or bit of porcelain, after he had been all day at a Board meeting of avaricious business men. It was no affectation with him that he felt he was going into an atmosphere in which he belonged. "I always assume that Royalties are gentlemen," he would say, "until I find that they are not; and as long as they conduct themselves as such I am perfectly at ease, but as soon as they begin to behave like bounders I am uncomfortable."

He was not one of those Americans who insist at all times and under all circumstances that he is as good as any man, simply because in his heart of hearts he knows that he is not, but hopes by this bluster to deceive the world. On the contrary, he was a firm advocate of an aristocratic form of government, and did not hesitate to say that he considered the Declaration of Independence, wherein it refers to the absolute equality of man, as a joke.

He was a most thorough believer in class and class distinction and said that he hoped to see the day when the world would be ruled by an upper class who would see that the lower classes had all that was good for them, but would not be allowed to turn the world upside down with their clumsy illogical reforms and new religions, Saint-Simonianism, humanitarianism, or as a matter of fact with any of the old established *isms*. They already have several hundred forms to choose from, he would say; they should not be allowed to make any more new ones until one single one of these has been universally accepted. The glamour of royalty had no effect upon him. Its solidity, dignity, and gentility did.

When he saw the royal livery standing before the hotel, he had rather surmised that it was being used by some Indianapolis heiress who had married a title which carried the privilege of using it and was getting her money's worth. He therefore took no interest in looking into the carriage, but he would have been glad to have gone up to the men and said: "A nice pair of horses you have there. How well they are turned out, and how very smartly you wear your livery."

The equerry, Colonel Stewart, was very simple and direct. He treated Edestone with consideration, but did not forget to let him understand that the King was showing great condescension in inviting him so informally.

"A carriage will be sent for you at four o'clock, and if there is any apparatus and you have men to install it they will be looked after by an officer of the Royal Household who will call in about an hour."

He said that the King wished to have it understood that he was not receiving Edestone in any way as representing the United States of America, since no credentials of any kind had been presented, but simply as a gentleman of science whose achievements warranted the honour.

In the course of their conversation, Edestone referred to his recent unpleasant experience in the spy-driven taxi, and he was assured by Colonel Stewart that he need entertain no further apprehensions on that score as thorough protection would be given him and every single one of these men would be and already were under espionage. Bowing then, the equerry left as quietly as he had come.

Edestone went up to his apartment and issued his instructions to James, his valet.

"Send Mr. Black and Mr. Stanton to me at once. Then fix my bath, send for the barber, and lay out my clothes. I am going out to tea"—he paused— "with His Majesty, King George V. of England," while he enjoyed the effect on his snobbish English servant.

"Mr. Black," he said when his electrician and operating man came in, "will you and Mr. Stanton go to Grosvenor Square and bring over the boxes with the apparatus and films. They will have to be back here by 3:15, as there will be an officer of the Royal Household here at that time. Go with him to Buckingham Palace and install the instrument and screen where he directs you; then wait there until you hear from me."

While he was dressing and being shaved he ran over in his mind what he should say to the King. He knew that either Rockstone or Underhill had engineered this audience, and he wondered whether it foreboded good or evil. At any rate it was progress, and that was all-important.

Colonel Stewart had certainly been most cordial, and the fact that he was to meet the King without the delay of presenting credentials through the American Embassy, rather argued that England felt the necessity for prompt action.

The barber almost cut his ear off when James came to announce the fact than an officer of the Royal Household was downstairs and that Mr. Black and Mr. Stanton had returned from Grosvenor Square with the apparatus and films, and when Edestone stopped him long enough to say through the lather: "Tell Mr. Black that I will be at the Palace and shall want everything in readiness by 4:30 at the latest," the man gave such a start that he almost dropped the shaving mug. He set it down with a bang on the marble washbasin.

"I go," he said. "My nose bleeds. I will send you another barber." And he rushed out of the room.

"What is the matter, James?" exclaimed Edestone indignantly. "Why didn't you insist on their sending up the head barber instead of that fool? Come finish this thing up yourself, I can't wait." Recovering his equanimity he added: "Time flies and the King waits."

James, who in his time had valeted princes, after he had finished shaving him and had turned him out as only a well-trained English valet can, glanced with satisfaction at his work. "I think, sir, when His Majesty sees you, sir, he will ask, sir, who is your tailor, sir. A buttonhole, sir?"

And so with a light step and buoyant spirit the American went down, when word came up that Colonel Stewart had called for him.

"Mr. Edestone," said the Colonel, "I am glad to tell you that your apparatus has arrived safely and has been installed in the Green Drawing Room. The King is deeply interested, and judging from a mysterious pair of curtains in the gallery I think that other members of the Royal Family intend to see this wonderful American with his wonderful invention. As to your friends, the German spies, I made due report of the matter and shall probably have something to tell you later."

It was a beautiful spring day and as Edestone was driven through Berkeley Square, up Piccadilly, and down Grosvenor Place he saw London at its best. Then, as he crossed the park with its beautiful old trees and lake and flower-beds, approaching Buckingham Palace from an entirely different angle than he had ever seen it before, he realized for the first time that it was in the midst of a beautiful sylvan setting. The Buckingham Palace that he knew had always suggested to him one of the Department Buildings in Washington in their efforts to look as much like a royal palace as possible.

When he stopped under a porte-cochère simple little entrance, he felt that he might be making a call at some rich American's country home rather than on the King of England in the middle of London. There were no soldiers and no extraordinary number of servants. He had seen as many and more at some of the houses at Newport. He was shown into a long, low, and rather dark room on the ground floor, where a lot of young officers were lounging about. Colonel Stewart introduced him to several of them and a smarter lot of young fellows Edestone had seldom seen.

He had not been waiting more than fifteen or twenty minutes when he heard Colonel Stewart's name called. His pulse quickened for he knew that this was a signal for him. Colonel Stewart, bowing to the other officers, said to him: "Will you please come with me, Mr. Edestone?"

Passing out of the room and up a short flight of stairs they came to a broad corridor about twenty feet wide which ran around three sides of a court, opening out upon the gardens to the west. They were conducted around two sides of the square and taken into a large reception room in the opposite corner where there were perhaps a dozen officers of high rank, ministers and statesmen, standing about in groups. They spoke in voices scarcely above a whisper and when the door on the left, which evidently led into a still larger room, was opened there was absolute silence.

Colonel Stewart, who up to this time had been quite affable, now seemed suddenly to be caught by the solemnity of the place, and stood like a man at the funeral of his friend.

In one of the groups, Edestone saw Colonel Wyatt, who gave him a little nod of recognition. In a few minutes the door to the larger room opened and Lord Rockstone coming out walked straight up to where he and Colonel Stewart stood.

"His Majesty wishes to waive all form and ceremony, and has ordered me to present you to him at once," he said. But when he saw the cool and matter-of-fact way in which Edestone received this extraordinary announcement his expression said as plainly as words: "These Americans are certainly a remarkable people." He merely bowed to Colonel Stewart, however, and continued: "Will you please come with me," and leading the way to the door, spoke to an attendant who went inside. In about five minutes the man returned, and announced to Lord Rockstone: "His Majesty will receive you."

CHAPTER X
HE MEETS THE KING

The room into which they were shown was large and well-proportioned, but was furnished and decorated in the style of the middle of the nineteenth century—that atrocious period often referred to as the Early Victorian, a term which always calls forth a smile at any assembly of true lovers of art and carries with it the idea of all that is heavy and vulgarly inartistic. But on the whole the room had an air of comfort, flooded as it was with warm sunlight that streamed through the four great windows on the right and those on each side of the fireplace at the opposite end.

Around the large table, sat a gathering of the most distinguished men of the Empire drawn from the Privy Council. They had evidently finished the work of the day, as was shown by the absence of all papers on the table and the precise manner in which the different cabinet ministers had their portfolios neatly closed in front of them. One would say that they had settled down to be amused or bored as the case might be. They looked like a company of well-bred people whose host has just announced that "Professor Bug" will relate some of his experiences among the poisonous orchids of South America, or like a lot of polite though perfectly deaf persons waiting for the music to begin. Some were talking quietly, while others sat perfectly still. The servants were removing writing materials, maps, etc., and a cloud of clerks and undersecretaries were being swallowed up by a door in a corner of the room.

At the end of the table opposite the door through which Edestone had entered, sat the King. He looked very small as he sat perfectly still, his hands resting listlessly on the arms of his great carved chair of black walnut picked out with gold. His face with its reddish beard, now growing grey, bore an expression of deep sadness, almost of melancholia. His expression became more animated, however, when Edestone entered, and he sat up and looked straight at the American as he stood at the other end of the table.

"Your Majesty," Lord Rockstone bowed, "I beg to be allowed to present to you Mr. John Fulton Edestone of New York of the United States of America."

The King rose and, as his great chair was drawn back, walked to the nearest window and stood while Rockstone brought Edestone up to him. Extending his hand he said:

"Mr. Edestone, Mr. Underhill tells me that you are from New York. It has been a source of great regret to me that I have never been able to visit your wonderful country. I recall very distinctly, though, a stay of several weeks that I made in Bermuda, and of the many charming Americans whom I met there at that time. I was, then, the Duke of York," he sighed.

His manner was cordial and he seemed to wish to put Edestone at ease, assuming with him an air rather less formal than he would have shown toward one of his own subjects of the middle class—the one great class to which the nobility, gentry, and servants of England assign all Americans, although the first two often try hard to conceal this while the last seem to fear that the Americans may forget it.

"I am rather surprised to find you so young a man after hearing of your wonderful achievements in science," the King went on, adding with rather a sad smile: "It seems a pity to take you from some charming English girl with whom you might be having tea this beautiful spring afternoon and bring you to this old barracks to discuss instruments of death and destruction." And his face seemed very old.

After a pause he turned to Rockstone and directing him to introduce Edestone he went back to his seat and with a slight gesture ordered the rest to resume their places. He fixed his eyes on Edestone, who had been taken back to the other end of the table where he stood perfectly still. Not once had the American spoken since coming into the room. He had acknowledged the King's great kindness with a bow which showed plainer than words in what deep respect he held the head of the great English-speaking race. This seemed to have made a good impression on some of the older men, who up to this time had not deigned to look in his direction. One of the younger men murmured in an undertone: "Young-looking chap to have kicked up such a rumpus, isn't he? He has deuced good manners for an American."

Meanwhile Lord Rockstone, bowing to the King and then to the rest of the company, was proceeding with the introduction, briefly explaining that Mr. Edestone had requested to be allowed to appear before His Majesty and explain certain inventions which he claimed to have made.

The King, however, seeming determined to make it as easy as possible for the American, chose to supplement this formality.

"Mr. Edestone," he said with a smile, "since this meeting is to be, as you say in America, 'just a gentlemen's meeting,' you may sit down while you tell us about your wonderful discovery."

Edestone acknowledged the courtesy with a slight bow but declined. "Your Majesty, with your kind permission, I should prefer to stand," and, then, without the slightest sign of embarrassment, he continued:

"I thank Your Majesty for your kindness. I will as briefly as I can explain that to which you have so graciously referred as my wonderful discovery, but before doing this, I beg to be allowed to set forth to you my position relative to Your Majesty and Your Majesty's subjects. Should I in my enthusiasm at any time violate any of the established rules of court etiquette, please always remember that it is due to my ignorance and not to any lack of deep and sincere respect or that affection which I and all true Anglo-Saxons have for your person as representing the head of that great people and the King of 'Old England.'"

A thrill went through the room. The King was evidently affected. One old gentleman, who up to this time had taken absolutely no notice of Edestone, turned quickly and looking sharply at him through his large eyeglasses, said: "Hear! Hear!"

The speaker acknowledged this and then proceeded. "I am an American and I am proud of it. Not because of the great power and wealth of my country, nor of its hundred and odd millions of people made up of the nations of the earth, the sweepings of Europe, the overflow of Asia, and the bag of the slave-hunter of Africa, which centuries will amalgamate into a *cafe au lait* conglomerate, but because I am proud of that small group of Anglo-Saxons who, under the influence of the free air of our great country, have developed such strength that they have up to this time put the stamp of England upon all who have come in contact with them. And while it is not my intention to sell my invention to England, I will give you my word that it shall never be used except for the benefit of the English-speaking people."

He then raised his right hand as he added very slowly and distinctly: "In your presence and that of Almighty God, I dedicate my life to my people, the Anglo-Saxons!"

This was received with a general murmur of applause, although there were a few dark-skinned gentlemen with curly beards and large noses who seemed uncomfortable. Edestone had caught that group of unemotional men and against their will had swept them along with him, and it was only with an effort that some of the younger men could refrain from giving him three cheers.

Underhill, who was smiling and gesticulating at Rockstone and Graves, applauded violently, while the King made no effort to hide his pleasure. There was something about this man that left in no one's mind any doubt of his sincerity, and on looking at him they felt that he was not the kind of a man who would so solemnly and in the presence of the King and all of the greatest men of England dedicate his life to a purpose if he did not know that therein lay a real gift to mankind. His sublime confidence was as convincing as his simplicity was reassuring.

Seeing that the ice was broken he turned now to the serious business of the afternoon.

"Mr. President," he commenced, "now that I have shown you how I stand on international politics, I shall proceed——"

He was astonished to see the King put his head back and laugh, while the rest, made bold by the royal example, joined in heartily.

The King seeing that Edestone was innocent of any mistake and was blankly searching for an explanation of their mirth leaned forward and not altogether lightly said:

"The King of England accepts the Presidency of the Anglo-Saxon people!"

"I beg Your Majesty's pardon. I am sorry. I have forgotten myself so soon: what shall I do when I get into the intricacies of mathematics, physics, and mechanics to explain to you my invention?"

"Mr. Edestone," said the King, "we understand perfectly. Go on."

Recovering himself quickly and assuming a thoroughly businesslike air, snapping out his facts with precision, speaking rapidly without notes or memoranda, he said:

"The physical properties of electrons form the basis of my invention, and it cannot be understood except by those who have studied the electron theory of matter, according to which theory the electron or corpuscle is the smallest particle of matter that had, up to my discovery, been isolated. They are present in a free condition in metallic conductors. Each electron carries an electric charge of electrostatic units and produces a magnetic field in a plane perpendicular to the direction of its motion. This brings us to the atom, which may be described as a number of electrons positive and negative in stable equilibrium, this condition being brought about by the mutual repulsion of the like and attraction for the opposite electrification so arranged as to nullify each other. Having thus established the law of the equilibrium of electrons, corpuscles, atoms, and molecules, I found that the same law applies to the equilibrium of our solar system, and, in fact, of the universe, and, by the elimination of either the positive or the negative electron, this equilibrium is altered or destroyed.

"I then sought to nullify the attraction of gravity by changing the electrical condition of the electrons of an object, which until that time was attracted by the earth, as is shown by the formula, *V equals the square root of (s times 2g)* for falling bodies, and by using the formula *Y equals the square root of mx divided by (pi times g)* I found— —"

But at this point he was interrupted by the King, who said, with a gesture of supplication: "Please! Please! Mr. Edestone do not go so deeply into science, for, for my part, I regret to say that it would be entirely lost on me. Save that for my men of science," and he waved his hand in the direction of his rough and rugged old Sea Lord, Admiral Sir Wm. Brown. "Just tell us what you have accomplished and then show us some of these marvellous things that Mr. Underhill has told us you can do. Besides, I understand that you are to show us moving pictures of the actual working of your machine, boat, or whatever it is."

The inventor was disappointed; for he had wished to set all minds at rest and to establish the fact that he was no trickster but a scientist. With a deprecating smile he said: "As Your Majesty pleases."

Then, without the slightest sign of condescension, and selecting with the greatest care only words that the man in the street could understand, he proceeded with his exposition.

"I have discovered that gravitation is due to the attraction that two bodies in different electrical condition have for each other, and that by changing the condition of one of these bodies so that they are both in the same electrical condition this attraction no longer exists. I have also discovered that the earth is, so to speak, as far as the laws of gravity are concerned, in a state of what we might call for lack of a better name, 'positive electrical condition,' and that all objects on the earth, as long as they are not in contact with it, are in what we may call 'negative electrical condition.' These remain in this condition so long as they are not in actual electrical contact with the earth and are separated from it by a non-conducting medium such as the atmosphere, glass, hard rubber, etc., and are attracted by it, as is shown by the formulae which I will gladly explain to your gentlemen of science." And he turned with a bow to Admiral Sir William Brown, who was leaning across the table frowning at him and who with his scrubbing-brush hair, long upper lip, and heavy brows looked more like a Rocky Mountain goat than ever.

"I have invented an instrument," continued Edestone, "which I call a *Deionizer*. With this, so far as regards any phenomena of which we are conscious, I am able to change the electrical condition of an object, provided this object is insulated from electrical contact with the earth. That is, I can change it from the so-called minus condition, which is attracted by the earth, to the plus condition, which being the same condition as the earth, is therefore not attracted by it. The object in that state can be said to have no weight, although frankly for some reason which I have not yet discovered it does not lose its inertia against motion in any direction relative to the earth."

He then took from his pocket the leather case which Underhill readily recognized, and, turning to Lord Rockstone, he said with a slightly quizzical expression:

"If your Lordship will be so kind as to stand on a glass plate or block of hard rubber I can with this little instrument which I have in my hand alter your electrical condition from its present minus to that of plus. I can then place you anywhere in this room and keep you there as long as you do not come in contact with any object that, electrically speaking, is in contact with the earth."

This caused Lord Rockstone to give a grim but thoroughly good-natured smile, and Edestone, feeling as if he had somewhat settled scores with the "Hero of the Nile," continued: "As a less valuable object than one of the most brilliant stars in Great Britain's crown will answer my purpose just as well, may I ask that one of the servants fetch the glass plate that was brought to the Palace this afternoon with my apparatus."

The glass plate having been brought in by a flunkey, he repeated the experiment with which he had so astonished Underhill at the Admiralty, using the flunkey however in place of the cannon ball, and leaving the poor unfortunate creature suspended in mid-air while he himself replied to the many questions that were put to him.

Finally he touched the man's hand, and taking the shock through his own body let him drop to the floor. The fellow remained there in an almost fainting condition, but, recovering and finding that he had sustained no injuries except to his dignity, which in his state of great excitement had fallen away from him, he rushed out of the room without asking for or receiving permission to do so. His panic-stricken exit would at any other time have been most amusing, but the audience just then was in no humour for levity.

Edestone next repeated the same experiment, utilizing different small objects that were handed to him by the gentlemen about the table, and soon had suspended above the glass plate an assortment of pocket-knives, watches, and a glass of water, while he chatted with those who were nearest to him, and handed to the scientific members of the council diagrams and mathematical formulae which he hastily scribbled on bits of paper.

CHAPTER XI
THE DEIONIZER

After the different objects had been returned to their respective owners, the King by a slight gesture called the meeting to order, for all had left their seats and were crowding around Edestone in what, for Englishmen, was a state of violent excitement. Even the more self-contained were unable to conceal the fact that they were impressed by these experiments as well as by the quiet dignity of this young man. They seemed to realize that he had them figuratively if not literally in the palm of his hand. The dullest and least imaginative saw the endless possibilities in the application of his discovery to the arts and sciences. During all of this time the young American had kept himself under perfect control and had answered all questions in the most deferential and respectful manner; and now, having received from the King permission to continue, he went on:

"The secret of my discovery lies in this little instrument, the construction of which is known only to myself. The application of this newly-discovered principle can be best understood by viewing my moving pictures, which show it in actual operation. Now, with your most kind permission I should like to inspect my apparatus to see that everything is all right."

And then, as if some sudden impulse which pleased him had flashed across his mind, like the big healthy-minded boy that he was, and with an irresistible smile on his face, he dropped into a more familiar tone than he had allowed himself up to this time.

"And to show you what I think of Englishmen," he said, "I will leave this Deionizer in your keeping until I return. A gentle tap or two on that hard-rubber shell and you will know its secret." He laid the instrument with its little case beside it on the table in front of the King and left the room escorted by a member of the Royal Family, young Prince George of Windthorst, who insisted upon acting as his guide to the Green Drawing Room.

As the door closed upon them, the King rose, saying as he did so, "Please remain seated." He walked into one of the windows and stood for some minutes looking out over the park. Whatever it was that was passing through his mind, it was not a pleasant thought, as was shown by his hands, which were clasped behind his back so tightly that the fingers were perfectly white; and the veins of his neck swelled, while the muscles of his jaws were firmly set. No one dared to move. The silence in the room was so intense that the men about the table, as if caught by a spell, sat with unfinished gestures, like the figures in a moving picture when the film catches. The clock on the mantel seemed suddenly to have waked up and to be trying by its loud ticking to fool itself into thinking that it had been ticking all the time. When the time came for it to strike five o'clock, it went at it with such resounding vim that Admiral Sir William Brown, who had served his apprenticeship in the turrets, seemed to think that he had better open his mouth to save his ear-drums.

"War is war! All is fair! War is war! All is fair!" it seemed to say.

The King finally turned, and walking back to the table picked up the innocent-looking instrument. He turned it over and over in his hand and then slowly and carefully wound the platinum wires about it as a boy winds a top and placed it back into its leather case. As he put it down on the table, he said, almost as if to himself:

"We have come today to one of the turning points in the history of the world. This is a remarkable man."

After a moment, he turned to Underhill: "I think you have done your country a great service today in averting what might have been an appalling catastrophe. Do you not agree with me, Sir Egbert?" he glanced toward the Minister of Foreign Affairs.

"I do, Sire," the minister acquiesced thoughtfully. "If this man represents the United States of America, it will not be long before she will insist that this war be brought to an end upon her own terms, and it would have been almost suicidal on our part to antagonize him. She doubtless controls this instrument whose practical application will probably be shown us by his pictures."

"But what this man has just said to you, Sire," suggested Underhill, "does not seem to bear out the idea that he is acting under instructions from the present State Department at Washington."

"If it please Your Majesty," interposed one of the statesmen of the old school, "should we not make some formal representation to the United States of America before this man be allowed to go to Berlin?"

"I should not approve of that," dissented the King. "In the first place, as far as we know, Mr. Edestone may have already communicated with Berlin, Paris, and Petrograd. I do not think he would put himself so completely in our power if he thought he was risking the destruction of his entire scheme."

"I believe, Your Majesty," said another sneeringly, "that this melodramatic exit is just another Yankee bluff. You will probably find in looking into it that the fellow has palmed the real instrument and has forced this one on us by clever sleight of hand."

"I disagree with you entirely," said the King, frowning and bringing his hand down on the table as if to put an end to the discussion. "I believe this man to be a gentleman and a thoroughly good sportsman."

CHAPTER XII
FIRST SHOW OF FORCE

On entering the room, when he returned, Edestone, although he was aware that the King had been notified and the attendants been given orders to admit him, did not advance, but took his stand near the door, looking neither to the right nor to the left. He permitted the young Prince, his escort, who had discovered that they had many friends in common, and whose sister it was that had been his fellow-passenger on the *Ivernia*, to inform His Majesty that everything was in readiness for the exhibition of the moving pictures.

The King immediately beckoned the inventor forward and, picking up the little instrument from the table, thrust it into Edestone's hands, almost with an air of relief.

"We appreciate the compliment you have paid us in believing that we still play fair." There was in both his tone and action a touch of the bluff heartiness of the naval officer, which was natural to him, and showed that he had thrown off all restraint. "But do not, I beg of you, do this again, even in England. These are desperate times; and nations, like men, when fighting for their very existence, are quite apt to forget their finer scruples.

"My cousin in Berlin, I am convinced," and there was perhaps a hint of warning in his smile, "would give the souls of half his people to know what that little box contains; and, in his realm, it is the religion of some of his benighted subjects to give him what he wants."

Bowing slightly, Edestone took the little case, and, without even looking at it, slipped it carelessly into the inside pocket of his coat.

"I knew that Your Majesty would understand me," he said in a tone intended for the Royal ear alone, and with more emotion than he had yet displayed. As he spoke, too, he lifted his hand in obedience to an involuntary and apparently irresistible impulse.

The King met him more than half-way. Reaching out, he grasped the extended hand in his own, and standing thus the two men looked straight into each other's eyes.

The suppressed excitement which the scene created was so intense that some of the spectators seemed to be suffering actual pain; and when, after a fraction of a moment which seemed an age, the King released the American's hand and spoke, there was an audible sigh of relief that pervaded the entire room.

"We will now look at the pictures," said His Majesty simply, and, leading the way, he set out in the direction of the Green Drawing Room.

Edestone fell back and bowed respectfully in acknowledgment of the pleasant glances which were thrown in his direction, as the Lords, Generals, Admirals, and Ministers of State took their places in line, clinging with an almost frantic tenacity, in response to the teachings of the Catechism of the English Church, to their position "in that state of life unto which it had pleased God to call" them.

Thoroughly amused at the situation which compelled him to bring up the rear of the procession like the piano-tuner or the gas-man, Edestone marched along at the side of an attendant in livery, who evidently looked upon him as a clever vaudeville artist that had been brought in to entertain the company. He told the visitor, with a broad grin, that he had frightened the other flunkey almost out of his wits with his magic tricks. Edestone, his sense of humour aroused, thereupon gravely offered to give a show in the servants' hall at two shillings a head, half the receipts to be donated to the Red Cross, provided he was given a guarantee of ten pounds; and when the fellow promised to consider the proposal, pretended carefully to take down his name.

The King, who, in the meantime, seemed to be in a sort of brown-study, passed down the corridor with the long file of dignitaries following him in order of precedence. But when His Majesty reached the Green Drawing Room and, looking around, saw nothing of the American, he gave a slight frown of annoyance. Immediately he directed that Edestone be brought up and placed in a chair near himself, while the attendants drew the curtains and extinguished the lights.

After the room had been made perfectly dark, and the buzzing of the cinematograph in its temporary cabinet indicated that everything was in readiness, Edestone's operator, in response to a word from his employer, threw upon the screen two or three portraits of the King and various members of the Royal Family. This was not only by way of compliment, but also to give assurance that the machine was in proper working order. Edestone proposed to run no chances of a bungling or incomplete presentation of his pictures.

Satisfied at length, he rose and faced about toward his audience.

"Ladies and Gentlemen," he said, after addressing the King,—for from the gallery had come sounds which showed that, as Colonel Stewart had suggested, some of the ladies of the Court were taking an interest in the exhibition,—"I shall not trouble you to listen to a long, scientific discourse on the theory of my discovery, nor how I have made practical application of it. I shall simply throw the pictures on the screen, letting them speak for themselves; and then, with His Majesty's kind permission, shall be glad to answer any questions that may be put to me. The first picture I shall show you is one of my workshop in New York."

There appeared on the screen a dark, somewhat indistinct interior, which seemed to have been photographed from high up and looking down through a long, shed-like building lighted from the roof. The immense height of this roof was not at first apparent until it was compared with the pigmy-like figures of the workmen who were busily engaged about a great, black, cigar-shaped object, which had the general appearance of a Zeppelin. In the dim light, there was nothing about its aspect to distinguish it from the latest models of the German air-ship, save that it seemed to be of heavier construction, as shown by the great difficulty with which the men were moving it toward the farther end of the shed, which was entirely open.

"I would especially call your attention to the track upon which moves the cradle that carries the large black object in the centre of the picture," said Edestone. "The tires are made of hard rubber, and the rails which are of steel rest on glass plates attached to each of the tires. Thus, any object placed in the cradle becomes absolutely insulated, and has no electrical connection with the earth, which, as I have explained, are the requisite conditions to permit of 'Deionizing' by the use of an instrument similar to the one I have in my pocket. Of course, though in actual operation we use a much larger 'Deionizer' than the little model I have shown you, and run it with a hundred horse-power motor, instead of with a small spring and watchworks. This track and cradle at which you are looking, although they weigh many tons, can be easily taken apart and transported in sections, as I stand ready to demonstrate."

The film ended as he finished, and for a moment the screen was blank; then with a little splutter from the cabinet, another picture appeared.

This was of a great open space, the most desolate and lonely stretch of country that could well be imagined, a broad, open plain that stretched on for miles and miles, perfectly flat, treeless and uninhabited. The wind apparently was blowing violently, judging from the way it tossed Edestone's hair about as, hatless, he walked back and forth in the near foreground, shading his eyes from the sun with his hand while he looked into the lens and called his directions to the man who was working the camera.

"That disreputable-looking individual is myself," he confessed. "My hat had blown away, a circumstance quite inconvenient at the time, but not without a certain element of present interest, as showing that a high wind was blowing at that time."

Behind him in the middle distance was a track and cradle similar to the one shown in the first picture. The machine in the cabinet buzzed, and clicked, and made a noise like that of a small boy rattling a stick along a picket fence. A draught from some open window blowing against the linen screen caused the flat, deserted plain to undulate like the waves of the sea. The horizon bobbed up and down, showing first a great expanse of sky, and then the foreground ran up to infinity. The cradle was seen first at the right, and then at the left of the picture. The clouds in the sky kept jumping about, as if the operator was trying to follow some object aloft, but was unable to get it into the field of his camera.

The audience began to grow impatient. Had the apparatus got out of order, they wondered, and were they to be cheated of the promised sensation? But just then the screen steadied, and there appeared in the upper left-hand corner of the picture a faint, far-away dot which gradually assumed the form of a dirigible. Across the desolate landscape it sailed, growing more and more distinct as it drew nearer. It circled, turning first to the right and then to the left, rising and descending, as if responding willingly to the touch of its unseen pilot, until with a majestic swoop it hovered like a great bird exactly over the cradle, and came to a standstill.

To those among the spectators who had witnessed the evolutions of the great battleships of the air over Lake Constance, there was nothing notable about either the vessel or its performance, except that it seemed larger, more solid, and had four great smoke stacks. In the gale which was blowing, the volumes of inky smoke which poured from the four great funnels were tossed about and flung away like long, streaming ribbons; yet the ship itself was as steady as a great ocean liner on a summer sea.

On closer inspection, too, it was seen that on the upper side of the craft there was a platform or deck running its full length, where men were working away like sailors on a man-of-war, and from portholes and turrets protruded great black things which looked like the muzzles of guns.

All at once, as if acting under an order from within, these were trained on the spectators and simultaneously discharged, belching out great rings of smoke. There was a stifled scream from the gallery at this, but immediately the room grew quiet again, and the audience sat as if spellbound awaiting further developments. A small door in the starboard side now opened, and the figure of a man came running down a gangway to a platform suspended under the ship, where, silhouetted against the sky, he occupied himself in signalling to some one on the ground. He was joined from time to time by others of the crew as the vessel settled slowly toward the earth.

When it was about one hundred and fifty feet above the cradle, Edestone was seen to walk out with a megaphone in his hand, and through it communicate instructions to the man on the bridge, in evident obedience to which the airship settled still lower, until it was not more than twenty feet above the top of the cradle.

A ladder having then been lowered to Edestone, he climbed up it, ascended the gangway, and disappeared into the interior of the great cigar-shaped object, it all the time remaining absolutely stationary. But he was not long lost to view. In a few minutes he re-appeared on the top deck and a man by his side energetically waved a large flag.

And as the two stood there, the airship began to move.

Slowly at first, but gradually gaining momentum, it soared away across the wastes, and soon was lost to sight.

There was a moment after that when the room was dark, while horizontal streaks of light chased each other from bottom to top across the screen, and disappeared into the darkness from which they had come.

Another picture followed, taken from the same viewpoint as the last.

"Here she comes!" cried Edestone, seeming to forget for the moment where he was, as a small speck which represented the approaching airship disclosed itself. "This time in the upper right-hand corner of the picture. See! I am on board, and I am driving her at one hundred and ten miles." And he followed with his pointer the swift course of the vessel, as it shot down the screen like a great comet, leaving a long tail of smoke behind it. To the overwrought nerves of the audience, the buzz and splutter of the moving-picture machine seemed to increase in volume, and thus lend a semblance of reality to the monster as it swept nearer and nearer.

Straight for the camera it was headed, grim, threatening, irresistible, as if it were preparing to rush out of the screen and destroy Buckingham Palace. The spectators with difficulty kept their seats, and when the formidable thing dashed by and disappeared at the side of the picture, they settled back in their chairs with an unmistakable sigh of relief.

It appeared again, after making a great circle, returning slowly now, and dropping lightly as a feather to the cradle, where it remained perfectly still, while the black smoke enveloped it in a veil of mystery.

The machine in the cabinet stopped, and some one was heard to say in a loud whisper, "Lights!" Admiral Brown was the first of the assembly to recover. He sprang to his feet and like a wounded old lion at bay stood glaring at Edestone. His rugged weather-beaten face convulsed with suppressed rage, which but for the presence of the King would have exploded upon Edestone after the manner of the old-fashioned sea-dog that he was, but holding himself in check he said loudly and challengingly:

"If there is no objection I will ask the young man to repeat the last picture, and I would also like to inquire with what material the framework of this ship is covered, and what is the calibre of those large guns—if they are guns?"

"Will you please be so kind as to answer the Admiral's questions, Mr. Edestone?" said the King.

"The material which I used through her entire length of 907 feet, both top and bottom, is Harveyized steel, six feet thick; and the largest gun is sixteen inches," replied Edestone slowly, enjoying the look of blank amazement which spread over the Admiral's face as he dropped back into his chair gasping and mopping his brow.

"This is the end of everything. I wish I had never lived to see the day!" The old sailor sat like a man who had seen a vision so appalling that it robbed him of his reason.

CHAPTER XIII
"THE KING IS DEAD; LONG LIVE THE KING!"

The King, of all the company, seemed to be the only one who had remained perfectly cool. He was like a man who realizing the gravity of the situation yet had nerved himself to meet it.

"Mr. Edestone," he said, as if speaking to one of his own naval officers, "you will please show the last two pictures again, and for the benefit of Admiral Brown you might give us some further details in regard to the ship's equipment and armament. May I also ask you where these pictures were taken?"

"On the flat plains in the centre of the island of Newfoundland," Edestone informed him, "between the White Bear River and the east branch of the Salmon, and from fifty to seventy-five miles from the seacoast on the south. If Your Majesty will look into the middle distance when the second picture is again thrown on the screen you will see some small, dark objects; these are one of those immense herds of caribou, which happen to be moving south over this vast barren at the time of year that these pictures were taken—that is, in October."

He observed that the face of the King took on an expression blended partly of astonishment and partly of resentment when he mentioned the name of one of the Colonial possessions of the Empire, and hastened to add:

"You will find, Sire, if you inquire of the Governor of that Province that I was there with the full knowledge and consent of Your Majesty's Government to carry on certain scientific experiments. I selected this deserted spot, so far removed from all human habitation, because there I should not be disturbed. Until I showed these pictures here today no one outside of my own men knew the nature of these experiments. The guns were loaded with nothing more harmful than several hundred pounds of black powder to produce the display of force which you have just seen. I will admit," he granted with a smile, "that if the newspapers had got word of what was going on there they might have made some excitement; I can assure you, however, that no act of mine could be construed even by our most susceptible and timid State Department as a violation of neutrality."

"But where is your ship now?" asked the King, while the rest of the company held their breath, awaiting the answer.

"That, Your Majesty, for reasons of state, I regret I cannot at this time tell you, but you have my word and that of our Secretary that wherever she may be, her mission is one of peace."

"Peace!" snorted Admiral Brown. "With a six-foot armour-belt and sixteen-inch guns! It is a ship of war, Your Majesty. We have the right to demand whether or not it is now on or over British soil, and if it is, to make such representations to the United States Government as will cause her to withdraw it at once and apologize for having violated the dignity of Great Britain."

"And if they should refuse, Sir William," asked the King, with a weary smile, "would you undertake to drive it off?

"No, Admiral," he continued, "up to this time we have no official knowledge of this airship's existence. Until we have, we will take Mr. Edestone's assurance that his own and his country's intentions to us are friendly."

A wave of hot indignation had swept over the entire assembly, and it was with some difficulty that the King was able to restore order.

"Please continue with your pictures, Mr. Edestone," he said in a tone of authority.

The lights again went out, the machine in the cabinet began to turn, and as the dramatic scene was re-enacted before them his audience sat in perfect silence while Edestone, as though he were recounting the simplest and most ordinary facts, gave out the following information:

"This ship has a length over all of 907 feet. Its beam is 90 feet. Its greatest circular dimension is described with a radius of 48 feet. She would weigh, loaded with ammunition, fuel, provisions, and crew, if brought in contact with the earth, 40,000 tons. Her weight as she travels, after making allowance for the air displacement is generally kept at about 3000 tons, which automatically adjusts itself to the density of the surrounding atmosphere, but can be reduced to nothing at pleasure. Its full speed has never been reached. This is simply a matter of oil consumption; I have had her up to 180 miles. Her steaming radius is about 50,000 miles, depending upon the speed. She carries twelve 16-inch guns, twenty-two 6-inch guns, sixteen 4-inch anti-aircraft guns, eight 3-pounders, four rapid-fire guns, six aerial torpedo tubes, and six bomb droppers, which can simultaneously discharge tons of explosives. She has a complement of 1400 officers and men. She required three years and eight months to build at a cost of $10,000,000. In action her entire ship's company is protected by at least six feet of steel, and there is no gun known that can pierce her protection around the vital parts. As you have seen, she can approach to within a few feet of the surface and remain perfectly stationary in that position as long as she is not brought in electrical contact with the earth."

The machine in the cabinet had stopped. As the lights were again turned on, Edestone, glancing in the direction of the gallery and seeing that there was no one there, bowed merely to the company before him. "I thank Your Majesty, Lords, and Gentlemen for your very kind attention," he said. He then stood quietly, waiting respectfully for the King to speak.

"Mr. Edestone," said the King as he rose, "you have certainly given us a most instructive afternoon, and you must be exhausted after your efforts." He turned to Colonel Stewart, "Please insist upon Mr. Edestone taking some refreshments before he leaves Buckingham Palace."

He grasped the inventor firmly by the hand. "Good-bye, Mr. Edestone. I shall probably not see you again," and bowing to the rest of the company he left the room deep in conversation with Sir Egbert Graves.

Edestone immediately became the centre of attraction.

"The King is dead; long live the King!" expresses the eagerness with which man adapts himself to a new order of things. The older men were stunned and seemed unable to throw off the gloom that had settled upon them. They bowed to the inevitable fall of the old and its replacement by the new. They were not buoyed up by the elasticity and confidence of youth; they seemed to realize that their race was run and that it were better that they step aside and give to younger men the task of solving a new problem in a new way. They sat perfectly still with dejected faces that seemed to see only dissolution.

The younger men were quicker to recover, and as they felt the old foundations crumbling under their feet, saw visions of a new and greater edifice. They gloried in the development of the age as they did in their own strength to keep abreast of it, and rushed to meet progress, to join it, and to become one with it. They did not stop to think what the future might have in store for them, but seemed to be intoxicated by its possibilities.

Crowding around Edestone they probed him with questions which he answered with the greatest patience and in the most modest, quiet, and dignified manner. When asked a question almost childish in its simplicity, he appeared to acknowledge the compliment in the assumption that he knew the answer, and gave it with the same precision as one which called for the most complicated mathematical calculation and reference to the most intricate formulae of the laws of mechanics and physics. He was rescued and borne away by Colonel Stewart who announced that, acting under His Majesty's order, he was obliged to give him some refreshments, whether he wanted them or not, and if he did not come at once to his quarters and have a drink he would be forced to order out the Guards. Drawing him aside the Colonel whispered, "I must see you alone before you leave the Palace."

Edestone turned and slowly left the room, bowing to each of the separate groups.

"Now," said Colonel Stewart, "come to my quarters first, as I have something rather confidential to tell you. You can come back and join the others afterward, if you care to."

When they were comfortably seated in the Colonel's private apartments, and had provided themselves with drinks and cigars, the equerry leaned toward his charge a trifle impressively.

"Mr. Edestone," he said, "you do not look like a chap who would lose his nerve if he suddenly found himself in a position that was more or less dangerous. Indeed I rather gather that you are like one of your distinguished Admirals—ready at all times for a fight or a frolic."

Edestone smiled.

"The facts are, Mr. Edestone, that you are in a pretty ticklish position, and had not Mr. Underhill notified Scotland Yard when he did, I do not know what might have happened. These German spies who have been following you all day are well known to them, and when our men picked you up, which was when you left the Admiralty and were talking to the taxi-chauffeur, they were convinced that you were in real danger. Then when you were directed to the German restaurant and afterward left it in the taxicab with this man Smith they had your cab followed, at the same time notifying Mr. Underhill, and covering your hotel."

"This is most interesting," said Edestone; "but if the business of these men is known why are they not arrested?"

"Mr. Edestone," said Colonel Stewart, "we Englishmen are not credited with any sense by our friends the enemy, and relying upon our supposed stupidity their work, which they take so much pride in, is by no means as secret as they suppose it to be. There have been in London thousands of what the Germans term 'fixed posts.' These are men who have established places of business and have lived in the community from ten to fifteen years. They receive a salary from the German Government running from two pounds to four pounds a month and all incurred expenses. The 'fixed post' men report to men higher up, who, in turn, report to the Diplomatic Service. Under them, too, are all of the patriotic emigrants from Germany, who act as spies without being conscious of the fact that they are doing so. These receive no pay for bringing in the bits of scandal or other information which is all carefully noted and kept on file in Berlin under a system of card indexes.

"That man Munchinger who keeps the restaurant where you lunched, and the barber Hottenroth at your hotel, are both of them 'fixed post' men. This American architect was new and had not been quite placed as yet. The chauffeur also seems to be one of them, although he is entirely unknown to Scotland Yard.

"When you discharged your first taxi and took another, Smith and the chauffeur spy followed you until they were frightened off by seeing my carriage with the royal livery in front of your hotel. They drove off then with such a rush that the chauffeur must have lost control of his car, for it plunged into the Thames with Smith inside it, and before he could be reached and rescued he was drowned. The chauffeur was either drowned or ran away, as nothing has been seen of him since."

Edestone rose, his face stern as he learned the news of Smith's fate. "Colonel Stewart," he declared sharply, "that poor devil was murdered." And to support his accusation he told briefly of Smith's confession and behaviour in the cab.

The Colonel bowed. "I shall see that these facts are turned over to the authorities," he said, "but at present I am more concerned in regard to you. These men are fanatics, you must understand, whose faith teaches them to do anything that is for the benefit of the Fatherland. We know most of them. We do not arrest them because they are more useful to us as they are. As soon as one is arrested he is immediately replaced by another, and it takes some little time before we can pick up the new one. We have received reports to the effect that a small army of them have been around Buckingham Palace all afternoon, as well as at your hotel; so it is evident that Smith's story was no fancy and that these men are after you in desperate earnest. Would you mind telling me, Mr. Edestone, what are your plans for the future?"

"Not at all. My movements are extremely simple. I shall return to my hotel, where I expect to remain until I retire. A friend of mine, an American, Mr. Rebener, whom I have known for a great many years, will dine with me there this evening."

"An old friend of yours you say?" The Colonel's eyes narrowed slightly.

"Yes," replied Edestone. "I have known him for fifteen years." For reasons of his own he had made it a point not to include Rebener's name among those mentioned by Smith in his confession, nor did he refer to it now.

Colonel Stewart hesitated a moment. "Of course, Mr. Edestone," he said finally, "you Americans are neutrals and are at liberty to select your friends where you please, but my advice to you would be not to take London as the place to entertain people with German names. You will probably understand that we cannot take any chances."

"I have known Mr. Rebener," repeated Edestone, "for years. He is one of our most prominent men, and I am confident that he would not lend himself to any of these Middle-Age methods."

"You can never tell," said Colonel Stewart darkly. "Germany holds out to the faithful the promise of great rewards at the end of this war, which she has convinced them cannot fail to end successfully for her."

"No," the American insisted stubbornly. "Mr. Rebener might readily sell to Germany a few million dollars' worth of munitions of war, and likewise tell his friend, Count Bernstoff, anything that he might hear. I will even go so far as to say that he might make an especial effort to pick up bits of gossip here in London; and he will almost certainly endeavour to use his influence with me in favour of Germany. But that he would take part in a plot to kill, kidnap, or rob me is incredible."

"I see you are determined to have your own way, Mr. Edestone," the Colonel smiled, "so I come now to the most difficult part of my mission. What do you propose to do with that instrument which you now carry so carelessly in your coat pocket? You can readily understand that it is not safe in your hotel, or, in fact, at hardly any other place in London outside of the vaults of the Bank of England. We are put in the delicate position of having to protect it without having the privilege of asking that it be put in our charge."

"I appreciate all that you say and have considered destroying it, but have now come to the conclusion to keep it always with me, for, after all that you tell me, I think that I am in pretty safe hands in London."

"But think, my dear fellow," cried the Colonel jumping up, "what might happen if this thing falls into the hands of the Germans! To prevent that it would be my duty to shoot you on the spot."

"Good work! Right-o!" laughed Edestone. "You have my permission to shoot whenever it goes to the Germans. Don't worry. They'll not murder and rob me in the middle of dear old London with all your fellows about, and I do not expect to leave the hotel tonight."

CHAPTER XIV
THE ROYAL TEA-TABLE

As Edestone and Colonel Stewart were leaving the Palace, they were met by the young Prince of the Blood, who seemed bent upon renewing his acquaintance with his American friend.

"I say, Edestone," he greeted him, "you really must not leave before giving me an opportunity of presenting you to some of the ladies of the Court. You are the lion of the day and they are anxious to meet you. My sister, Princess Billy, is almost in tears and hysterical. She insisted upon seeing your pictures because she said that you were an old friend of hers she had met on the steamer coming over from America."

Accepting, Edestone smiled as he thought of the undignified manner of their meeting, and was taken in charge by the young man.

Colonel Stewart made his excuses when the invitation was extended to him, saying: "Mr. Edestone, I shall wait for you in the Guards' Room," and, turning to the young man, he added: "I deliver him into your hands, and I hold you responsible for his valuable person which must be delivered to me there."

Edestone was then taken in charge by the young Prince, who proudly bore him off to deliver him into the hands of the ladies. He was rather bored with the idea, and would have preferred to have gone directly to his hotel, as he had had an eventful day and he did not feel in the humour for the small talk of the tea-table.

He was taken into one of the smaller rooms where several ladies and young officers in khaki were just finishing their tea. The atmosphere of the room was offensively heavy with the strong odour of iodoform. His pity was aroused when he suddenly realized that almost every man in the room bore the unmistakable mark of service in the trenches. It was the first time that he had been brought violently into contact with the far-reaching and horrible devastation of this cruel war. One pitiful figure, a young man of about twenty-two who sat apart from the rest, so affected him that he scarcely recovered himself in time to acknowledge the great kindness of the Duchess of Windthorst, who was receiving him in the most gracious manner. This boy was totally blind. Edestone was filled with admiration for these descendants of the Norman conquerors, who in their gallantry and patriotism responded so quickly to the call of their country, while the miserable swine whose homes and families were being protected by these noble men were instigating strikes and riots under the leadership of a band of traitors who hid their cowardice behind labour organizations, or attempted to mislead the disgusted world by windy speeches on the subject of humanitarism into which position they were not followed by the very women that they were giving as their excuse for their treasonable acts.

The Duchess presented him to Princess Wilhelmina and the others. In the soft and rich voice of the Englishwoman of culture and refinement, which always charmed him, she said:

"Mr. Edestone, my daughter tells me that you came over on the *Ivernia* with us."

"No, no, mamma!" interrupted the Princess, with a frown and nervous little laugh. "I said that Mrs. Brown said that she thought that Mr. Edestone was on board."

The Duchess acknowledged this correction, and with the cool effrontery that only a woman can carry off to her entire satisfaction, she then pretended that this was the first time that she had ever laid eyes on him, when as a matter of fact she and the Princess had discussed this remarkable, independent individual, who had so quietly and alone occupied the large suite adjoining theirs.

"Do sit down, Mr. Edestone," she smiled, "and tell us about your wonderful electrical gun or ship. I really know so little about electricity that I could not understand what my daughter has just been telling me." And then, as if to save him from the great embarrassment of speaking, which she felt that he must have in her presence, she hastened to continue: "I am really so sorry that I did not know you were a fellow-passenger or I should most certainly have had you presented. I am very fond of you Americans, I find them most charming and so original, you know."

Edestone bowed.

"I really became quite attached to your Mr. Bradley, who was on board. I think you call him 'Diamond King John.' He was most attractive," and, with a charming smile, "he showed me his diamond suspender buttons; and he dances beautifully, my daughter tells me. I understand that Mr. Bradley is one of your oldest Arizona families—or was it Virginia?—I am so stupid about the names of your different counties. But I agree with him that family is not everything, and that clothes make the gentleman. He tells me that he gets all of his clothes from the same tailor as the Duke. Do you get your clothes in London, Mr. Edestone?" And then, seeing an expression on Edestone's face which indicated to her that he was going to be bold enough to attempt to enter into the conversation, hastily added: "No, of course not, you would naturally get yours in New York, where Mr. Bradley tells me that the finish of the buttonholes is much better on account of the enormous salaries that you very rich Americans are able to pay your tailors. No tea, Mr. Edestone? How foolish of me to ask! You would like to have one of those American drinks; what is it you call them? Cockplumes? My son could make one for you. Madame La Princesse de Blanc taught him how to make one."

Edestone smilingly declined.

The Duchess, who by this time was beginning to feel that perhaps Mr. Edestone would not insist upon taking off his coat or squatting Indian fashion on the floor, continued:

"My son tells me that it was at her house in Paris that he had the pleasure of making your acquaintance."

"Yes, Duchess," nodded Edestone.

"She is a most delightful little American," continued the Duchess. "So bright, natural, unconventional, and original. And she chews tobacco in the most fascinating manner."

Edestone all this time had been debating in his mind whether this silly prattle was the result of real ignorance, snobbishness, or kindness of heart. He gave her the benefit of the doubt, however, and, wishing to show her that she might put her mind at rest as to his ability to overcome any embarrassment that he might have had, said with a perfectly solemn face:

"You should have asked your friend, Mr. Bradley, to show you his suspenders themselves, Duchess. They are, I am told, set with rubies, sapphires, and diamonds, and cost, I understand, $10,000."

"How very odd," said the Duchess.

"And I am sure," he continued, "that he feels as proud of having danced with the Princess as she could have been at having been the recipient of so much attention at the hands of 'King John,' who apparently is also a Prince Charming."

And then ignoring their pretence of having just seen him for the first time, in a most natural manner Edestone referred to the episodes of the crossing.

Turning to the Princess, who all this time had vainly endeavoured to check her mother, and changing his manner out of deference for her youth and inexperience, and assuming a more humble demeanour, he continued:

"I sincerely hope, Princess, that I did not hurt you when I was forced to handle you so roughly, but it was blowing almost a hurricane."

"I forgive you, Mr. Edestone," she said with a charming smile, "for hurting my arm; but," with a little pout, "I don't think I can forgive you for hurting my feelings. Why did you not ask Mr. Bradley to present you? He said that he knew you very well."

"Oh, I was rather afraid," laughed Edestone, "to suggest this to him. You know we do not move in exactly the same set, and I did not wish to give him an opportunity to snub me. Now that he does speak so familiarly of his royal friends, I thought that he might consider me a bit presumptuous."

"You don't mean to say," snorted the Duchess, "that that creature would dare to speak of me as a friend?"

"Well," said Edestone, "I shall do him the justice of saying that I am quite certain he would not if he did not believe that you were, and did not think that it was perfectly natural that you should be."

The Princess, who was looking at Edestone with an intense look, of which however she was absolutely unconscious, broke in impatiently:

"Oh, mamma, do stop talking about that dreadful man and ask Mr. Edestone to tell us something about his wonderful work." A light came into her eyes which would have alarmed an American mother had she seen it in the eyes of her daughter at a mixed summer resort.

Edestone was anxious to get away as he took absolutely no interest in this particular phase of life; yet he did not wish to appear unappreciative of the great honour that had been conferred upon him by these ladies of such high rank. However, an opportunity soon presented itself which permitted him to retire, and he bowed himself out of the room, but not, it must be admitted, until he had answered a number of questions which the Princess insisted on putting to him. He did this with perfect deference, yet in such a businesslike way that she was convinced, should a year elapse before he next saw her, he would probably not recognize her.

CHAPTER XV
SURROUNDED BY SOLDIERS

As Edestone left the Palace in company with Colonel Stewart, and the two took their seats in the waiting carriage, he was amused to see a troop of cavalry, which had been drawn up before the entrance, fall in about them as an escort. The men were all dressed in khaki, and, judging from their equipment, they were fixed for business more than a mere guard of honour. A smart, young officer rode up and, saluting the Colonel, asked: "Where to, sir?"

"To Claridge's." The Colonel saluted in return.

The carriage started, and the troopers, clattering out of the courtyard, closed up about it in a fashion which showed that they were going to take no chances with their valuable charge.

Edestone laughed at himself with his high hat and frock-coat as a centre for all this military panoply. It recalled to him an old-fashioned print he had seen when a boy, representing Abraham Lincoln at the front.

"You don't mean to tell me that you really consider this necessary?" he chaffed his companion.

Colonel Stewart nodded gravely. "They will make no attempt on your life, Mr. Edestone," he added reassuringly, "except as a last resort; but they are determined to have your secret. They prefer to get it with your co-operation and assent. If not, they want it anyhow. Finally, they stand ready to accomplish its destruction and your own rather than permit England to obtain it."

Arriving at the hotel, the soldiers were drawn up in line while he entered the door. To his surprise, moreover, the Colonel and two of the cavalry-men accompanied him to the door of his apartment.

"Mr. Edestone," said the Royal Equerry, "I am sorry, but my orders are to place a sentry at your door. You are not of course to consider yourself in any sense a prisoner, but an honoured guest whose safety is of paramount importance. Should you at any time wish to leave your apartment, notify

Captain Bright by telephone at the hotel office where he will be stationed, and he will act as your escort. My advice, however, is that you remain in the hotel." Giving a military salute, he retired, leaving the two soldiers posted in the corridor.

A moment later, Edestone was summoned to the door to find that the sentries had halted Black and Stanton whom he had directed to report to him immediately on his return to the hotel.

A word from him proved sufficient to secure the admission of his moving-picture experts; nevertheless, the three gazed at one another uneasily as they stood within the room.

"What is it, Mr. Edestone?" Black's eyes rounded up. "They haven't placed you under arrest, have they?"

Edestone shook his head. "Apparently not. At least they tell me I am under no restraint, and, as they might say to a little boy about to be spanked, that this is all for my own good. Whether or not this is merely a polite subterfuge, and they intend to postpone my departure from London from time to time in a way that can give no offence to our Government, yet would spoil all my plans, I am still uncertain."

"By Jove, it might be worth while trying to find out," flared up Stanton, bristling at the very suggestion of an indignity to his adored chief. "If they've got anything of that kind up their sleeves, we could soon show them that— —"

"No." Edestone spoke up a trifle sharply. "I have decided to let the situation develop itself."

His manner indicated that he wished the subject dropped; but, after he had given the two men the orders for which he had summoned them, and dismissed them, he fell into a rather perturbed reverie.

After all, might it not be well, as Stanton had urged, to assure himself in regard to John Bull's honourable intentions? His mind reverted to an expedient which he had already considered and cast aside. It was to communicate with the American Ambassador, get his passports, and start for Paris at once. Then, if he were halted, the purpose of the British Government would be made plain and its hypocrisy exposed.

But, to tell the truth, he rather shrank from such a revelation. Suppose he forced their hand in this way, and they should retaliate, either by attempting to detain him in England, or insisting upon his return to his own country? Was he prepared to— —?

As Underhill had said, blood is thicker than water; and there were in his nature many ties that bound him to the mother-country.

No, he concluded; if there was cause to worry, he would meet the emergency when it arose. Anyhow, he was not of the worrying kind. He threw himself down upon the sofa, since even for him it had been a rather strenuous day, and soon was fast asleep.

He was awakened by James. "It is 7:30, sir, and you are dining at 8 o'clock." Then with a perfectly stolid face: "I beg pardon, sir, what clothes will you take to the Tower, sir? The hall porter says, sir, that with all these soldiers around, they are certainly going to stand you up before a firing squad. And Hottenroth, the barber, says as how every American that comes to London is more or less a German spy. But he is a kind of a foreigner himself, sir. A Welshman, he says he is, and he talks in a very funny way."

"No, they are not going to stand me up before a firing squad," Edestone halted this flood of intelligence, as he sprang up from the sofa; "but I shall turn myself into one, and fire the whole lot of you, if you don't stop talking so much. Now hurry up, and get me dressed. I don't want to keep Mr. Rebener waiting."

Yet even with James's adept assistance, he found the time scant for the careful toilet upon which he always insisted; and it was almost on the stroke of the hour when at last he was ready.

Snatching his hat and cane from James, he started hurriedly out of the door, but found himself abruptly challenged by the sentry just outside whose presence he had for the moment completely forgotten.

"Excuse me, sir," the soldier saluted, "but my orders are to notify Captain Bright, if you wish to leave your rooms."

He blew a whistle, summoning a comrade who suddenly appeared from nowhere.

"Notify Captain Bright," he directed; then, in response to Edestone's good-humoured but slightly sarcastic protests: "I'm sorry, sir, but those are my orders."

"Has England declared war on the United States?" said Edestone.

"I don't know, sir," the sentry grinned. "We seem to be taking on all comers." Then standing at attention, he waited until the soldier, who had returned from telephoning, came forward to announce that the Captain presented his apologies and would be right up.

A moment later Captain Bright himself came panting down the corridor. He expressed profound regret that any inconvenience should have been caused, but explained, as Colonel Stewart had already done, that he was held personally responsible for Edestone's safety, and had instructions to accompany him wherever he might go.

"Very well, Captain; I bow to the inevitable. May I trouble you to conduct me to the dining-room?" And he strolled toward the lift at the side of the tall cavalryman.

But in the office they encountered Rebener himself writing a note on the back of his card.

"Oh, there you are, Jack?" he hailed Edestone. "I was just sending you a note asking you if you wouldn't come and dine with me at the Britz instead of here. It is too damn stupid here. Not that it's very bright anywhere in London at present, but at least there's a little bit more life at the Britz."

"Who is stopping here anyhow? Royalty?" he interrupted himself. "There are soldiers all over the place."

"Yes; I am the recipient of that little attention," laughed the young American. "Let me introduce Captain Bright here, who is acting as my especial chaperon."

"What? You surely haven't run afoul of the War Department?" Rebener rolled his eyes. "That sounds more like our friends, the barbarians, than Englishmen. But, say, you are joking of course; you're not really in trouble? Seriously is there anything you want me to do for you? I have quite a little pull over at the War Offices, you know."

"No, thank you; I am leaving for Paris tomorrow." He looked straight into Rebener's eyes, without giving the slightest hint in his expression of the disclosure which had been made to him by the unfortunate Smith. "It is simply that Captain Bright thinks there are some people who might do something to me. I don't know exactly what it is, but he insists on preventing them anyhow; so there you are. How about it, Captain? Am I permitted to dine with Mr. Rebener at the Britz? I think the Britz is a perfectly safe place for two American business men."

"As you please, Mr. Edestone." The Captain drew himself up. "My orders are to escort you, though, wherever you go." He raised his hand toward a sergeant who was standing just inside the door.

"What! You are not going to take all the 'Tommies' along too?" expostulated Rebener. "Oh, I say; you come along yourself, Captain, and dine with us, but leave the men behind. I will see that Edestone doesn't come to any grief."

"Sorry." The officer's tone ended any further argument. "I shall keep my men as much out of sight as possible; but it will be necessary for them to accompany us."

"You see." Edestone smiled somewhat ruefully. "I can't even go out to buy a paper, without turning it into a sort of Fourth of July parade."

On going to the door they found that one of the royal carriages was waiting for them, and after the two men were seated, and the Captain had given the directions to the coachman, they dashed off in the midst of a cavalcade.

"By the way," Rebener vouchsafed as they drove along, "I have taken the liberty of inviting Lord Denton and Mr. Karlbeck, two friends of mine, to dine with us tonight, and as Lord Denton is in mourning, he has asked that I have dinner in my apartment. I hope that is all right?"

"Certainly," assented Edestone. "Lord Denton, you say? I don't think I have ever met him, have I? And isn't he just a little supersensitive to raise a scruple of that sort? It seems to me that practically everybody over here is in mourning. Fact is, I don't feel like going to a ball myself." His face saddened, as he thought of the many good fellows he had met on former visits to London who now lay underneath the sod of Northern France and Belgium.

But by this time they were at the Britz and the proprietor was bowing them inside, apparently so accustomed to receiving men of distinction with military escort that he did not even notice the lines of trim cavalrymen which drew themselves up on either side of his entrance.

"Will you gentlemen dine in the public restaurant?" asked Captain Bright, stepping up to Edestone.

"No," Rebener took it upon himself to answer. "We are going to have a little *partie carrée* in my apartment."

"In that case," said the Captain, "I regret that I shall have to station men on that floor."

Rebener frowned as if he were about to voice a protest, but at that moment the proprietor called him over to consult with him in regard to the menu.

For a moment or two they discussed it calmly enough; then as the proprietor began to gesticulate and wax vehement, Rebener spoke over his shoulder to his guest.

"Excuse me, Jack," he said, "but M. Bombiadi insists that I hold a council of war with him over the selection of the wines. He declines to accept the responsibility with such a distinguished personage as you seem to have become." Then lowering his voice, he added with a wink: "He is evidently impressed with that military escort of yours, for all that he pretended not to notice it. I won't be away a minute."

He was hurried by the proprietor through the office and into one of the small duplex apartments on the main floor. Passing through the pantry and dining-room of the apartment out into the little private hall with its street door on Piccadilly, and up a short flight of marble steps with an iron railing, he was ushered into a handsomely furnished little parlour.

There, standing in front of the mantelpiece was a man who did not look like an Englishman, but more like a German Jew. He was perfectly bald and had a black beard which was rather long and trimmed to a point. His nose was unmistakable, and taken with his thick, red lips showed pretty well what he was and whence he came. Talking to him very earnestly was another man, who was much smaller, and who was also German to the finger-tips.

Pausing on the threshold, M. Bombiadi with the servile and cringing tone always assumed by those frock-coated criminals, European hotel proprietors, asked humbly: "May we come in, Your Royal Highness?"

But Rebener, with the air of a man who was not accustomed to, or else declined to consider, such formalities, unhesitatingly brushed the proprietor aside, and walked up to the two men.

"I am sorry to be late," he said in a thoroughly businesslike manner, "but Bombiadi here has doubtless explained the reason for it." Then, as if he purposely refused to acknowledge the high rank of either of the two men by waiting for them to speak, he said brusquely, even with a slight touch of contempt: "Bombiadi tells me that you want to speak with me, before we meet at the table."

"Yes, Mr. Rebener," said the smaller man, bowing with exaggerated ceremony. "If it is not asking too much of you, I am sure that His Royal Highness will appreciate your kindness."

The silky smoothness of his manner seemed to disgust Rebener.

"Now, look here, Karlbeck, don't try to get friendly with me," he drew back as the other attempted to lay a hand upon his arm. "I am not in love with this business, anyhow. I am German, and I am proud of the Fatherland, as she stands with her back against the wall, fighting the entire civilized world—and some of the barbaric;—but you two fellows are Englishmen, and——"

"Pardon me, Mr. Rebener," the man with the beard broke in angrily. "You seem to forget to whom you are speaking."

"No, that is just the trouble," cried Rebener with a loud laugh. "I can't seem to forget it. And if Your Royal Highness insists upon keeping on your crown, you had better let Mr. Edestone and myself dine alone."

"Please, Mr. Rebener. Please not so loud," cautioned the proprietor, pale with terror. "One never knows who may be listening."

"I have a word for you too." Rebener turned, and shook a threatening finger in his face. "If I find that you cut-throats have murdered Schmidt, I will turn you over to the London police, and let you be hanged as common murderers without having any of the glory of dying for your country. I distinctly told you, that I would not stand for that sort of thing. He was a miserable creature, but he was an American, and we Americans, even if we have got German blood, are not traitors to the country of our adoption." And he looked with a sneer at the two Englishmen. "Now, if any of you are planning to indulge in any of your pretty little tricks with Mr. Edestone tonight, I give you fair warning. I will call Captain Bright in, and turn the whole lot of you over to him. I think he would be rather surprised to find His Royal Highness in such company."

The man with the beard was literally white with rage. The thick veins swelled along his neck, and his lower lip was trembling. But he controlled himself with an effort, and endeavoured to speak calmly.

"Now, now, Mr. Rebener," he said, "you are unnecessarily excited, and I therefore overlook your disrespect toward me. There is no intention whatever of doing any violence to Mr. Edestone. We hope merely to prevail on him to talk."

"What good will his talking do?" cried the smaller man before his associate could silence him. "We know all that he said today at Buckingham Palace. What we want is his instrument, and if we're not going after that, what use is this dinner, I would like to know?"

"I can't tell you," rejoined Rebener, "unless His Royal Highness would be willing to show his hand, and try to persuade Edestone to take our view of the matter."

A sharp retort trembled on the lips of the Jewish-looking man, but just then he caught sight of Bombiadi out of the corner of his eyes gesticulating and making signs to him from behind Rebener's back.

"I suppose that is the only chance left us," he pretended to consider. "We can try it at any rate. I suppose, too, we had better come to your apartment immediately. Remember, though, we are to remain incognito until I give the word. In the meantime, we are simply 'Lord Denton' and 'Mr. Karlbeck.'"

On that agreement, Rebener left; but the proprietor, after following him far enough to make sure that he was out of earshot, returned to the little parlour where the other men waited.

"We will have to leave him out of our calculations," he shook his head. "He is not heart and soul in the cause as is your Royal Highness. However, it can be managed without Rebener.

"Hottenroth has telephoned me that he thinks Edestone has the instrument on his person, but cannot make sure, as his rooms at Claridge's are too closely guarded to permit of a search. We must go upon the assumption that he has it with him, however, and get it away from him. That plan of Your Royal Highness's will work perfectly, I am sure. I will call Edestone to the telephone while you are at dinner, and since the rest of you will all remain at the table, how can Rebener suspect either of you gentlemen any more than he would suspect himself.

"Now, I will return in a few minutes, and take you up to Mr. Rebener's apartment. No one knows of your presence in the house so far, I can assure you, and the servants on that floor may be thoroughly depended upon."

CHAPTER XVI
A DINNER AT THE BRITZ

When Rebener got back to the entrance hall he found Edestone standing talking with an American newspaper correspondent, and as he came up heard the inventor say: "Well you can say that if I sell my discovery to anyone it will be to the United States, and that rather than sell to any other nation I would hand it over to my own country as a free gift."

"Here, here," Rebener joined in laughingly as he came up, "don't you offer to give away anything. Just because your father left you comfortably well off is no reason that you shouldn't sell things if people want to buy. Sell and sell while you've got the market, and sell to the highest bidder. Look at me, I am selling to both sides; that is my way of stopping this war." He turned to the young newspaper man. "Is there anything new, Ralph?"

"Nothing, Mr. Rebener, except that there is a story out in New York that Mr. Edestone here has been sent over to act as a sort of unofficial go-between to bring England and Germany to terms; but he denies this. Then there is another story that he is trying to sell this new invention of his to England and that the German agents are trying to get it away from him before he does. You've just heard what he has to say on that subject, so I seem to have landed on a 'Flivver' all around.

"Say, Mr. Edestone, you'll give me the dope on this lay-out won't you, before the other boys get to it?" he wheedled. "We all know that something is going on, and she's going to be a big story when she breaks, and it would be the making of me with the 'old man' if I could put it over first.

"I saw you, sir, this afternoon coming home from the Palace," he chuckled, "and the President, going out to the first ball game of the season, surrounded by the Washington Blues, to toss the pill into the diamond, certainly had nothing on you."

"You've struck it," said Edestone, with a good-humoured laugh at himself. "I have been trying all day to think what I looked like, and that's it."

Rebener laid his hand upon his arm. "Well, Jack," he said, "hadn't we better be getting up to my place? I don't want to keep the other gentlemen waiting, and these Europeans have an awful habit of coming at the hour they are invited, and do not, as we do in America, in imitation of the 'Snark,' 'dine on the following day.'

"Good-night, Ralph," he waved his hand to the correspondent. "Drop around tomorrow; I may have something for you."

Then as they were going up in the elevator he confided to Edestone: "I am not so crazy about these two chaps that are coming to dinner tonight, but you know most of the good sort are at the front, or, if they happen to be in London, are too busy to waste their time on us Americans. Do you know, Jack, there is at this time quite a bit of feeling against us in England? Exactly what it is they resent it is hard to say. I certainly do not understand how they can expect us to take any part in this war with our population composed of people from every one of the countries that are engaged."

They had scarcely had time to take off their coats when Lord Denton and Mr. Karlbeck came in through the private entrance. Edestone was introduced, and after the two Americans had had their cocktails, both Englishmen having declined to indulge in this distinctly American custom, the four sat down to dinner. Rebener put "Lord Denton" on his right, Edestone on his left, while "Mr. Karlbeck" took the only remaining seat. The conversation was general, and Edestone found that both the Englishmen were evidently making an effort to be agreeable.

"You are quite like an Englishman," said "Lord Denton" addressing him. "I have known so few really nice Americans that I must say it is a most delightful surprise. When I was told that you were a great American inventor, I was prepared to see a fellow with the back of his neck shaved, who, while chewing gum, would seize my lapel and hold on to it while he insisted on explaining how I could save time and money by using his electrical self-starting dishwasher or some such beastly machine. When I visited New York two years ago, a committee had me in charge for three days. Their one idea seemed to be to force large cigars and mixed drinks on me at all hours of the day and night. One of these charming gentlemen, a particularly objectionable fellow, although he seemed to be very rich, was covered with diamonds and wore the most ridiculous evening clothes topped off with a yachting cap fronted with the insignia of some rowing club of which he had been admiral. He always referred to his one-thousand-ton yacht as his 'little canoe,' and took delight in telling exactly what it cost him by the hour to run, invariably adding that this amount did not include his own food, wines, liquors, and cigars. 'We always charge that up to profit-and-loss account,' he would say with a roar of laughter, in which he was joined by a group of his satellites."

"I'll bet I can call the turn, eh, Jack?" Rebener glanced across the table to Edestone, with a twinkle in his eye. "Didn't the chap also tell you with great seriousness, 'Lord Denton,' that he had pulled off more good deals in his 'little canoe' than in all the hotel corridors put together?"

"Well, I sincerely hope it's the same," said 'Lord Denton'. "You can't have two such creatures in your country?"

"Was that the chap, 'Denton,'" broke in "Karlbeck," "who said to you, the day that he slapped you on the back, that he was not so strong for making all this fuss over Princes and things, as in his opinion it wasn't democratic?"

"Yes, that was when I was on board his yacht, but he said I was all right and he didn't mind spending money on me. 'This is my pleasure today,' he said, 'although the Boss did say he wanted you treated right, and his word goes both ways with me. See!'"

"Tell them about your experience with the New York newspaper men," suggested "Karlbeck."

"Oh, that was very amusing! The whole committee would stand around and laugh while the 'boys,' as they called them, had a chance, which consisted in my being asked the most impertinent questions by a lot of objectionable little bounders whom they constantly referred to as 'the greatest institution of our glorious country,' at times allowing also that the country was 'God's own.'

"When I objected, some of your most powerful men would say: 'You had better tell the reporters something or they'll get sore on you and print a lot of lies about your women-folk.'

"The particularly offensive gentleman of whom I have spoken, after telling me what he thought of the British aristocracy, which was not always flattering, though I seemed to be exempt, said as he bade me good-bye: 'By the way, don't forget that my wife and two daughters will be stopping in London next spring.'"

"Well," inquired Edestone with a faint smile, "you did forget that his wife and two daughters were stopping in London in the spring, I am quite sure, and sure that he is convinced you got the best of it."

"Oh, I say, Mr. Edestone, that was a nasty one! You really would not have expected me to introduce that fellow at my clubs, would you?" "No," said Edestone, toying with something on the table to hide the smile that played across his lips. "No, no, not at all. The Lord Mayor of London would have satisfied him."

He would have dropped the subject there, but pressed by the other man he continued rather seriously: "Since you ask me, 'Lord Denton,' I do think that you should not have accepted that man's hospitality unless you were prepared to return it to a certain extent."

"Well, what would you have expected His Royal Highness to do—I mean 'Lord Denton?'" "Karlbeck" corrected himself hastily. Edestone set his glass down, and looked at the man for a moment. When he finally spoke it was with a touch of asperity. With a sarcastic smile he said:

"The quiet way in which you Europeans accept everything from us and return nothing, is being resented, not by the lower classes for they read in our papers how the King shook hands with Jack Johnson; not by the *nouveaux riches*, for they are perfectly satisfied with the notoriety they get at the hands of your broken-down aristocracy who spend their money,—no not by these classes, but by our ladies and gentlemen."

"Then why do you entertain our Princes so lavishly?" sneered "Karlbeck."

"It is our sense of humour, which allows us to be imposed upon. That sense of humour is often mistaken for hysterical hospitality by the distinguished stranger. We—and when I say we I mean people of breeding which does not include the vulgarian who knows nothing and may be the son of your father's ninth gardener—we know that the more ridiculous we appear to you, the better you like it. Not to appear ridiculous offends you, as it arouses a feeling of rivalry to which you object, but with your lack of that same sense of humour, this you deny."

Again he would have willingly dropped the subject, but "Lord Denton" once more insisted upon keeping up the discussion.

"You must remember," said he, "Prince Henry's visit to America. You don't mean to tell me the Americans were not complimented and pleased at a visit from a Royal Prince?"

Edestone laughed. "You mean when Prince Henry of Prussia came over to bridge the chasm which had formed between the German and American nations over the Manila episode, by the interchange of courtesies between the two ruling families, the Hohenzollerns and the Roosevelts?

"I was surprised that the Kaiser was so poorly informed as not to know our attitude toward him and his Divine Right and mailed fist. Why, everybody laughed except the Kaiser and the President—they were the only ones who were fooled: the Kaiser, because he could not help himself, it was in his blood; and Roosevelt, because he was at that time in a most septic condition and was suffering from auto-intoxication at the hands of that particular form of microbe."

"Edestone entertained Prince Henry himself at his Little Place in the Country," said Rebener, who saw that "Lord Denton" was losing his temper.

"Yes, I did," said Edestone. "Not that I thought he would enjoy it, but somebody—and now when I come to think of it, you were the man, Rebener—insisted that he would like to visit my machine shops. And he did seem to enjoy seeing them very much, and Admiral Tirpitz and his staff took all kinds of notes while asking all kinds of questions." The reminiscence seemed to make the three other men a trifle uncomfortable.

"Oh! what difference does it make after all?" said Rebener. "Let's get down to business.

"Now, Edestone," he turned to the inventor, "you know me, and I'm not much for beating about the bush. When I want something, my motto is, 'Go to it.' My object in inviting you here to meet these gentlemen tonight was to see if we can't get together. As I understand the situation, Jack, you have something that you think is pretty good. You have lots of money, and you don't want to sell it. You don't have to, but you want to get England to use it, and if she won't, you will try Germany. Now is not that just about the size of it?"

"To a certain extent, yes," replied Edestone.

"Then why in the name of common sense don't you let 'Lord Denton' and me have it and we will guarantee to have it used where it will do the most good. He has more pull with the Government than any man in England. I think you know pretty well now who he is," he added with a wink. "If it is the war you want stopped, he is the best man outside of the King or Kaiser."

"Well, yes, Mr. Rebener," said Edestone, "I do know who 'Lord Denton' is and had the pleasure of seeing him this afternoon at Buckingham Palace, but I thought perhaps he would prefer that I should preserve his incognito and, following the example of his most charming Duchess, permitted myself to forget. I shall be most happy to——"

He halted and turned as a waiter stepped up behind his chair to interrupt him.

"I beg pardon, sir, but the Marquis of Lindenberry wishes to speak to you on the telephone.

"I am sorry, sir, but you will have to go to the booth in the room behind the stairs. Mr. Rebener's telephone is out of order."

"What do you mean, 'my telephone is out of order'?" Rebener glanced up sharply. "I used it not twenty minutes ago." And going into the adjoining room he tried to speak to the floor switchboard.

"The fellow's right," he admitted on returning to the table. "You'll have to use the booth, Jack. Waiter, show Mr. Edestone where to go."

"This way, sir," said the waiter, and he conducted Edestone down the long corridor, passing one of Captain Bright's cavalrymen at almost every turn. Just around the foot of the stairs the waiter showed him a door.

"There it is, sir," he pointed.

Edestone went in and found himself in a room that was almost dark. It was lighted only by a shaded electric bulb used by the man at the switchboard, who sat facing the door but hidden from anyone entering by the high instrument in front of him. Edestone walked over to him, finding him almost obscured by the huge green shade pulled down over his eyes, and seemingly very much occupied with both incoming and outgoing calls.

"Is there a call for Mr. Edestone?" he asked.

"Yes, sir," said the man without looking up from his plugs. "The second booth from this end, No. 2."

Edestone, turning, saw in the dim light a row of booths against the wall over beyond the door. It was quite dark in that corner, but he could see that the door of the second booth was open. He went inside, muttering as he did so, "I think they might give a fellow a little more light."

As he sat down and took up the receiver, he put out his hand to stop the door from slowly closing, apparently by itself. It was one of those double-walled, sound-proof, stuffy boxes, and he did not want the door shut tight, so he put out his foot to hold it open. But he was just a moment too late. The door shut with a little bang, and when he tried to open it again, he found that it seemed to have jammed.

CHAPTER XVII
THE VOICE IN THE TELEPHONE

Edestone waited. He thought he heard, or rather he felt, a vibration as if someone were moving in the next booth. He tried the door again, but found that it held fast.

He was about to signal the switchboard operator and tell him to come and open up the booth, when an, "Are you there, Mr. Edestone?" came to him from across the wire, and caused him for the moment to forget the refractory door.

"Hello!" he answered. "Yes; I am Mr. Edestone. Who is this?"

The voice, instead of replying directly, spoke as if to another person with an aside. "Mr. Edestone is on the wire."

A moment, and then a second voice spoke. "Are you there, Mr. Edestone?"

It was not the voice of his friend, and he answered a trifle impatiently: "Yes. Who are you? Are you speaking for the Marquis of Lindenberry?"

"No, I am not," came the reply. "And I must apologize for having used his name."

The voice bore the unmistakable intonation of an English gentleman.

"I am the Count Kurtz von Hemelstein. I regret that circumstances compel me to force myself upon you in this caddish manner. But my duty as a soldier in the service of His Majesty, the Emperor of Germany, demands it. I shall not delay you long, however, if you will only do what I ask."

There was a moment's pause. Involuntarily Edestone drew back slightly from the instrument.

"Count Kurtz von Hemelstein, did you say?" He spoke with a touch of sternness. "I do not think that I have ever had the pleasure of meeting you, sir. I did meet a Count Heinrich von Hemelstein last summer."

"Yes; that was my brother. He has often spoken of you, Mr. Edestone. If I am not mistaken, you were rivals for the attention of a pretty, young matron with a good-natured husband?"

"Not rivals, Count von Hemelstein." Edestone laughed, but under the laugh he was doing some rapid thinking. "Your brother was the favoured one, and when the war broke out, and he had to leave for the front, the lady was almost inconsolable.

"But, Count von Hemelstein," he continued, "what can I do for you? We Americans, you know, do not always insist upon a formal introduction. As we say, 'Any friend of a friend of mine.'"

"Also, you are wrong on one point," said the Count, with a little chuckle. "I have had the pleasure of meeting you. It was a trifle informal, I must admit, but you were just as charming as you are now, and I think I am indebted to you to the amount of several shillings. In the end, you did leave me rather abruptly, and seemed offended at something I had done; but I trust you have recovered from that by this time." Edestone could hear him laughing heartily.

"You have met me?" repeated Edestone, completely mystified. "When and where?"

"Today; in London. Indeed, I am in London now."

"In London, Count von Hemelstein?" Involuntarily Edestone lowered his voice. "But I say, isn't that taking a bit of a chance for a German officer? Where are you speaking from now, may I ask?"

The Count was laughing so, that just at first he could not answer; but after a moment he managed to control his amusement.

"I am in the next booth to you," he said.

When he spoke again, his tone had lost all trace of levity and become hard and direct like that of a man charged with a distasteful duty, yet with which he was determined not to let his feelings interfere.

"In regard to our meeting today," he said; "I was in disguise. In short, I was the taxi-driver whom you gave the slip this afternoon by the aid of that cur, Schmidt. And now, Mr. Edestone, you must realize what it is I want." In a more conciliatory tone, he added: "I can see no reason, however, why we should not settle this matter as between gentlemen."

"Please be more explicit," returned Edestone, quietly.

"In brief, then, I am authorized by my Government to meet, and even double or quadruple any offer for your invention made by the English Government. I will take your word of honour. All that you have to do is to say now, on your word as a gentleman, that you will sell it to my Government, and you can return to your friends. My Government will then communicate with you, and close with you at your own price."

"And if I decline the proposition?" said Edestone.

"Then I fear I shall be compelled to use force; and much as I may regret to do so, I will tell you that I am prepared to stop at nothing.

"You are now," he went on, "locked in that solid oak booth, with its strong double doors, perfectly sound-proof. The operator at the switchboard is my man. He can by pulling a wire uncork a bottle which is concealed in your booth and asphyxiate you in one half minute."

But if he had expected the American to show any trepidation as a result of his threats, he soon found out his mistake. Edestone's reply was as insouciant as if he had been merely commenting on the weather.

"Really, this is quite interesting, Count von Hemelstein," he said. "I might almost call you a man after my own heart. That bottle trick is so simple and yet effective that I, as an inventor, cannot help but compliment you. I am wondering just what chemical you have employed. There are of course a dozen or more that would answer your purpose; but as their action varies greatly in the effect upon the victim, I am naturally curious."

"Does that mean that you are about to decline my offer?" demanded the Count sharply. "Have a care, Mr. Edestone. I am not merely trying to frighten you, as you may suppose. The facts are just as I have stated them, and I shall not hesitate to— —"

"Assuredly, my dear Count," Edestone broke in. "I have never doubted that for a moment. Nor am I going to refuse your proposition—that is, not definitely. Instead, I have been so pleased by the charming manner in which you have presented this little matter that I desire to submit a counter-proposition. Only, I must beg you to urge your modest friend with the weak eyes out there at the switchboard to be a little careful with that wire. Judging from the atmosphere in this booth, his bottle has been leaking for some time."

"Come, come, Mr. Edestone." The Count's voice rose nervously, showing the strain under which he was labouring. "I have already told you that this is no joke. If it is your game to play for time, in the hope that some one may come to release you, or that you may discover the manner in which the bottle is secreted, you are going to be disappointed. I must do my work quickly. If I do not have your answer at once, I will give the signal and take your instrument away from you by force."

"It is not time I want, but air." Edestone gave a little gasp. "You yourself have spent more time than I, with your kind explanations as to how I may avoid what would be to me a most distressing accident. However, since celerity is what you want, I hasten to say that I have not my instrument, nor indeed any instrument with me."

"Not with you?" snapped the Prussian angrily. "Where is it, then?"

"Ah! That is my counter-proposition. Count von Hemelstein, if I promise to tell you, on my word of honour, where you may find this instrument of mine that contains the entire secret of my invention—and it is near at hand where, if you are a brave man, you can easily get it,—if I do this, will you, on your side, give me your word as a gentleman, that you will immediately open this booth?

"I may add," he went on, as von Hemelstein seemed to hesitate, "that this is my last and only proposition, and you can take that or nothing. I will die here in this box before I will sell my invention to any European Government; but you may have it as a free gift, Count, if you have the nerve to go after it. There is a challenge to your boasted Prussian valour! Are you a sport, Count von Hemelstein, or are you not?"

Von Hemelstein wavered no longer. From what Edestone told him, he argued that the inventor must have left his instrument with some of his subordinates, probably Black and Stanton, and relied upon them to protect it; and it stung him to think that the American should believe a German officer would falter at such odds—a couple of electricians, mere Yankee artisans.

"Yes," he growled hoarsely. "I accept your terms. It is a bargain."

"On your honour?"

"On my word of honour as a Prussian officer and a gentleman."

"Well, then, hurry up and open this door. It is getting stifling in here; and, besides, Rebener will be growing anxious about me."

"But, first, your information. Where is the instrument?"

"Oh, the instrument?" It was now Edestone's turn to laugh. "Why, that is lying on the floor under the table in Mr. Rebener's dining-room. I dropped it there, when I came out to answer your telephone call, and I also gave instructions to the sentries on guard at the door of the apartment to shoot any one who attempted to pass in or out during my absence. You are doubtless a brave man, but I do not think you are prepared to tackle a whole company of British cavalry.

"And now," he concluded, "I have kept to my bargain. Will you kindly open the door?"

A muttered German imprecation, like a snarl of baffled chagrin, was his only answer. But a moment later the door to his booth swung open, and he was free.

As he stepped out, he found the lights in the room turned on, and the man at the switchboard gone. He also noticed that the door to the adjoining booth was shaking, as if someone had just jerked it open and had passed out hurriedly, and, as he came out into the corridor, he thought he glimpsed the figure of a man hastily disappearing down the staircase. So far as any other evidence went, except for his wilted collar and heaving lungs, the whole experience might have been a dream.

He returned quietly to the dinner table, and stooping over, as if to pick up his napkin, recovered the instrument and slipped it into his trousers pocket.

"Lord Denton" and "Karlbeck" kept staring at him with puzzled, almost incredulous faces.

"Did you find your friend on the wire?" finally ventured "Lord Denton," leaning across the table toward him.

"No; it was another gentleman speaking for him," smiled Edestone, "a mere visitor to England like myself. I took the liberty of asking him to join us, but he declined. He is, I fancy, leaving the country very shortly — probably going to Berlin."

A little gasp from behind him caused him to turn in his seat. It came from the hotel proprietor who, entering the room by the rear door, stood rooted in amazement at the sight of Edestone, his jaw dropping, his eyes as big as saucers.

Edestone regarded him a moment; then turned to his host.

"What silly-looking waiters you have in this hotel, Rebener," he said. "That fellow yonder doesn't appear to have brains enough to be even a German spy."

The real waiter, overhearing this compliment to his employer, clapped his hand over his mouth and dived for the pantry, just managing to get through the swinging door before he exploded.

The self-satisfied Bombiadi also overheard, and although he endeavoured to appear unconscious, a dull red flush crept up over his cheeks, and after shifting for a moment from one foot to the other, he left the room.

"Lord Denton" and "Karlbeck" exchanged glances out of the corners of their eyes; and Rebener, although he made out to grin at the speech, shifted a little uneasily in his chair.

But Edestone, who, under his quiet exterior, possessed a rather mischievous spirit, was not yet through with them.

"As I was saying when I was called to the telephone," he leaned across the table toward the *incognito* Royal Duke, "the desire of Your Royal Highness— pardon me, I mean, of 'Lord Denton'—is of course to see England victorious in this contest; but that may mean years of fighting and an appalling loss of men and money. Such true patriots as yourself and 'Mr. Karlbeck' must see that it would be far better to end the war now, provided that a lasting peace can be ensured, and that I think I can guarantee with my discovery. I should be delighted, therefore, to co-operate with you gentlemen to that end, and if you would advocate the proposition that England allow me to go to Berlin with something to show that she is willing to enter into *pour parlers*, I shall bring pressure to bear on Germany to make some liberal answer."

"Lord Denton," however, seemed no longer interested in the matter, and was unable to concentrate his attention; while "Mr. Karlbeck" made no attempt to hide the fact that he was disgusted gusted with the evening, and wished to see it end as soon as possible.

Rebener, seeing his dinner a failure, although not quite understanding the cause, like many a nervous host compelled to face a tableful of distinguished guests who do not hesitate to show that they are bored, did the silliest thing possible under the circumstances, and drank more than he should.

Presently he began to talk in such unrestrained fashion that "Mr. Karlbeck" looked as if he would faint with apprehension, while His Royal Highness sought by every possible means to divert Edestone's attention from the broad hints and imprudent revelations that were thrown out.

They were still engaged at this, when suddenly the door was thrown open, and some one announced in a loud voice, "The King's Messenger!"

"Karlbeck" and "Lord Denton" sprang to their feet, their faces ashy pale, as they stood grasping the backs of their chairs. When, a moment later, Colonel Stewart, the Equerry, appeared on the threshold, they both crumpled up, and dropped into their chairs, fit subjects for the starch-pot.

The Colonel stared at them in undisguised surprise, a slow frown gathering between his eyes.

"Your Royal Highness did not mention to me this afternoon that he was dining with Mr. Edestone tonight," he drew himself up stiffly. And it was in his mind that, on the contrary, His Royal Highness had inveighed against the American inventor as a fraud and a fakir, and had loudly urged that no attention be paid to him or his claims.

Neither did Colonel Stewart forget that certain ugly whispers had been in circulation regarding the loyalty of these two high-born Englishmen with the Teutonic names. What did it mean, then, when he found them here in the apartment of a man practically known as a German agent, and in conference with the possessor of the secret which Germany was seeking so eagerly to obtain?

Whatever his suspicions, though, he said nothing further at the time, but turned to Edestone.

"I am sorry to disturb you, Mr. Edestone, but His Majesty, the King, has ordered that certain messages be delivered to you without delay, and I should appreciate it, if you would give me a few minutes of your time."

Then, when Edestone, after requesting Rebener's permission, had withdrawn with him into the salon, he explained that the King had instructed Sir Egbert Graves to call the following morning at nine o'clock and to state the decision of the Government in answer to the inventor's proposition.

"Will that hour be convenient to you?" asked the Colonel.

"Perfectly," Edestone assented. Then on an impulse, he added: "I do not leave for the Continent until eleven."

The Equerry extended his hand. "In that case, I shall probably not see you again. Good-bye, Mr. Edestone; I trust you will have a pleasant journey and good luck when you reach Berlin."

It was evident that he was not to be detained. He was in no sense a prisoner, but free to go or stay as he chose. With a smile of gratification, he responded to Colonel Stewart's parting salute, and returned to the dining-room.

There he found the two discomfited members of the nobility just taking their leave; while Rebener, his earlier ill-humour put aside, was playing the rather too strenuous host, and with his flushed face and over-loud manner urging them to stay and "have another." Wouldn't they try one of his wonderful cigars? Just one pony of his marvellous brandy?

But His Royal Highness, pale as death, was bent on getting away, and turned a deaf ear to all these hospitable suggestions; and although "Mr. Karlbeck" did consent to gulp down a large glass of Rebener's very fine brandy, he immediately hurried off in the wake of his royal associate.

Edestone left almost immediately, and his "guard of honour," to which he was getting quite accustomed by this time, having been duly assembled, he was escorted back to the hotel and a sleepy-eyed James.

CHAPTER XVIII
IN THE HANDS OF THE GERMANS

The next morning Sir Egbert Graves called. He touched first upon the occurrences of the evening before at Rebener's dinner, and Edestone was surprised to learn how fully the Government was informed concerning all that had transpired.

"His Majesty begs that you will, if possible, forget the whole distasteful episode," Sir Egbert said, with a stern face, and a flash of contempt in his eye. "His Royal Highness has been relieved of his commission and is in retirement, and the Duchess of Windthorst together with Princess Wilhelmina is leaving to join the Princess Adolph, in Berlin. By these means, and of course with your silence, upon which he counts, His Majesty hopes to keep England in ignorance of the fact that such rottenness exists in his immediate household."

"And so that pretty young girl who crossed with me on the *Ivernia* is in the mire too," thought Edestone; for it seemed to him that the King's order of exile against the Duchess and herself could mean nothing else. Yet somehow his feeling of disdain and aversion for the traitor did not extend to the feminine members of the family. For them he had only sorrow and sympathy.

Meanwhile, Sir Egbert, as if glad to be rid of so disagreeable a subject, had taken up the direct purpose of his call.

He said that, whereas the King was unwilling to offer any terms of settlement that Germany in her present mood would be apt to consider, His Majesty thought that after she understood the position of the United States, and after her spies had reported the nature of Edestone's reception in London, and especially after the inventor should have had an interview with the Emperor, the Berlin Government might suggest something which could serve as a basis upon which to open negotiations. In such a case, His Majesty was of the opinion that Edestone, if he were willing to undertake the delicate task, would be the most suitable person to act as a go-between.

The Foreign Minister made it plain that England could promise nothing at that time; but that he had her friendly interest upon his mission, and that she would listen in the most conciliatory spirit to any proposition he might bring back.

He brought letters to the President of France, General French, General Joffre, and others, which would guarantee Edestone's safety up to the German line; but suggested that it would be well not to show the French too much, since they were such a volatile nation that they might readily decide to retire from the field and allow the United States and England to settle the matter. On account of the long and sincere friendship which had existed between the French people and those of the United States, France might feel that she could depend upon the United States to recover her lost territory, together with Alsace and Lorraine, and that was all she wanted.

In leaving, Sir Egbert, upon behalf of the King, insisted on placing a torpedo boat at Edestone's disposal. Then, with the assurance that anything he might have to communicate to the British Government would be given most careful consideration, the Foreign Minister bowed himself out.

Edestone could not but compare this interview with the one he had held with Lord Rockstone—the opening gun of his campaign. Verily, twenty-four hours had made a vast change in the attitude of the British Cabinet.

His journey to Paris was uneventful except for one incident.

In the middle of the Channel, as he leaned against the rail, gazing back toward the white cliffs of Dover, he drew the Deionizer from his pocket and quietly dropped it overboard. With scarcely a splash the little instrument, for which the warring nations were willing to barter millions and commit almost any crime, disappeared beneath the waves.

He did not, however, intend giving any further demonstration until his arrival in Berlin, and there he thought he might have a larger and better one; while, in the meantime, and especially since his encounter with Count von Hemelstein had shown him how far the Germans were prepared to go, he did not feel like taking any unnecessary chances.

At Calais, he was received by the representative of the President and other high officials, and when they had seen some of his photographs, and had heard an outline of his plans, they readily followed the lead of England in accrediting him as a sort of unofficial peacemaker. Indeed, the Frenchmen looked upon Edestone as someone almost superhuman—a being who had come to establish on earth the dream of their philosophers, "Liberté, Égalité, Fraternité"—and they gloried in the good fortune of their sister Republic in having produced and sent to their rescue such a son.

When he left for Berlin, he was conducted to the Swiss frontier like a conquering hero, and, with prayers that he would be careful while in the land of the Huns, was turned over to the Swiss Government. The latter also accorded him every consideration and courtesy; but when he finally left their outposts behind and arrived on German soil, he found a different story.

Here, he was immediately taken in charge by the frontier military authorities, and practically held a prisoner for three days under the excuse that instructions in regard to him had to be asked for from Berlin.

He was incensed at the petty annoyances to which he was subjected by his jailer, a fat old German martinet.

Under one pretext or another he and his men were constantly being interrogated, and his baggage, which they insisted upon opening, was thoroughly and repeatedly searched.

When they discovered among other things something that suggested a miniature wireless plant, they would not let him or any of his men out of their sight. His letters were so strong, however, that they would not dare to do anything with him without instructions.

He let it be known that he had absolutely nothing hidden on his person by taking off all of his clothes and going to bed, and would apparently sleep while watching the spies go through them. They seemed to enjoy this little game so much that he would sometimes play it once or twice a day, varying it by taking a bath or having James give him massage.

They never seemed to suspect that he was playing with them, but would stand around and pounce down on his clothes, each time searching them thoroughly as if they had discovered something entirely new, when they had just turned the same things inside out within an hour.

While waiting here, too, he came to learn how intensely bitter was the feeling against Americans among Germans of all classes. They regarded themselves as superior beings, he found, and when they first noted his splendid physique, would not believe but that he must have German blood in his veins. When he convinced them, however, that he was of pure Anglo-Saxon stock, Virginia bred—a thorough-paced "Yankee," as they called it—even the peasants treated him as the dirt beneath their feet.

But at last word came from the German General Staff. He was "sealed, stamped, and marked, 'not to be opened until after delivery in Berlin.'" He was shown greater consideration now; but it was a consideration which rather unpleasantly reminded him of that shown by the keeper to a condemned prisoner in presenting him with his new clothes in which to be executed.

He and his men and all his belongings—the latter carefully listed in triplicate—were put into a private car, and locked in, like a rich American with the smallpox whom they were sending out of the country; while, to add to his comfort, he was told that Count von Hemelstein was to act as his escort.

As they started on the journey, Edestone had an opportunity of seeing in his true character for the first time the man whom he had so cleverly outwitted in the telephone booth, and he found it hard work to identify the smart cavalry officer as the grimy London taxi-driver of a few days before.

The Count was a big, splendid-looking fellow, who rather affected an American manner in order to hide the fact that he had been educated both at school and college in England. Without his uniform, he would have been taken anywhere for an Englishman, blond, blue-eyed giant that he was, with as beautiful a moustache and as winning a smile as was ever given to the hero of a love story. He wore the uniform of a Colonel of Uhlans, which well set off his handsome figure. In fact, he was as noble-looking an Uhlan as ever, either before or after marriage, broke the heart of a rich brewer's daughter.

"Delighted to meet you again, Mr. Edestone," he grasped the American's hand, with a hearty laugh. "Ever since our last encounter, I have been wanting the opportunity of asking how you knew that I would keep my word and release you, when you divulged to me the whereabouts of your instrument there in the telephone booth? Didn't you realize that, by 'putting you out,' and then having the switchboard man raise an alarm, I could in the resultant confusion, easily have secured the instrument?"

"But I also realized that I was dealing with a soldier, not a burglar; and I took a chance," said Edestone with a smile.

"Well," said the Colonel, "now that you are safe in Germany what difference does it make? We mean to keep you here."

"The United States might have something to say to that," suggested Edestone.

"The United States? Bah! One more country to fight; what difference would it make to Germany, especially one that could make so little showing? You have no army. Your navy could do no more than England is already doing. We are at present cut off from your supplies as much as if we were at war with you. Finally, the German-Americans would put the brakes on you, now that another Presidential election is approaching.

"No, Mr. Edestone," he shook his head triumphantly; "you are making a bad mistake, if you are relying on the protection of the United States, now that you have stuck your head into the tiger's mouth."

"Do I understand, Count von Hemelstein, that Germany proposes to hold me a prisoner? Are you telling me that she would dare do such a thing?"

"Ah, do not put it so crudely." The Count raised his hand a trifle mockingly. "Let us say, rather, that we expect you to become so convinced of the righteousness of our cause that you will gladly turn over your instrument and render us any other aid you can toward the crushing of our enemies."

The smile faded from his lips, and for a moment he, "showed his teeth."

"Take my advice, my friend," he said sharply. "Don't try to frighten the Wilhelmstrasse with your moving pictures and your covert threats of intervention by the United States as you did at Buckingham Palace. We are made of sterner stuff here. We know the nature of your invention, and just what you can accomplish with it; and our gifted men of science are now hard at work in the effort to duplicate your achievement.

"My brother brought back word a year ago," he disclosed, "that you were building a super-dreadnought 907 feet long, 90 feet beam, 35 feet draught, 40,000 tons displacement. We also know that you are now working full blast night and day at your 'Little Place in the Country.' We know about the tricks you played with that flunkey in your audience with the King. A hint to us Germans is all that is needed.

"We know further," he went on in a sterner voice, "the sentiments of love and devotion toward England that you expressed to the English King, and we know the tenor of the answer that was returned to your proposition.

"But do you imagine that you can come here, sir, and dictate terms to our Emperor, or arrange a peace for us, which would mean anything less than the absolute humbling of England? Do you think we would run the slightest risk of letting this invention of yours fall into England's hands?

"Your question was expressed very undiplomatically, Mr. Edestone, for one who is arrogating to himself the prerogatives of an envoy and ambassador. Nations in speaking to one another use language that is lighter than fairy's thought, and sweeter than a baby's dream, but more deadly than a pestilence. But I will answer you on this occasion just as bluntly and baldly.

"We do propose to hold you virtually a prisoner on German soil until such time as our men of science have completed their labours. If they succeed in solving the secret of your discovery, we shall be ready to try conclusions with the United States, and shall deal with you personally as may seem most advisable, dragging you by force from the very Embassy itself, if you attempt to take refuge there. If, on the other hand, our men of science fail, your position will be in no way preferable. We will simply compel you to disclose your secret to us, and, as I told you once before, we stop at nothing to gain our ends. Your best plan, therefore, and I believe I am your sincere friend when I tell you this, is to sell to my Government at once."

A slightly amused smile flitted over Edestone's lips from time to time as he listened; but when he spoke it was quite seriously.

"I have no doubt," he said, "that everything you tell me is absolutely true. Germany is undoubtedly thorough, whether her thoroughness take the form of the destruction of Louvain, or of sewing two buttons where only one is needed on the trousers of her soldiers. But I pity her for not finding a larger way to gain her ends in the first place, and for her conceit in thinking that a lot of little thoughts and extra buttons when added together make a great nation. Germany may know exactly how many gold and how many amalgam fillings there are in the teeth of the German army, but she does not know that thousands of men leave Germany and come to the United States simply because they do not want their teeth counted. Germany may know what I have done and am doing at my place on the Hudson, but she does not know that she has so incensed me by her methods of obtaining this information that it were better for her if she had never known, or you so boastful as to have told me of it.

"Yes," and he spoke almost with the fervour of an inspired prophet; "Germany may know her alphabet of war from end to end, forward and backward, but she does not know that she and it are doomed to destruction, because she thinks that she can drive the intelligent modern world with a spear, as her forefathers did the wild beasts of the Black Forest."

Von Hemelstein started and laid his hand indignantly to the hilt of his sword. His instructions to bring Edestone safely to Berlin alone prevented him from punishing then and there such insult to his country and his Emperor.

"My orders prevent me from killing you!" he said hoarsely, as he straightened up and, drawing his heels together with a click, turned and stalked away.

He took a seat at the other side of the car, and as if utterly oblivious that such a creature as Edestone existed, produced and deliberately adjusted the two parts of a very long and handsome cigarette holder, and with much straining of his very tight uniform restored the case to the place provided by law for its concealment on his glittering person. He then took out his cigarette case, and after selecting a cigarette, he gently tapped it on the gold cover, glaring all the time quite through and beyond the unspeakable American. With more absurd contortions the cigarette case was disposed of, and matches produced. Then, stretching out his beautiful patent-leather boots, he finally lighted his cigarette.

He took a deep inhalation, and blew from the very bottom of his lungs a thin cloud of smoke in Edestone's direction, while with much rattling he unfolded a newspaper, and pretended to read it.

Edestone, who was with difficulty keeping a straight face, sat all this time solemnly watching him with the expression of a schoolgirl looking at her matinee idol at about the juncture in the last act when that hero puts on his kingly robes which have been hidden for a hundred years in the moth closet of his twenty-story apartment house on upper Riverside Drive.

When the Count finally peeped cautiously over the top of his paper to see what effect he was producing, he felt almost tempted to applaud and blow him a kiss.

"Count von Hemelstein," he said lazily, when finally the Prussian had put down his paper, and was sitting glaring in front of him, "I was just thinking what a stunning book-cover you would make for a cheap novel, or how many thousands of bottles of beer your picture would sell in Hoboken. Hoboken, you know, is the headquarters of the German-American standing army, and your second largest naval base. Or you might serve as——"

He halted in some anxiety, for it seemed as if the Count were about to choke to death.

CHAPTER XIX
THE GERMAN POINT OF VIEW

They sat this way for some time, Edestone looking thoughtfully out of the car window and rather disgusted with himself for having lessened his dignity in the eyes of the other man.

He was broad enough to be able to put himself in von Hemelstein's place. He knew that by birth, education, and example the man's attitude to him, in fact to the rest of the world, was that of a superior being looking down upon those immeasurably beneath him. For him, a Prussian nobleman, to be spoken to in this way by one of a lower sphere was bad enough, but when that one was of the very lowest of spheres, an American, it was acute pain. He looked upon Edestone as a low comedian rather than as a gentleman in the hands of a chivalrous enemy, which the officer considered himself to be.

Edestone himself felt no resentment but the sort of pity that he would feel for one who was born with an hereditary weakness that he could no more control than the colour of his eyes. He was as sorry as he would have been, had he been guilty of laughing at the irregularity of another man's teeth which were not so perfect as his own.

He got up and walked slowly over toward his travelling companion. The handsome warrior quickly let his hand fall to his loaded automatic as if he expected to be attacked, but when he saw Edestone standing quietly before him, and with a rather sad smile on his face, he turned back to his reading and refused to look up, even after Edestone had begun to speak.

"I am sorry, Count von Hemelstein," said the inventor, "to have offended you, and I beg that you will accept my most humble apology. We Americans, I fear, are too much inclined to let our sense of humour run away with us."

The soldier raised his eyes with a threatening look, not knowing but that Edestone was still poking fun at him, or else, fearing the consequences of his rashness, was trying to ingratiate himself with his jailer. But after that glance at Edestone's face he felt confident that his apology was sincere. The Prussian's pride was too deeply wounded, however, for him to give in at once.

"I am glad, Mr. Edestone," he replied stiffly, "that you realize that it is not customary to speak lightly of Germany in the presence of one of her officers."

"I know," exclaimed Edestone, "it was extremely bad taste for me to criticize a civilization so much older than my own, but you will," he smiled, "forgive the cowboy I am sure when he tells you he is sorry." Then seeing by the expression of the officer's face that he had won the day: "Come now, Count von Hemelstein, let's be friends. I would not have liked you had you not resented my remarks, and I was a cad to take advantage of your absolutely defenceless position."

The Count broke out into a hearty laugh, and jumping up took Edestone's extended hand.

"You Americans," he vowed, all traces of his ill-feeling gone, "are the most remarkable chaps. I never saw a cowboy, but if they are anything like you they must be descended from some branch of the Hohenzollern family."

"No, I cannot claim that distinction," laughed Edestone; "but I think perhaps there are many cowboys who if they knew and knowing cared to could boast of as distinguished a lineage. Did you ever breed dogs, Count? Well, if you have, you would know that the good points of the champion do not always appear in the oldest son of the oldest son, but spring up where we least expect to find them. And so it is I think with men; the good points are in the blood and will appear long after the man has lost his family tree. Sometimes they appear in individuals who show so strongly the traits of the champion that they scorn the existence of musty documents to tell them who they are."

"Then, Mr. Edestone, you do not believe in our method of keeping our best blood where it belongs—at the top?"

"Yes, I do most thoroughly approve of some of your methods. They are perhaps the best that have yet been devised, but you have not yet found the true method of following the centre of the stream. You sometimes dip from an eddy, simply because you believe that at some time it might have been in the middle, and you allow the deep dark red torrent to carry its saturated solution by you."

"Well, Mr. Edestone," the Count smiled, "whether you are descended from a cowboy king or a business baron, you are deuced good company. I am glad that if I am to be cooped up here for two days it is with you instead of some conceited English duke, whose English grandfather was a fool and whose American grandfather was a knave—oh, I beg pardon. I am like poor little Alice in Wonderland when she was talking with the mouse. I seem always to insist upon talking about cats."

Edestone laughed.

"And now, Mr. Edestone, that you have been such a brick and apologized to me, I shall have to admit that I was rather rude in what I said to you. I think that the German Government has every intention of treating you fairly, and if you will only listen to reason, you will find that they are as anxious to bring this war to a close as is the United States. I know, however, that Germany intends to have her fair share of the earth; we are righting for our national existence, and we will not, and in fact we cannot afford to, stop at anything. If you really do not intend to sell your invention to any of the countries of Europe, you can at least use your influence with the United States to keep out of this muss, and let us settle our little difficulties in our own way."

Edestone became serious. "My sole object, Count von Hemelstein," he said, "is to stop this war and settle these 'little difficulties,' as you call them, without further loss of life. If your Government will allow me to take back to England some assurance that it is now willing to discuss a settlement, I know that my Government will keep out of the discussion."

The conversation was interrupted at this point by the stopping of the train at a station where the Count said he expected to take on the lunch baskets. With a comfortable lunch between them, and a bottle of wine to divide, they soon forgot their differences and laughed and joked like old friends.

"It is a great pity, Mr. Edestone," said the Uhlan, "that you are not a German. I am sure the Kaiser would like you. He might even make you a Count, and then you could marry some woman of rank and with all your money you could be one of the greatest swells in Europe. He might make you an officer, too, so that you could wear a uniform and carry the decorations which he would confer upon you. Then when Americans came over to Kiel in their big yachts, you could tell the Emperor which were the real cowboy families and which were the Knickerbocker noblemen."

"Well, that is exactly what I was thinking about you, Count von Hemelstein," Edestone chuckled. "If you would only come over to America I would get you a nice position in one of our large department stores, where your knowledge of German would be of the greatest assistance to you and soon put you at the top. Your German-Jew boss would invite you to his palace at Long Branch to dinner some night before a holiday and you would meet his beautiful daughter. She would take you into the big parlour, which would be open that night, and say to all her friends: 'I want you to shake hands with Count von Hemelstein, who is head salesman in Pa's M. & D. Department.' And she would be corrected by Ma, who would say: 'No, dearie, you mean the M. & W. Department.'

"With your military training you would, by this time, have undoubtedly become a second lieutenant in one of our exclusive National Guard regiments, and after marrying 'Dearie,' you would come over to Germany and visit me at one of my castles on the Rhine. I would now have gambled away my entire fortune, and my son, the Baron von Edestone, would marry 'Dearie's' daughter."

So they passed the time with good-humoured chaffing, carefully avoiding more serious subjects, and when they reached Berlin they had become fast friends.

But as the train pulled into the German capital the Count leaned forward a trifle persuasively. "Now, Mr. Edestone," he said, "we have had a deuced good time together, and to tell the truth I am sorry to turn you over because I do not believe these old fellows on the General Staff will understand you as I do, but don't be an ass, I beg of you, and stand up against these wise old chaps. Do what they want you to do—they know better than you how to handle this complicated European situation. You will get no thanks for your trouble if you do not, and you may get your fingers rapped or even pretty severely pinched. My orders are to see you to some comfortable hotel, any that you may select. I would suggest the Hotel Adlon as perhaps the most comfortable.

"After that I am to take you to call on General von Lichtenstein, who will hear what you have to say, and if in his judgment you should go higher he will pass you on."

"I am to see nothing more of you?" asked Edestone.

"My duty finishes when General von Lichtenstein takes you up. You will, of course, be watched and your every movement will be recorded, but that will not be my duty, nor here in Berlin will you be at all annoyed by it. Now that you are in Germany, you will be looked upon as a friend and treated accordingly, unless you are found not to be. I have given you my card, and I will take great pleasure in introducing you at the clubs or helping you in any way so long as it is consistent with my duty."

"You are extremely kind, and I appreciate it very much, Count von Hemelstein."

"Now above all things," warned the Count, and his tone was very impressive, "if by any chance you should be ordered to appear before His Imperial Majesty, please be careful what you say. You have said things to me in the last two days which, understanding you as I do, I could overlook, but I would no more think of repeating them while you are in Germany than I would think of flying. They were not of a nature that would make it my duty to report them, but they might get you into no end of trouble. For instance, you would not be so foolish as to intimate that the Hohenzollern family is not in the middle of the 'big stream.'" He smiled in spite of himself.

Then as the train rolled into the station he took Edestone's hand and said: "*Auf wiedersehen*, my friend. I must now assume my other role of your escort of honour. Speak German," he suggested quickly as the guards came into the car; "you will be less apt to be annoyed."

Edestone was conducted hastily through the station, where automobiles waited to whisk him and his entire party off to the hotel. At his request, the trunks containing all his apparatus were sent to the American Embassy. He was not as familiar with Berlin as he was with the other capitals of Europe, but if he had not known that Germany was engaged in a most desperate war, and millions of her sons were being sacrificed, there was nothing that he saw as he rushed through the city that would have suggested it.

He was received at the hotel with extreme politeness, but it was the politeness that was insulting. The proprietor, waiters, and even the bell-boys treated him with poorly concealed contempt, and though he spoke to them in perfect German, would always answer in English, as if to show him that they knew he was of that despised race.

Count von Hemelstein left him with the understanding that he would call for him in the morning and conduct him to General von Lichtenstein.

CHAPTER XX
GENERAL VON LICHTENSTEIN

That afternoon, Edestone took occasion to call at the American Embassy, where he found that Ambassador Gerard, broken down by the strain of the first few months of the war, during which he had accomplished such wonderful work, had been forced to go to Wiesbaden for a rest.

The Ambassador had left in charge Mr. William Jones, First Secretary of Legation, who with his wife was occupying the Embassy and representing the United States. The doctors had warned the Secretary that the Ambassador's condition was such that he must have absolute quiet, and that he should under no circumstances be troubled or even communicated with in regard to affairs of state. Jones was, therefore, to all intents and purposes the Ambassador.

This suited Edestone's plans perfectly, for Jones was only a few years older than himself and he had known him intimately since boyhood.

His friend received him with almost the delight of a man who has been marooned on a desert island and was pining for the sight of a friendly face.

"Well, well, Jack," he said, "what foolish thing is this that you are up to now? We have received the most extraordinary instructions from the State Department—I gather that the Secretary of State has either lost his mind or that you have got him under a spell, and then with your hypnotic power have suggested that he order us to do things which we could not do in peace times and which are simply out of the question now. Don't you people over home understand that these Germans, from the Kaiser to the lowest peasant, are all in such an exalted state of Anglophobia that they regard everyone with distrust, and are especially suspicious of us. My advice to you, as Lawrence would say," —referring to one of his under-secretaries, a college mate and intimate friend of Edestone's, —"is to 'can that high-brow stuff' and come down to earth."

"Now, speaking for myself as your friend, I advise you to go and see General von Lichtenstein, whom you will find a delightful old gentleman but as wise as Solomon's aunt. Talk to him like a sweet little boy, and then come back to the Legation and stop with us while you see something of the war. I can take you to within one hundred and fifty miles of the firing line and show you the crack regiments of Germany looking as happy and sleek as if they were merely out for one of the yearly manoeuvres. I would have difficulty, though, in showing you any of the wounded, as they are very careful to see that we are not offended by any of the horrors that one reads of in the American papers."

"Berlin is being forced to fiddle, eh, while Germany is burning?"

"Yes, she suggests the hysterical condition of Paris just before the Reign of Terror, while I, like Benjamin Franklin, in 'undertaker's clothes' in the midst of barbaric splendour, wait for the inevitable."

"Is your face, like his, 'as well known as that of the moon'?" asked Edestone.

"Yes, but a thing to be insulted, not like his to be painted on the lids of snuff-boxes, as souvenirs for kings.

"Or if that does not amuse you, Mrs. Jones can introduce you to some of the prettiest girls you ever saw."

"Big, strong, fat, and healthy, I suppose, with red faces looking as if they had just been washed with soap and water."

"Well, then we might have some golf, and if you will give me half a stroke, I will play you $5 a hole and $50 on the game. Or if that is too rich for your blood, I will play you dollar Nassau. In fact, Jack, I will do anything to get this foolish idea out of your head. These people can't see a joke at any time, but to try one now might put you into a very serious if not dangerous position. Now you go along and see Lawrence, as I have to look after some American refugees who are waiting in the outer office. You will dine with us tonight, of course."

Lawrence Stuyvesant, to whom the Secretary had referred, appeared at the door at that moment and beckoned to Edestone. He was one of those irrepressible Americans, born with an absolute lack of respect for anything that suggested convention, at home in any company and showing absolutely no preference. He would be found joking with the stokers in the engine room when he might be walking with the Admiral on the quarter-deck, flirting with a deaf old Duchess when he might be supping with the leader of the ballet. With a sense of humour that would have made his fortune on the stage, he spoke half-a-dozen languages and a dozen dialects. He could imitate the Kaiser or give a Yiddish dialect to a Chinaman. Light-hearted to a fault, he would make a joke at anyone's expense, preferably his own. An entertaining chap, but a rolling stone that could roll up hill or skip lightly over the surface of a placid lake with equal facility. He had already run through two considerable fortunes, and had been almost everything from a camel driver to a yacht's captain. Now he imagined himself to be a diplomat.

"Behold the dreamer cometh," he said in Yiddish dialect as Edestone approached, and grasping the inventor by both hands, dragged him into the other room, and began to ask questions so fast that a Chicago reporter, had he heard, would have died of sheer mortification.

After he had gotten all the information that he could pump, pull, and squeeze out of Edestone, he shook his head discouragingly.

"I am darn glad to see you, old chap," he said, "but I am sorry to hear that you have come over to try and reason with this bunch of nuts. Don't you know they are so damn conceited that if you were to tell them that every time you look at a German you see two men, they would believe you; and then as if they hated to lie to themselves, they would say perhaps it was an optical illusion. Tell them that God did not create anyone but the Germans and that he left the rest of the world to the students in his office, and they will give you a smile of assent." Edestone smiled indulgently. "Tell them that when the Kaiser frowns every wheel in the United States stops and refuses to move until reassured by the German papers that it is but the frown of an indulgent father and not the thunder of their future War Lord, and they will give a knowing look. Tell them that only German is taught in our public schools, and that any child who does not double-cross himself at the mention of the name of any of the North German Lloyd steamers is taken out and shot, and they will say, 'Ach so?'

"But just you pull something about what a hit Brother Henry made in the United States, especially with the navy, and what a swell chance he would have of being elected Admiral when Dewey resigns, then look out! Get under your umbrella and sit perfectly still until the storm passes. Keep well down in the trenches and don't expose anything that you do not want sent to the cleaners. For when one of these Dutchmen begins to splutter, there is nothing short of the U-29 that can stand the tidal wave of beer and sauerkraut which has been lying in wait for some unsuspecting neutral in their flabby jowls like nuts in a squirrel's cheek. They back-fire, skip, short-circuit, and finally blow up, and if you don't throw on a bucket or two of flattery quick, you've got a duel on your hands, which for an American in this country means that you get it going and coming."

Edestone, knowing Lawrence well, took what he said largely as a joke; but from his own observations and from what Jones had told him he felt convinced that there did not exist the kindest feeling for Americans in Berlin. Brushing all this aside, he turned to Lawrence with a businesslike air:

"Where are the trunks that I sent to the Embassy?" he asked. "Have they got here yet?"

"Down in the basement," Lawrence nodded.

"I'd like to get something out of them."

"Well, why look at me?" inquired Lawrence. "I'm no baggage smasher."

"It's a pity you're not," rejoined Edestone. "You would be better at that than you are at diplomacy. However, all I want is for you to have someone show me where they are."

"Fred, show the King of America where his royal impedimenta await his royal pleasure," Lawrence directed a young man with the manners of a Bowery boy, who appeared in answer to his summons.

With him Edestone went down to the trunks and took from one of them a small receiving instrument with a dial attachment similar to the one on top of the Deionizer, which he had dropped into the Channel. Then after a few words with his other friends in the Embassy, he went back to the hotel.

The next morning Count von Hemelstein called, and it was quite like meeting an old friend. Edestone was really sorry when, the Count leaving him at the door of General Headquarters said: "This is where I turn you over to my superiors. These are times that try men's souls, and you are now dealing with men who must win."

They had arrived on the stroke of the hour, and Edestone was quickly taken in charge and shown without a moment's delay into the presence of General von Lichtenstein. The General was a man whose age was impossible to tell. He was over sixty, but how much over one found it hard to estimate. He was erect and rather thin, and he wore his uniform with the care of a much younger man. The lines about his mouth and chin, which are such a sure index, were hidden by a full beard, white as snow and rather long. His high forehead was half covered by a huge shock of hair, also perfectly white, which was parted neatly on the side. His steel-blue eyes, looking out through a pair of gold-rimmed spectacles, were bright, but were set so far back under his heavy brows that they looked very old, very wise, and almost mysterious.

When Edestone was brought into the room without any form of introduction, the General rose and greeted him in the most kind and fatherly manner.

"Good-morning, Mr. Edestone," he said in English with a marked accent. "I am very glad to see you," and, putting out his hand with an air of simple kindness as if to lead him to a chair, he said: "Won't you sit down, sir?

"You must not mind if I treat you like a boy," he went on with a gentle smile; "you are about the age of my own son who was killed at Ypres. I am too old to fight any more, so they keep me here to entertain distinguished strangers like yourself," and he laughed quietly to himself, looking at Edestone as he might at a little boy whom he had just told that he had on a very pretty suit of clothes.

He picked up from his desk, a box of very large cigars, selected two, and, after looking very carefully at one to see that it was absolutely perfect, handed it without a word to Edestone. After he had watched with great interest to see that Edestone had lighted his cigar properly, he lighted his own.

"I see by the way you smoke that you are a good judge of tobacco. I have always understood that you Americans like very fresh cigars and smoke them immediately after they are made. I like them old myself."

"You are thinking of Cuba, perhaps," suggested Edestone.

"Oh, that is true," admitted the old gentleman. "The Americans live in the United States and you do not allow the other inhabitants of the hemisphere to the north or to the south of you to use that name. You are perfectly right; you are—what do you call it?—the boss," and again he smiled his gentle smile.

"I get all my cigars from England," he continued. "The English and I have very similar tastes—in cigars. I have a very old friend, Professor Weibezhal, who lives in England, and he sends them over to me. I just received these a few days ago. He is not having a very good time over there now, he writes me. He can't get what he wants to eat, and he says he misses his German beer."

Edestone could scarcely realize that he was sitting in General Headquarters, the very heart of German militarism, talking to General von Lichtenstein, the most powerful and astute man in all Europe. But for the German accent and magnificent uniform it might have been in the Union Club in New York, and he himself talking to a very nice, rather simple-minded old gentleman, who was flattered by the attention of a younger man.

After the General had inquired about a friend of his who lived in America—he said he did not know exactly where, not in New York, but some town near there, Cincinnati or perhaps St. Louis. This struck Edestone as strange when he thought of the springs on his father's old place which were marked on a German map that he had seen, although he himself did not know of their existence, and he had spent his entire childhood roaming all over it.

Finally, when he had told him one or two stories about an American woman whom he had been quite fond of when he was a young man, the General said in a most apologetic manner:

"Now I must not keep you. I suppose you would like to go out with some of the younger officers and see something of this war, now that you are over here. Or, by the way, it was about some discovery or invention you have made that you called to see me, was it not? What is this invention, tell me, and exactly what is it that you want the German Government to do? If you will explain to me and I can understand, I will be glad to help you in any way I can. Of course you know that I am a very small part of the German Empire. I am, however, in a position to bring your wishes to those who are above me and are all-powerful."

Then, while Edestone explained to him everything in regard to his mission except the actual construction of the Deionizer, the old General sat quietly smoking, smiling occasionally and listening with the attention that a man might show who was being told of an improvement in some machine in which he had no personal interest but was glad to be enlightened, although up to that time the matter had been something he had never thought much about.

He would now and then say, "How very interesting!" "Can that be possible?" "Is that so?" Not even when Edestone described the pictures shown to the King of England did he manifest any feeling except that of kindly interest in a most charming young man, who was taking a great deal of trouble to explain his youthful hopes to a rather slow-thinking old one.

He allowed Edestone to talk on, not even interrupting him, to ask a single question, and when the visitor had finished by expressing the hope that he might be instrumental in bringing the war to a close, General von Lichtenstein replied with apparent sincerity:

"I really see no reason why you should not. You are a brilliant inventor, apparently a hard worker, and above all you seem willing to give your talents to the world for the benefit of your fellow-men. The only thing that you lack is age and experience. I am not an inventor, I cannot work hard any more, and I am not known as a philanthropist, but I have age and I have experience, so I think that you and I might make a good combination. Leave this to me, and I think I can show you how all that you wish to accomplish can be accomplished, if not exactly in your way, in a way which I think you will agree with me is a better way. Whereas I should not dare to speak for His Imperial Majesty, the Kaiser, I believe I am perfectly safe in saying that he will see you and inspect your photographs, drawings, and anything else that you may wish to show him. I will see him and let you know when and where."

He laid his hand on Edestone's shoulder and walked with him as far as the door.

"You are a fine young fellow," he said with a hearty grasp of the hand as he bade him goodbye, "and all you want is an old head on your broad young shoulders. Let the old man help you, and everything will be all right."

When Edestone was on the outside and thought over all that the General had said, he would have been delighted with the turn things had taken had he not been warned by Jones and did he not recall what Count von Hemelstein had said.

Being so straightforward himself, he could not understand deceit in others, and when he recalled the almost inspired expression on the kind old gentleman's face when he spoke of his son so recently killed in battle, he could not bring himself to believe that this was the trained diplomat of iron who covered with that gentle exterior a determination to crush and kill anything that came between him and the accomplishment of the great purpose, the great cause to which he had gladly sacrificed his first-born and the heir to his name and title.

It was nearly noon, Greenwich time, now, so Edestone hurried back to his hotel to receive from "Specs" the daily signal: "Awaiting orders. All is well."

With the forethought of a good general he wished to be prepared for any emergency, and when the needle of the receiver, which he had taken from the trunk at the Embassy, recorded the reassuring message, Edestone thoroughly satisfied with the work of the morning returned to the Embassy to keep his appointment with Lawrence.

CHAPTER XXI
HE INSTALLS HIS WIRELESS

Lawrence was on the lookout for him when he arrived at the Embassy, and conducted him at once to his own private quarters, where they could be absolutely alone.

"Now, Lawrence," said Edestone, when they had made themselves comfortable, "I want your assistance. Are you game?"

"Well I ask you, you old simp! Did you not initiate me, in my freshman year, in the Ki Ki Ki, and do you think that I have forgotten the oath that I took while sitting with my naked back within a foot of a red-hot stove, my fingers in a bucket of red ink, and you branding me with a lump of ice?" He went through with some ridiculous gesticulations to prove the honours that had been bestowed upon him.

"I know, old man, but this is no college boy performance. Before you commit yourself I want you to understand that you are running great danger. Besides, I don't think that the Acting Ambassador would exactly approve, as it might involve the United States. Desperate situations, though, have to be met sometimes with desperate measures."

"Yours is a noble heart, Lord Reginald Bolingbroke, and the child is safe in the hands of Jack Hathaway, the Boy Scout. Go on, I listen. Your story interests me strangely," said Lawrence.

Edestone paid no attention to this, but went on in the same manner: "I can assure you that, except as a last resort, you will not be called on to do anything that will be an actual violation of our neutrality, and not even then until I have obtained the permission of the Secretary of the Embassy. But from now on, Lawrence, you will be looked upon with great suspicion, and you may have trouble explaining yourself out of a German prison, if not from in front of a firing squad." He eyed the younger man keenly as if questioning whether or not he could rely upon him, and upon seeing this, Lawrence altered his light tone and for once spoke soberly.

"Jack Edestone, you know perfectly well that you can depend upon me, while I know that you will not do anything that is not strictly on the level, so what's the use of saying anything more. I'm with you. What is it you want?"

"Well, take me up on the roof," said Edestone.

"Say, Bo, is that all?"

"Now be quiet, Lawrence; do what you are told. You will get a good run for your money, so for Heaven's sake do be serious."

The roof, which was reached by elevator, was flat, covered with cement, and but for the chimneys, a few skylights, and the penthouse over the elevator shaft, was unencumbered.

Edestone first went over and examined this penthouse with great care. He found as he expected a small free space over the machinery which was entirely hidden from view and could be reached only from the roof of the car when it was run to the top of the elevator shaft, and then by climbing over the big drum around which the cable ran. It was perfectly dark inside and one could remain there for days without being discovered.

After thoroughly inspecting this, the inventor went over and examined the tall flag-pole, first saluting the stars and stripes which were waving from it. Finally, appearing satisfied, he led Lawrence to the edge of the roof and stood for a moment looking over the coping wall at the city below. He seemed to be establishing his bearings, but seeing one of the soldiers who was stationed in the street near the Embassy, he stepped back quickly.

"Come below," he drew Lawrence back. "We must not be seen."

Lawrence, who by this time was satisfied that there was going to be some real excitement, led the way back to his apartments.

"Little did I think," said Edestone with a smile when they were once more settled, "when I used to chase you out of the wireless room on board the *Storm Queen*, Lawrence, that I would some day make use of the information which you got there, and which cost me a new instrument and one of the best operators I ever had, but that is the reason I am calling on you now."

"Good," cried Lawrence. "I am the best little sparker that ever sent an S. O. S. over the blue between drinks of salt water, while swimming on my back around the wireless room chased by a man-eating shark. And as for a catcher, why, my boy, I can receive while eating a piece of toast."

"All right," said Edestone with a laugh; "as your references from your last place are so good you shall have the job. You took charge of my trunks, did you not?"

"Yes," replied Lawrence.

"Well, in the one marked 'Black,' there is a small wireless instrument. The Germans know that I have it, and I realize that they let it get through in the hope of picking up any messages I may send out. They do not know, however, that I intend to send but two, and these will be both of but one word each. If they can make head or tail of these, they are welcome. Still, on Jones's account, I want them not to know that I am sending from here, nor do I care to have Jones know that this instrument is in the Embassy. I want you to install it in the penthouse above the drum, and I will assure you that if I ask you to send out my two messages, it will not be until after Jones has given his consent. Do you think that you can do this?"

Lawrence pondered for some moments. "Of course I can send the messages, and I can install the instrument too, but how to do it without letting the Secretary know or keeping the damn German servants from catching on I don't quite see."

"I have thought of all that. The elevator is an electric one and any person can run it by pushing the button. All you have to do then is to unpack the wireless instrument here in your room, and after you have adjusted it you can certainly arrange in some way to get it on top of the elevator car?"

"Yes," Lawrence nodded.

"Now my Mr. Black, who is at the hotel, is one of the best electricians in America. He can install the instrument easily, and I will tell you how. In the other trunk I sent up is a moving-picture machine— —"

"Oh, I say, come now!" said Lawrence. "I suppose you are going to tell me next that you've got a setting hen in another trunk and that you are going to bribe Fritz and Karl with fresh eggs. And that's no merry jest; we haven't seen a fresh egg in Berlin in six months."

"No, Lawrence, I'm not joking. I mean exactly what I say. I have a moving-picture machine with me and lots of films, interesting ones too, and I propose to give a show right here in the Embassy. I will ask the Secretary to allow every servant in the house to come in and see it. I can keep them quiet for an hour, and during that time you can get Black, who will be acting as my helper, into the elevator shaft and run him up to the top of the penthouse. You can depend upon him to do the rest, and all you will have to do after that is to see that he gets down before I turn up the lights, when your absence might be remarked. Isn't that simple enough?"

"But how am I to get up there to send the messages when the time comes?" asked Lawrence.

"I have not thought of that yet. You may not have to send any messages at all, and if you do, it will not be for some little time, so perhaps it's just as well that you can't get up there without my assistance."

Then with a jolly laugh, which showed that although he was pitting his strength and wits against the great General Staff, the most wonderful machine on earth, he was as light-hearted as a boy, he said:

"You might, as you did on the yacht, want to see the wheels go 'round, or else you'd be sending messages off to a lot of girls.

"Now, make haste," he directed, "send for the trunk marked 'Black.'"

With the arrival of the trunk the machine was soon adjusted, and Edestone having tested Lawrence's knowledge, and explained to him again exactly what he was to do, gave him orally all that was necessary for him to know about the code that was to be used.

A little later, when they rejoined Jones, the Acting Ambassador, he wanted to know what they had been up to. "Has Lawrence been giving you the telephone numbers of some of these prospective war brides," he asked, "or does he want you to take tea with some Royal Princess? You know, Jack, Lawrence seems to be quite a favourite in the very smart army set. It appears that they have heard that his grandfather was the military governor of New York. That makes him eligible. And besides, he is teaching the entire royal family the latest American dances."

"Well, if you care to know what we have been up to," said Edestone, "I don't mind telling you that we have been arranging for a little moving-picture entertainment here at the Embassy. Have we your permission to go ahead with it? It would be a little treat for the people here in the house."

"Certainly," consented Jones. "Go as far as you like. I myself will be glad to see something beside battles and dead men. But why in the name of common sense have you lugged a moving-picture machine all the way over from America when you might have brought us some potatoes? I suppose, of course, it has something to do with your fool scheme. Well, as long as it doesn't get us into trouble, and helps to take our minds off this war, I haven't any objection. When do you propose to have your show?"

"I can't exactly say as to that," Edestone answered. "It all depends upon Lawrence, who is to be my trap-man. He had better fix the date." He looked at the other conspirator with a questioning glance.

"We'll have it tonight then," said Lawrence. "I think I can get up my part by that time." He made significant faces at Edestone behind the Secretary's back.

"Tonight's the night, eh?" said Jones with a smile. "Very well, we'll all be on hand."

Edestone, after his experiences on the frontier, and his two days' journey shut up in the railroad car, greatly enjoyed these evenings with his old friends, the Joneses; and found pleasure in meeting some of Mrs. Jones's young friends, who were delighted when they heard of the moving-picture show.

Later, while the Secretary of Legation and Edestone were alone, Lawrence having insisted upon helping Black install the moving-picture machine, Jones turned to his guest.

"I saw General von Lichtenstein at the club this afternoon," he said. "He seemed to be delighted with you, Jack. Said you were a fine young man, and will not believe that you are not of German descent. He hopes to present you when the Emperor returns to Berlin, which he says will be in a few days. When I told him that you had not told me what your invention was he merely laughed. I know he did not believe me. He seems to think that the United States has something to do with sending you over here. He is a sly old fox and I tell you to look out for him."

He might have added more but Lawrence appeared just then and, imitating a barker in a sideshow, announced that everything was ready for the performance.

The entertainment proved a brilliant success. Edestone showed some scenes from America which he had brought over to amuse the distinguished audiences he had expected to meet in Europe. The pictures showing him tossing great weights and men about the room delighted the servants, but the Secretary only looked bored and Mrs. Jones did not hesitate to say that she thought Edestone must be losing his mind, travelling all around the world with such silly things.

But it answered his purposes. Lawrence soon came in and whispered to him that Mr. Black and the wireless machine were safely up in the penthouse, and if Edestone could hold his audience for a half-an-hour longer the work would be finished.

Edestone then threw on the screen all the crowned heads of Europe, taking tea, playing tennis, and laying corner-stones. He had some especially fine pictures of the German Emperor. He was getting a little nervous though as he found his supply of films running short, but at that moment he spied Lawrence entering the door, who gave the signal "All is well."

The Secretary, after the entertainment, pressed Edestone to tell him something more about his invention, but Edestone shook his head.

"I am purposely keeping you out of this, William," he said, "for if I get into trouble I don't want to drag you and the Missus in with me."

Then with the promise that he would move around to the Embassy in the morning, he left for his hotel.

CHAPTER XXII
KAFFEE KLATSCH

Edestone had now been at the Embassy for about a week and was wondering what would be the next move on the part of the German General Staff.

He knew that General von Lichtenstein was not waiting for the return of the Emperor, for he was in Berlin. In fact he had seen him driving past the Embassy in his big automobile with the General. Edestone was just coming out, and although he was not certain, he thought that the General had recognized him, for he leaned over and spoke to the Emperor, who looked straight at the American.

He had heard nothing, but from what the different officers at the clubs had dropped, he was confident that he had not been forgotten. These had all received him with great show of cordiality, and among Count von Hemelstein's friends there had sprung up a certain friendliness, which he knew was due to the Count's influence. The Count himself, on the other hand, seemed now to be a little bit ill at ease when in his presence. He said to Edestone one night after he had been drinking quite heavily:

"Mr. Edestone, it is a great pity that you have come over here and mixed up in our troubles. It is too late now, however; you could not get out if you tried," and then with a sneer, "not even if you called to your assistance Princess Wilhelmina, who seems to take so much interest in you."

Edestone decided that the German General Staff were preparing their answer to the new condition that had been brought about by his invention, and that they were waiting for additional information before delivering it. He knew that they must realize that some action must be taken, but with the forethought for which they were so celebrated they were preparing the way. When they had satisfied themselves that they were in possession of all of the facts that could be gotten without his assistance, and had looked at these from every possible standpoint, he would be sent for, and not until then.

Several days after his sight of the Emperor, Edestone, in passing through the halls of the Embassy, was approached by one of the German servants, who in a rather mysterious manner handed him a note, which read as follows:

"Dear Mr. Edestone: Please have Mr. Stuyvesant bring you to tea on Tuesday afternoon. It is a matter of the greatest importance. I must see you.

"PRINCESS WILHELMINA."

He knew that Princess Wilhelmina was in Berlin. Lawrence had seen her at the house of Princess Adolph, and in his joking way had said that she had inquired very particularly after the American inventor, and that Count von Hemelstein, who thought he was the "candy kid," was very jealous.

But why had she sent for him? he thought. When he spoke to Lawrence, he in his usual jocular manner exclaimed: "Ah, so now you are to have Kaffee Klatsch with the Princess. I told you so. The lady is in love with you, and the Emperor is going to offer you her hand in marriage after he has bestowed on you an Iron Cross in return for one of your quack medicines."

Edestone, who declined to take any notice of this, thoughtfully said: "Can it be possible that she also is a traitor? She cannot imagine for one moment that she will be able to accomplish what her father was unable to do, but God gives women confidence in themselves to compensate them for the fact that nobody else has." With an impatient gesture, "No, no, Lawrence, that is impossible! That sweet little child!"

"Ah!" said Lawrence, "so little Willie Westinghouse has fallen for the baby stare?"

"You are absurd, Lawrence," said Edestone with a rather embarrassed expression. "It is perfectly clear. She feels deeply her father's disgrace, and perhaps she thinks that I might do something to help her to exonerate him."

"Well," said Lawrence, "I don't think there is any satisfaction in being a hero in Berlin while being locked up in the Tower in London like her father, but you are the limit. You talk as quietly of using your influence for a Prince of the Royal Blood with the King of England as if she were asking you to get her brother a position on the New York police force. God certainly gave you confidence in yourself."

"There is nothing very strange about that," replied Edestone. "As I understand it, the only thing that they have against the Duke of Windthorst is that he was dining with Rebener and myself, and were I to state that at no time during the dinner had he shown any disloyalty to his King and country, it might do a little good. But whatever it is, we will go and see this afternoon."

About half-past five they were driven to the handsome residence occupied by Princess Adolph when in Berlin.

They were immediately shown into a large and beautiful room in the style of Louis XVI., which had evidently been designed and executed by a French artist. It was free from the brutal touch which the Germans show in their attempt at the refinement of the French Renaissance of that period.

They were received by Princess Adolph, a very striking young woman, who shocked all of Berlin by affecting French clothes, French language, and a French mode of life. She was surrounded by some of the dashing young officers of the very exclusive army set. These glared through their monocles when the Americans were announced and did not try to hide their annoyance.

Lawrence, without taking the slightest notice of these "Knights of the Butchered Face," as he called them, with his usual careless and frivolous manner, went over to the Princess and immediately began to shower upon her in the most effusive manner compliment after compliment, which she received with laughter. She rather prided herself on shocking Berlin by pretending to be tremendously interested in this wild young American.

The Princess turned to Edestone and extended her hand. He had hesitated; he resented the manner of her young gallants, and feared that they might, with their usual rudeness to Americans in the presence of women, put him into an embarrassing position. Smiling she said:

"I welcome you, Mr. Edestone, as the greatest lion of them all in this den of lions," and with a reproving frown she waved her hand at the officers who were so poorly hiding their annoyance.

She then turned to Princess Wilhelmina, who was seated behind a large table and was pouring out a cup of coffee, which she continued to do when she saw Edestone until it was called to her attention that the cup was full as well as the saucer.

"Billy," she nodded, "you and Mr. Edestone are old friends. Give him a cup of tea; I know he does not like *Kaffee und Schlagsahne.*"

The little Princess, who was very much embarrassed, extended her hand, which Edestone took and seated himself beside her.

This scene might have been enacted in an English country house if it had not been so entirely different. The Germans, in their effort to affect certain charming English customs and Germanize them, in the process lose the charm. Tea time for the Englishman is the hour of relaxation after a day in the open, when he can in his easy clothes receive the homage of the ladies in their beautiful tea-gowns. Whereas here, these men in their tight-fitting and uncomfortable uniforms, were attitudinizing and indulging in that military form of gallantry, which may be picturesque but certainly looks most uncomfortable.

The entrance of the Americans had thrown a chill upon the entire company. The officers simply refused to open their mouths, and sat glaring at the two intruders.

Edestone, after having made several attempts to relieve the situation, relapsed into silence. The feeble efforts of the Princess Wilhelmina but added to the atmosphere of restraint which she was unable to dispel.

Princess Adolph up to this time had been entirely monopolized by Lawrence, but catching an appealing look from her English cousin, came to the rescue at last. She was apparently in the secret, and in a most natural manner called upon Princess Wilhelmina to show Mr. Edestone her new French garden, which she said had been laid out by a young American studying at the École des Beaux Arts.

Princess Billy, who by this time was in such a state of excitement that she could scarcely get up from where she was sitting, and as if to postpone as long as possible the meeting which she had brought upon herself, managed to say:

"I don't think that Mr. Edestone is interested in such simple things as flowers," but catching the glance that was thrown at her by Princess Adolph she continued with a nervous little laugh: "Come, Mr. Edestone, I hope I shall be able to explain everything to you properly."

When the timid little figure led the way and was followed by that of the big man with his dignified bearing, one might almost imagine that it was an indulgent father taking his very frightened little daughter out to give her a lecture.

When they were on the outside and alone, as she stopped and grasped the balcony to support herself she said, looking up into his face with eyes in which tears were gathering:

"Oh, Mr. Edestone, I don't know what to say! I don't know what you will think of me. I know you hate all of us and especially me."

"Oh, don't say that, Princess!" interrupted Edestone, moved to pity for the poor little child who seemed to him, as he looked down into her sweet little face, almost young enough to have been his own daughter.

"Oh yes you do; I know you do! But I am not what you think I am," and in a very hurried manner, looking about her, she continued, lowering her voice: "I am no traitor to my country, and I know that what my father did he did because he believed it was his duty."

"Oh, Princess Wilhelmina!" said Edestone, as if to stop her on this most disagreeable subject.

"Please do not call me Princess in that sarcastic manner. I hate being a Princess! I know you hate all of our class, and believe that we are all as heartless as we are sometimes forced to appear. But it is not of that that I wish to speak. My sole object in sending for you is to tell you that I know you are in great danger, and to beg—I mean advise—you to leave Berlin at once. I know that you believe I am working for them, and in fact I could not have arranged this interview unless I had left them under the impression that I was, but I don't care. Please go before it is too late."

Edestone, who at first thought that she might have been playing a part, was now convinced of her sincerity. "My dear little Princess Billy," he said, leaning over and with great effort resisting his inclination to take her hand, "is that why you sent for me?"

"Yes," she blushed and smiled when he used the familiar form of address, "I have heard that you were going to be killed, and I was determined to warn you, so I pretended to be working for them. Now please go before it is too late."

"But, Princess, why did you take all of this risk for me?"

"Oh, I don't know; but I must show you the garden. I hope that you won't think I am very forward."

She then hurriedly passed into the garden and gave him in a very rapid and disconnected manner a description of the different plants, fountains, statues, etc. She hurried back into the drawing-room, but just before reaching the other group, she said in an undertone:

"Now, won't you promise me that you will leave Berlin at once?"

Before he had time to answer they were joined by Princess Adolph.

The Americans remained for a few moments and then took their leave. The little Princess, as she put her icy cold hand in his, gave him an appealing look.

CHAPTER XXIII
THE TWO-WHEELED MYSTERY

The Secretary came in with a very grave face one morning after having had a long talk with the German Chancellor.

"Do you know, Jack," he said, "I think the German Government intends to declare war on us, and I would not be a bit surprised if she proposes to strike first and declare afterwards. Their newspapers, and they are all inspired by the Government, you know, are working up a strong anti-American feeling, and this I think is done in order that when they do strike the Government may have the entire country back of it. Have you noticed, too, that they are constantly increasing the guard around the Embassy, which is either to save us or to catch us? Is it possible that your nonsense has got anything to do with all this? By Jove, Jack, I think it is about time that you told me what you are up to."

Edestone considered for a moment. "When you tell me that you are absolutely certain that they are going to strike, I will tell you, William, and not before. You know enough now, however, to realize that those soldiers outside are to catch and not protect. It is me that they want, though, and not you. Your position is perfectly safe and unassailable so long as you do not know too much."

That ended the discussion for the time, but Lawrence came in one night in a state of great excitement. He had just seen some woman who, he rather intimated, was a little bit fond of him, and who was also very closely connected with certain high officials. She had told him, he said, apparently joking although he knew she was in earnest, that she hoped her pretty boy would not mix up with this man Edestone, or he might get into trouble too.

"'They are only allowing us to stay in Berlin,' she said, 'until they get you, Jack,'" declared Lawrence, "and then we will have to go, the whole lot of us."

In the meantime things were going from bad to worse. The Secretary was getting more and more anxious. Reports of all kinds kept coming in from all sides. Americans were being insulted in the street. The officers at the clubs were a little more arrogant in their studied politeness toward

Edestone and his associates, the younger officers even taunting Lawrence with having to leave his girl in Berlin and go back to cow-punching.

Finally one of the papers reported that the entire American fleet was collecting at Hampton Roads, that all the German boats in New York had been dismantled by force, and broadly suggested that the Yankees were about to strike first and apologize afterward.

However, there came a slight rift in the clouds. Coming back one morning after a conference with the Chancellor, Jones was all smiles.

"Well, we are all right for a little while at least," he announced. "The Chancellor has just informed me that the Emperor has decided to see you, Edestone, and he wishes to inspect here, at the Embassy, anything that you may like to show him. The Chancellor intimated that it would depend entirely upon your attitude on this occasion whether or not your mission to Europe was a failure or a brilliant success."

"And when is he coming?" asked Edestone quickly.

Jones grinned. "With his usual impetuosity, he has selected tonight, and will pay the Embassy a formal call at nine o'clock, after the celebration at the Palace in honour of the birthday of one of the Royal princes."

Edestone was delighted with the prospect of some action at last, but he had long since lost all hope of an amicable settlement. They had waited too long. He felt that they were preparing to strike, and should they do so it made him sick to think of the awful consequences. He was almost tempted to tell Jones of the wireless instrument in the penthouse and his daily communications with "Specs," but he remembered that he had no right to involve him as a representative of the United States, and that, as the matter stood, he and Lawrence were the only culprits.

He did not care to destroy the roseate hopes of the Secretary after his conference with the Chancellor, and contented himself with saying: "William, I hope that you are right, but I have an impression that we are in for it. I am prepared to meet any game that they may play, but I do sincerely hope that I shall not be forced to it."

By seven o'clock that evening the streets for blocks around the Embassy were filled with soldiers, and Edestone smiled when looking from the window he noticed that the Germans were bringing up anti-aircraft guns.

"They are taking no chances," he thought to himself, his curiosity aroused as he noticed several large mortars being brought up and so placed that each battery of four could throw their shells in parallel lines over the Embassy to the north, south, east, and west. This struck him as very strange, but he became even more interested when he perceived that besides the ordinary ammunition wagon each gun was provided with a trailer that looked like a big wheel or drum on a two-wheeled carriage, although it was so carefully covered over that he could not make out exactly what it was.

"I have got to find out what those things are," said Edestone to himself, and taking his hat and cane, he left the Embassy as if for a short stroll before dinner.

The soldiers took no notice of him as he sauntered along, and allowed him to inspect everything at his will until he approached the strange-looking mortars. Then he was stopped by a young officer, who told him in a very polite but firm tone that he would have to pass on and could not go by that way, at the same time showing him where he could walk around the block.

"I would give a good deal to know what those things are," muttered Edestone to himself. "In fact, I must know before the night is over."

He went back into the house, after strolling about for a quarter of an hour, and for the first time since he had left the Little Place in the Country, he became really anxious.

"These are wonderful people. They evidently are satisfied now that they have the answer, and who knows but they may have. All may yet be lost."

He sat down and drove his brain as he had never driven it before. He wondered if he could get the Secretary to demand what all this preparation meant, and what these new death-dealing instruments might be that were threatening the Embassy of the United States; but that was useless, he knew. They would reply that it was to protect the Emperor, or would simply refuse to answer, or answering would lie.

After waiting until it was time to dress for dinner, in a fit of desperation he sent for Lawrence.

"Lawrence," he said, "have you seen those mortars out there?"

"Yes," replied Lawrence, "I did. They take no chances with the 'Big Noise.'"

"Don't joke, Lawrence. This is serious; very serious. Did you notice those two-wheeled wagons that are so carefully covered with canvas just behind each of the mortars?"

"No, to tell you the truth, I did not. They have so many travelling soup wagons and ice plants that I don't pay any attention to those things any more."

"Well, Lawrence, I've got to know what they are tonight in order that I may be prepared; otherwise we may find ourselves in a very serious situation, and what is much more important, my whole life's work may be absolutely lost."

"Now, since you put it that way," said Lawrence with a broad grin, "I will step out and in my most polite Deutsch inquire."

"They will not let you get within a block of them. Do you think it will be possible to persuade one of the German servants to find out from the soldiers? I would pay any price."

"Well, I will dress myself like the cook and go out and flirt with one of the soldiers for $2. I'm a little badly off for money myself just about this time."

"Lawrence, you must stop joking. I tell you, something must be done."

"Leave me think, leave me think," said the irrepressible. "*Donnerwetter*, I have it! What time does the Hohenzollern Glee Club arrive?"

"At nine o'clock."

"And you come on immediately after the 'First Part,' succeeding which I suppose Lohengrin will sing his Duck Ditty, while the Boy Scout, dressed as Uncle Tom's Cabin, after biting the triggers off all the guns, and pulling his wig well down over his eyes"—imitating the action—"will sally forth into the limpid limelights, and after he has been shot once in the face by a 16-inch howitzer and has been played upon in the rear by a battery of machine guns, he will limp on with the regular limp of the old Virginia servant and die at your feet, but not until I have whispered their secret into the heel of your boot."

Edestone had known Lawrence long enough to understand that all of this nonsense meant that his really bright mind was working, and that he had some definite plan in view. The best way to handle him, he had found out, was to let his exuberance of spirit have free swing, so he replied in the same melodramatic manner: "Good, my faithful District Messenger Boy. Now in what way can I assist you in your wonderful scheme?"

"Leave all to me, Lord Reginald Bolingbroke, and before the clock on yon 'back drop' strikes eight bells, you will know what is hidden beneath these veils of mystery."

"I can depend upon you," Edestone eyed him searchingly, "and no mistake?"

"On the life of me mother who lies dead beneath the sacred soil of dear old Idaho!" With a wave of an imaginary sword, and jumping astride an imaginary stick horse, he saluted and galloped from the room, singing "It's a Long Way to Tipperary."

"I wonder what that dare-devil is up to," thought Edestone. Nevertheless he believed that Lawrence would accomplish his purpose.

Presently his attention was attracted by the beams of a searchlight crossing the window, and looking out he saw those great white arms stretching up from every part of the city.

"They expect me to show my teeth tonight," he said.

The distant tapping of drums showed that troops were moving in all parts of Berlin, and they were beginning to form in the streets below. It was easy to see by which route the Emperor was coming, or at least by which route he wished the people to think he was going to arrive.

Edestone dressed hurriedly, although James seemed to think that something extra should be done.

"Beg pardon, sir," he pleaded in an accent which would have meant imprisonment for him if heard on the streets outside, "but these here barbarians likes a bit of colour, sir. I understands as how the Emperor calls the Ambassador the 'undertaker,' sir, and it's all on account, sir, of his not a-having any lace on his coat, sir. Don't you think you might wear some of your Colonial Society medals and decorations, sir?" and he tried hard to hide his contempt for these American signs of alleged aristocracy. "There is some as is bright in colour, sir, and he wouldn't know, sir, but as how you is a duke in America, sir."

"None of that nonsense, James, unless," he said with a quizzical look, "you give me the copy of the Golden Fleece, which shows that I am a member in good standing of the South Chicago Aero Club."

"Not that one, sir," protested James, "if you will pardon me, sir, I think it is a bit large, sir, for the waistcoat opening, sir. I think, sir, that the Order of the Cincinnati is very neat, sir. It is very much like one of the Greek Orders, I don't recall which, sir, but Lord Knott wore it once, I recall, sir, when the King of Greece was in London, sir."

"No, James," Edestone shook his head. "My father was a blacksmith, and I would not like to deceive the Emperor."

"How you do like your little joke, sir," said James, putting his hand to his mouth. "Won't you just use that button, sir, instead of a buttonhole? It ain't so frivolous like, sir, begging your pardon, sir."

"Oh well, yes; just to keep you quiet."

"Thank you, sir."

And Edestone left the room.

CHAPTER XXIV
DER KAISER

Downstairs, the household was in a state of suppressed excitement. The German men servants, without the usual protection of a brilliant uniform, looked as if they would like to drop everything and hide themselves in the coal cellar. The maids were almost on the verge of tears. Mrs. Jones, with all the jewelry on that she possessed, was moving about with a flushed face seeing that everything was in order.

"For Heaven's sake, hurry up, Jack," she said. "We must have a short dinner and be ready when the Emperor arrives. As for myself, I never can touch anything for hours before I meet him. He scares me almost out of my wits."

Her husband was walking up and down with the expression of a man who is the speaker of the evening, watching the waiters serving coffee and passing cigars. The only persons who seemed perfectly at their ease were Lawrence and his Bowery boy valet, Fred, who were holding a very serious conversation in the corner of the hall.

Dinner, it must be confessed, was very like the gathering of the distant relatives the night before the funeral of the rich old maid of the family. Lawrence's jokes were either not heard or were received with sad-eyed contortions of the face that were less like a smile than the premonition of a sneeze. The strain was so great that as they were having their coffee a sudden clatter in the street came as an immense relief.

The air was instantly filled with the subdued noise of the different members of the household taking their various places. The Acting Ambassador and Mrs. Jones went out of the dining-room and took a position near the door of the large reception room, leaving Edestone and Lawrence alone. They had previously explained to Edestone what he must do when they notified him that it was time for him to come in and be presented.

"Lawrence," he said when the servants had all gone, "won't you tell me what you have decided on? I am rather curious to know your plan."

Lawrence, who had grown quite serious for him, came around from his place and lighting a cigarette sat down close to him.

"You know Prince Fritz Funk?" he leaned over to whisper.

"Of course," said Edestone.

"Well," continued Lawrence, "I'm supposed to look something like him. I am just his height. He has, as you know, certain striking mannerisms, which when he is drinking are accentuated. I have all last year been amusing the officers at the clubs by giving imitations of him, and they do say I am better than he is himself.

"Now all the soldiers stationed in and about Berlin know Fritzie's peculiarities, so I propose to impersonate him tonight while he is in here drinking the Ambassador's champagne. My man is to get his helmet, '*avec le grand panache*,' and his long gray-blue military cape, and with my riding boots and spurs and a sword, I shall be able to fool those boobs out there; that is, if they don't throw on me one of those damned spot lights. If they do, G-o-o-d-n-i-g-h-t! Then I can only say that I am doing it on a bet. But I hardly think that would save me in these times. The least I could expect would be a term in prison for insulting the uniform. I will go down in history as 'Little Boy Blue up in the air.'"

"It's a big risk you're taking," frowned Edestone, "and were there any other way I would not allow you to do this. But if you do succeed, you will go down in history in a way you could never dream. Lawrence, if you get back safely with this information, I will make you a present of $1,000,000."

Lawrence looked at his friend as if he thought that he had lost his mind, but when he saw the look of determination on Edestone's strong face, which seemed to have aged within the hour, and when he felt the grip of his powerful hand, he knew that he meant every word he said.

"By God, old man," he said with a little break in his voice, "you should be the Emperor instead of his nibs out there."

"I may be yet," said Edestone smiling, and a look came on his face that Lawrence had never seen there before.

The servants were moving quietly about the room, but it was plain to see that they felt the presence of the Lord's Anointed. Through the house could be heard the clatter of many swords and the tramping of booted heels along the marble hall. It sent a thrill through Edestone that he would have had difficulty to explain. It was like the echo of some far distant past seeming to recall to life a sleeping spirit, which with great exultation was throwing off the fetters of its long slumbers. He seemed to be impelled by an almost irresistible force to rush into their midst and take his rightful position at their head.

He was recalled to himself by the sudden silence that had fallen on the entire house, as though some great army had been halted and was standing at rigid attention. Then he heard the silvery tinkle and metallic clink of sabre and spurs as of a single figure striding with military precision over the softest of carpets, and he could picture that majestic form advancing well in front of his glittering escort as they stood in breathless silence while he made his dramatic entrance.

Then the silence was broken by a voice which said slowly and distinctly: "His Imperial Majesty." An almost simultaneous click followed as if all had come to a salute and were waiting for the sign to relax and from automatons become human beings again.

Edestone was all alone in the dining-room.

The servants had left the room after removing the table decorations, covering it with a dark cloth and setting a large bowl of flowers in the centre; and Lawrence had gone out quietly on hearing the noise in the hall.

And so he sat, this young man in a strange land, thousands of miles away from his home, waiting to be called to a death struggle, without help from anyone, with the most powerful, arrogant, and relentless man on the face of the earth, an adversary surrounded by the most perfect fighting machine yet devised by man, with all the confidence, that tradition, success, and a brilliant mind could give. An Emperor with the sublime dignity of his position which he sincerely believed he held by Divine Right, and who had always lived surrounded by an atmosphere of absolute submission to his will.

Yet Edestone was not afraid. He was not even nervous. He was merely anxious to be up and doing. This show of force, those mysterious two-wheeled wagons, had roused his fighting blood. So assured was he of his own sincerity in his efforts for the good of all that he resented the attitude which they had taken. He knew they would try to get his invention peaceably, if possible, but would stop at nothing if they failed, and he expected some overt act of violence tonight that would mean war with the United States.

So when he was called by one of the under-secretaries of the Embassy he went with little charity in his heart, but with head erect and determination shown in his every movement, bearing on his face, which seemed to have grown very hard, a look that left no doubt of the fearlessness of the spirit that was behind it.

He was taken in at one end of the large room that vibrated with light and colour. Around three sides of it was banked the most brilliant array of uniforms that he had ever seen. There were white-headed generals ablaze with decorations and medals; there were young princes with simple uniforms and with but one handsome decoration to show their distinguished rank. There were Cuirassiers and Uhlans, and now and then he could pick out the sombre black and silver uniforms of the celebrated Death's-Head Hussars.

But the one figure which dominated all and held his attention was that of the Emperor.

He stood in the centre of the room with the Secretary and General von Lichtenstein, Mrs. Jones having retired as soon as she had received her distinguished guest.

He was a man of medium height but with a bearing which made him appear larger than he really was. He was dressed in the wonderful white uniform of the Garde du Corps, which carried with it the celebrated silver eagle helmet.

As this figure dominated and held the centre of this brilliant picture, so his face drew the attention from his magnificent uniform and held it as with a magnetic power. It was handsome, intelligent, strong, but above all it was commanding. There was little kindness but there was a merry twinkle in his sharp blue eyes which showed a human side and was most attractive.

These eyes could change, however, and when he saw Edestone and they were met by his perfectly fearless but respectful glance, they seemed to try by force to penetrate his very soul.

Edestone advanced alone until he came to within a few paces of the central group, and then stopped, standing with one knee slightly bent, his right hand held lightly in front of his body, which was inclined in a graceful and easy attitude of reverence, while his other hand hung naturally at his side.

After his first quick glance, Edestone dropped his eyes to about the Emperor's knees and held them there until the Secretary, with a slight gesture, called him to his side. The young man then straightened up and went slowly to the Ambassador's left, and there stood perfectly erect looking straight at the Emperor, while Jones with some show of embarrassment was saying:

"Your Majesty, may I present Mr. John Fulton Edestone, of New York."

The Emperor, with the hearty and easy manner which he always assumes with those he has been told are distinguished Americans and with that quizzical expression in his sharp eyes which, though attractive, is described as most disconcerting, replied.

"Mr. Edestone," he said, in a loud voice, "your fame has gone before you, and we are always glad to welcome distinguished men of science in Berlin, which we think is the centre of science and culture. Your name, that of a great lighthouse and suggesting the greatest of your inventions, electric lights, convinces me that you were born to blaze the way for us," and he laughed, in which he was joined heartily by his well-trained courtiers, who knew that nothing pleased him more than to appreciate his little jokes of which he was so fond.

With his quick eye for detail he had caught the Cincinnati button worn by Edestone, and said:

"I see that you are the descendant of a soldier, which gives you a greater claim upon my imperial favour. What was your ancestor's rank?"

"He was a general, Your Majesty," replied Edestone with a firmness that seemed to attract and slightly offend him.

He scowled. He was so accustomed to seeing strong men quail before him that the coolness of the other man shocked his sense of propriety. "General von Lichtenstein tells me," his face brightening up again, "that you have made a very interesting invention, which may be of great service to me in bringing to a successful end sooner than I had expected this cruel war, which has been forced upon me by those grasping English. He tells me that you have motion pictures of this invention in actual war practice, which the representative of the American Ambassador has so kindly invited me here to see."

Turning to Jones, he said with great show of condescension: "I thank you, Mr. Secretary." Then looking at Edestone sharply, and with rather a sarcastic turn in his voice, he continued: "I will gladly see your pictures, and what is perhaps of more interest to you, no doubt, I will, if I like it, buy your invention at a good price."

And then, as if addressing the entire company, who stood waiting to applaud his every sentiment, he said: "Germany expects and is able to pay large prices for American goods now." And then, as if to cut short any possible protest that Edestone might presume to make, he turned his back upon him and said very abruptly to the Secretary: "Where are these pictures?"

"In the next room," replied the Secretary, "and if you please, Mr. Edestone will show them to Your Majesty at once. Edestone," he said, "has everything been arranged?"

"Yes," nodded Edestone. Though boiling with rage he kept a perfectly calm exterior.

The entire company led by the Emperor and the Secretary moved into another room where Black had installed the apparatus.

Edestone, with his usual modesty, had obliterated himself, and bringing up the rear was about to go around through the other rooms to reach his place in front of the screen when his attention was called by General von Lichtenstein, who had fallen back apparently with the intention of speaking to him apart from the others.

"Mr. Edestone," he said, drawing him aside, "one would think that you had spent your entire life among us," and with a quizzical smile he added: "I think you rather astonished the Kaiser by your *sang-froid*. I have seen men of the highest rank stand speechless in his presence, while you are as finished as a courtier of the Grand Monarque and as cool as the Iron Chancellor.

"I admit," he said in his fatherly manner, "I had no authority from you to do so, but thought it best to leave upon the Emperor the impression that you would sell your invention. Had I not done so he certainly would have demanded the reasons for your presence in Berlin, and had I dared to suggest that you had been sent by the United States to coerce him he would have been thrown into such a rage that he might have declared war on your country, which I understand is the last thing that you want."

"I regret that you did this, General von Lichtenstein, if I may be pardoned for seeming to criticize a statesman of your experience and distinction; for I do not intend to sell and my country has not sent me to coerce. I have come instead to appeal to your reason, after showing you the uselessness of continuing this loss of life in the face of the great power in the hands of those who know the secret of my invention and intend to put a stop to it."

A cloud seemed to pass over the General's face, but he soon recovered his bland, almost Oriental smile.

"But, Mr. Edestone, you seem to forget that whereas others *may* have the secret, we know that you certainly have it, and you are still our most honoured guest in Berlin."

"Where I am also the guest of my own country, so long as the Acting Ambassador is so kind as to allow me to remain under his roof and our flag," replied Edestone pointedly, intending if possible to force the General's hand.

In this he failed as the old man only smiled through his glasses.

"A great statesman was lost when you turned inventor, Mr. Edestone," he said in a most complimentary tone. "But come, I fear His Majesty waits." And then changing his manner, he said with a knowing wink:

"Here is a note which Princess Wilhelmina asked me to deliver to you. She seems to be very much interested. Can it be possible that you are raising your eyes to a Princess of the Blood?

"Still, stranger things than that have happened," he half mused, "and His Imperial Majesty is always glad to recognize talent and reward it in a befitting manner."

They went into the other room where the Emperor sat waiting. Evidently impatient that Edestone was not at his position of parlour entertainer in front of the screen with his pointer in hand as soon as the Imperial eye should deign to be cast in that direction, he rose with exaggerated politeness when the American appeared and said in a most sarcastic manner: "Must the whole world wait while inventors dream?"

Then sitting down he added in a harsh and irritable tone: "With your very kind assistance, Mr. Edestone, we will now inspect these much talked of pictures."

There was a silence in the room that was like a gasp of horror, and the company all standing looked as if they expected to see Edestone sink to the floor with mortification; that is, all except Jones, who slow-moving had only gotten half-way to his feet when the Kaiser sat down, and who now dropped back into his chair with a quizzical little smile playing about the corners of his mouth.

But Edestone, with the respectful manner of a grown man answering his father, who still looked upon him as a boy, and who had reproved him unjustly, said with an indulgent smile that bore no trace of resentment:

"I beg that Your Majesty will forgive me, but I was held prisoner by General von Lichtenstein, and not until I waved the Stars and Stripes would he let me go."

The General hurried over to the Emperor. "Pardon me, Sire," he said, for he saw that the Emperor would fly into one of his fits of rage and might upset all of their well-laid plans if something was not quickly done to quiet him. "Pardon me, Sire, it was my fault. I did not know that I was keeping Your Majesty waiting."

"Go on with the pictures," said the Emperor, with an impatient gesture of his enormous right hand, and he sat glaring at the screen as the lights went out.

CHAPTER XXV
THE MASQUERADER

Lawrence waited until the room was dark and then slipped out unnoticed. He would have liked to remain and see the rest of Edestone's most interesting pictures which had started off with those taken in Newfoundland and included a series not shown at Buckingham Palace. But he had an exciting task before him. The idea of posing as a Royal Prince in the magnificent uniform of the Imperial Hussars with nodding plumes and flowing military cape, his coat-of-arms emblazoned on his left shoulder, appealed to his dramatic instincts, as did the danger to his passion for adventure.

He was brave, but unlike Edestone his was the bravery of an unthinking recklessness rather than that of a perfectly balanced mind which, contemptuous of the body that carries it, forces that body to do its bidding.

The fact that Edestone had offered him an unheard of reward had made little impression, going in one ear and out of the other. He would accept it as lightly as it had been offered because he himself would have made exactly the same offer under the same circumstances. Whenever he wanted anything he paid the price, even if it took his last cent. It was no incentive to action now, as he would have gladly paid for the privilege of playing this big part in this wonderful melodrama—a melodrama which he was prepared at any time to see change into a tragedy, with him the dead hero.

He found that his Bowery boy Fred, under the pretext that it was customary in the best New York "high society," had bullied the German flunkeys into bringing all of the officers' helmets and cloaks upstairs and laying them out on a bed in one of the chambers on the second floor, from which place it was easy for him to smuggle all he wanted into Lawrence's room. Lawrence found him there waiting to help him "make up."

Turning up the collar of his dress coat so as to hide his white shirt front, the masquerader buckled on the sabre that Fred handed to him. Without changing his trousers he put on his riding boots and spurs, which with the busby and cloak, a pair of white kid gloves, and a small blond moustache completed his disguise. Standing thus in the middle of the room with the door open, he waited until Fred signalled that the coast was clear. He then stepped quickly across the hall and into the elevator, closely followed by Fred, who closed the door. When they were perfectly safe from interruption, he adjusted his costume and his false moustache to his entire satisfaction, pinning the cloak securely together with large safety pins to prevent it from flying open. Then as the elevator passed the main floor on its way to the basement, he made a gesture of derision.

Fred got out of the car and again carefully reconnoitred. Finding that the passage leading to the garden was clear and that there was no one in the billiard room, which was between the elevator and the outside door, he signalled and Lawrence walked out into the garden at the side of the Embassy.

It was quite dark there, but not dark enough to prevent the soldiers, who were stationed about to watch this door, from seeing him as he stood perfectly still as if hesitating which way to turn.

Observing that he was an officer, they saluted and stood at attention. Then as he moved forward and they saw the insignia on his cloak they signalled in some mysterious manner to the next post, who in turn passed it down the line that Royalty was at large and that they must be careful not to be caught napping.

Accordingly, as Lawrence emerged from the semi-darkness and came around to the front of the Embassy, every soldier was standing at attention and the different officers, after looking searchingly but most respectfully at him to satisfy themselves who he was, stepped back and allowed him to pass, while they stood like pieces of stone.

Lawrence did not deign even to notice them, but, reeling unsteadily in his gait, passed them without even acknowledging their salute.

His presence having been reported to the Captain who had charge of the company that was stationed in the street immediately in front of the Embassy, this officer hastened up to him.

"Is there anything that you require, Your Royal Highness?" he saluted. Lawrence, carrying out his pretence of intoxication, gave a perfect imitation of the Prince when in that condition.

"I am making a tour of inspection to see that everything is all right," he said thickly.

The Captain saw his condition and showed an inclination to follow him, but Lawrence waved his hand with what was intended to be a regal gesture, although in fact it seemed to throw him almost off his balance.

The Captain stepped back most respectfully and saluted, but smiled as he followed with his eyes the young Prince.

Lawrence strutted quickly but unsteadily until he came to within about a hundred yards of the mortars, where a sentry challenged him.

"Pardon me, Your Royal Highness, but my orders are to permit no one to pass. If you will allow me, I will call the Corporal of the Guard, who will send for the Captain."

Lawrence interrupted him by bellowing:

"Get out of my way, you stupid blockhead, or I'll kick you out of my way! I have not time to wait for the lot of fools that you all are."

Then as the man did not move he gave him a tremendous upper-cut, catching his chin with the base of his open hand and sending his head back and lifting him off his feet. He fell sprawling about ten feet away against an iron railing, where he lay perfectly still with a nasty cut in the back of his head.

The Captain, who had been slowly following to see that nothing happened to his Royal charge, ran up quickly and, ordering another soldier to take the place of the fallen sentry, had the wounded man hurried quickly out of sight.

In the meantime Lawrence was strolling along, without even looking back at the poor fellow where he lay.

"I caught him just right," he muttered with a touch of compunction. "I hope I did not hurt him badly."

When he finally came to the mortars with the mysterious two-wheeled wagons attached to them, he walked around from one to the other, as if he were making a careful inspection to see that everything was all right. It was impossible for him even now to make out what was hidden under the canvas covers. One thing he could see, however, and that was, that from under each there ran a carefully insulated electric cable to the nearest fire hydrant where it was carefully attached.

After inspecting all four, Lawrence turned around and went back to the second wagon, the cover of which he had noticed was not on exactly straight. He hoped to be able to see what was underneath, but he found that the cover was strapped down so tightly that he could get no inkling.

During all this time the officers and men were standing at attention in their proper places, although they followed him with their eyes, an amused expression on their faces.

Finding that it was impossible for him to discover anything while the covers remained on the wagons, he bellowed in a loud and commanding voice, not forgetting to imitate Royalty in its cups:

"Lieutenant!"

And to the young officer who ran up to him he said:

"Why is not that cover on straight? Did you not receive orders that these—" and as Lawrence had not the slightest idea what "these" were, he substituted a loud hiccough for the unknown name, and contented himself with pointing with an unsteady hand. "Did you not understand these had to be perfectly concealed? Now that one is not perfectly concealed, for I can see perfectly what it is, so take that cover off and put it on straight. And be quick about it or I will report you for untidiness."

The Lieutenant, who was one of the very young recruits now officering the German Army, feeling overpowered by the presence of Royalty, had given the order, and the men were unstrapping the cover when the Captain came up.

"What are you doing there?" he demanded. Then turning sharply to the young Lieutenant he said in the most brutal manner:

"Don't you know that the orders are not to take these covers off, not until the very last minute, not until everything else has been tried and has failed to bring her down."

"But His Royal Highness," stammered the younger officer, "has ordered this cover off because it is not on straight."

"But, Your Royal Highness," expostulated the Captain, although in the most deferential manner, "don't you think that this cover is on straight enough?"

"What! Do you mean to contradict me?" Lawrence almost screamed. "I say that the cover is not on straight, and I have ordered this fool to take it off and put it on straight, perfectly straight."

"But that is impossible," said the Captain, warily keeping out of reach of His Royal Highness's fists. "The orders are that these covers are not to come off until the American flying machine makes its appearance, and if it does not appear, the covers are not to come off at all. These are the orders of the General Staff, and Your Royal Highness must realize that they have to be obeyed."

"Well," said Lawrence with the persistency of a drunken man, talking at the top of his voice, "if you do not put that cover on straight I will report you, and you will be court-martialled for insulting a Prince of the Blood."

All the while he kept swaying as if he were about to fall.

Straightening himself up with much difficulty and assuming a drunken dignity he started to go away; but as if he were unable to free his intoxicated mind from the one idea that obsessed it, he turned and changed his tone to a persuasive one.

"I don't insist that you take the cover off," he laughed, "I only insist that it be straightened, because you can see as well as I that it is not on perfectly straight, and your orders were to put these covers on straight, perfectly straight."

The Captain, now thoroughly amused, and deciding that the best way was to humour him, thought, since his orders were only not to remove, that he would be able to satisfy the Prince without directly disobeying his instructions. He therefore ordered the men to unstrap the cover and pull it around.

Lawrence seemed entirely satisfied with this, and took such interest in seeing that the cover was adjusted to exactly the right position, that he leaned over and took hold of it himself, as if to give his help. As he did so he gave a lurch, and grabbing at the cover as if to save himself, he went down in a heap with it on top of him.

The men helped him quickly to his feet and as quickly readjusted the cover, but not before he had seen that the drum-shaped objects were in fact great wooden spools on which were wound thousands and thousands of yards of large copper wire.

Having seen all that he wanted, he now turned his attention towards getting back to the Embassy, so taking the Captain's arm, and seeming either to have lost all interest or to have been overcome by his fall, made his way along. He swung and lurched so that it was with difficulty the officer kept him on his feet.

Then when they arrived at the front steps and the Captain was assisting him up, Lawrence, as if suddenly awaking from sleep, stopped.

"I am too dirty to go in by the front door," he protested, "I will go in by the garden. I am much obliged to you, Captain; don't come any farther."

Then laughing and shaking his finger in the Captain's face, he said in a tone of exultation: "I got that cover on straight, anyhow—perfectly straight."

Swaying as he rounded the corner of the house, he went in through the side door, where he found Fred waiting for him, who pulled off his boots and gave him his pumps.

He took off his busby, and handed it to Fred, unpinned the long military cloak, unbuckled his sword, turned down the collar of his evening coat, and "Richard was himself again."

Stepping into the elevator and letting himself off at the main floor, he went hurriedly into the room where Edestone was still showing his pictures, while Fred, after brushing and cleaning the royal paraphernalia, put them back in their place.

Lawrence moved quickly over to the cabinet where Mr. Black was working the machine and stepped inside. "I must speak to Mr. Edestone," he whispered. "Can't you stop the machine as if something had gone wrong? Then Mr. Edestone will come back here and see what is the matter."

"Not on your life!" Black shook his head violently. "The Emperor now is in a perfect fury. He and Mr. Edestone have had one or two 'set-tos,' and Mr. Edestone is beginning to put it back at him pretty strong, and if anything should happen to the machine I think it would end in a fight. I rather wish we were back in New York. If it is necessary for you to speak to Mr. Edestone before the lights go up, this reel that I am running off now will take just about eight minutes more, so if you will slip quietly back of the screen you can whisper to him from there without attracting much attention. I will make a little extra noise to help you out."

Lawrence worked his way unobtrusively through the room, and standing just to the side of the screen in a dark corner, called in a low voice:

"Jack, can I speak to you?"

Edestone, who had been deeply concerned about him, felt that a load was lifted from his mind when he heard the dare-devil's voice. He knew at least that Lawrence was back safely, and he was confident that he would not have come back without the information until he had made a good fight for it. So as everything was quiet on the outside he was reassured.

Lawrence very quickly explained to him exactly what he had seen, and Edestone, squeezing his arm, said quietly:

"Ah! That is their little game!"

CHAPTER XXVI
TWO REMARKABLE MEN

When the lights finally went up and the entertainment ended, perhaps the most surprised, almost dumbfounded, man in the room was Jones. He now had his first insight into the stupendous amount of work that had been done by his friend, and was completely overcome by the seriousness of the situation. He understood at last many things which had been lost on him before, as for instance the insinuating remarks of the Chancellor at their various conferences and why he had suspected the Secretary of lying to him.

Jones wondered also if his own Government had purposely kept the Embassy in the dark as to its relationship with Edestone. Not knowing the whereabouts or even the ownership of this frightful instrument of war, he was at a loss to know what he should say when certain pointed questions which were inevitable were put to him.

He realized now for the first time that the German General Staff was at work and would stop at nothing either to obtain the use of this great monster of the air or, by seizing Edestone himself, control its movements; that is, if Edestone and not the United States were operating it.

He could not blind himself to the air of confidence that pervaded the entire company, composed as it was of the highest men in the German Government, and this led him to believe that they knew Edestone held the key of the situation, and as long as they held him they occupied the strongest position.

But why, he could not help asking himself, had Edestone been such a fool as to put himself so completely in their power. Still, being a very astute man, and having the greatest confidence in his old friend, who he knew would do the straight thing in a strong position and the wise thing if he found himself in a weak one, he awaited developments.

Edestone, who had walked over to the Secretary of Legation, leaned down and said in a voice loud enough for the Emperor to hear:

"Will you please say to His Imperial Majesty that if there is any question he would like to put to me, or if he would care to have me repeat any of the pictures, I should appreciate the great honour."

The Emperor, who was just waking up to the fact that he had in this young American a very strong and clever man to deal with, was to a certain extent at a loss to decide just how he would treat him.

Without waiting to have the request conveyed to him in due form, and speaking directly to Edestone he said in an affable voice:

"I should like to see again the picture showing the working of the bomb-dropping device, and I would like to have the film stopped exactly at the moment that the projectile leaves the tube. I wish to examine the action of the ejector."

"I shall be most happy," replied Edestone, "to run that film again very slowly and repeat it as often as Your Majesty may desire. I can also run it backward very slowly, but I cannot stop the machine that I am using tonight without ruining the film, and I am quite sure," he bowed most respectfully, "that Your Majesty will not wish me to do that."

"Stop that machine as I order you to do, and ruin the film if it is necessary!" said the Emperor in his most commanding tone.

At last Edestone had the chance he had been looking for. He knew that he was perfectly in his rights, and if he refused and the Emperor still insisted upon his most unjust demand, it would open the eyes of his country's representative to the situation and the true attitude of the German authorities. Besides, he was incensed at the wanton destruction of other people's property to satisfy the whims of this absolute monarch.

"I am very sorry, Your Majesty, I cannot do that, and for state reasons that it is impossible for me to explain."

The Emperor turned perfectly livid. His face was painful to look at. He tried vainly to speak, but could not. It was plain that he was labouring under an emotion greater than his physical condition could stand. His mouth worked and each hair of his moustache seemed to stand on end, giving to his trembling lips an almost ghastly expression. He was seized with a violent fit of coughing which on account of the weak condition of his throat caused his doctor, without whom he rarely moved, to step forward, as if alarmed, to his assistance.

General von Lichtenstein leaned over as if to restrain him and whispered something in his ear, but this seemed only to infuriate him the more, and he waved his Councillor aside.

The Acting Ambassador, a lawyer of ability, felt strongly the justice of Edestone's position in defending his property rights, and had he been sitting on the bench instead of on the edge of a raging volcano would have ruled in his favour. As it was, he watched with intense interest this contest between these two remarkable men.

When the Emperor had recovered sufficiently to speak, in a way that showed his uncontrollable rage was battling with an inherited physical weakness, his voice, starting in a whisper, rose and broke, and, in his violent efforts to control the convulsive spasms of his throat, turned into a scream.

"Show that film!" he shouted, "and stop it where I command or I will confiscate everything you have and throw you into prison."

At this Jones rose quickly to his feet, a dangerous light in his eyes, and he was about to speak, but General von Lichtenstein rushed over and stopped him.

"His Majesty is beside himself," he urged in a low voice. "He does not mean what he says. When he is himself again he will regret the indignity that he has offered your country and will make reparation."

The Emperor had also arisen and was standing in the midst of as furious and warlike a looking lot of men as had ever grouped themselves around his wild barbaric ancestors, ready to pile their dead bodies about their master and give the last drop of blood for his protection.

They looked as if they approved and only waited for the word to rush in and avenge the insult to their beloved lord, and while waiting for this word they stood and glared at Edestone with a look of absolute contempt and undying hatred.

"Well, which shall it be?" said the Emperor, in a voice which was more under control but none the less determined. "Will you stop your film?"

Edestone, who all this time had stood perfectly still looking at the Emperor with eyes out of which had gone every vestige of deference and respect, showed in every feature a fixed and determined but absolutely cool defiance. The only time that his face had changed or his position altered since he last spoke was when the Emperor was apparently suffering, and then it had taken on an expression of deep pity and sincere sympathy and he too had made a step forward as if to render assistance.

This had quickly changed, however, when his glance caught the look of hatred that was riveted upon him. Declining even to glance at the Emperor, he addressed himself directly to the Secretary of Legation, speaking in a perfectly clear voice, which was a relief after the Emperor's painful and rasping efforts.

"Mr. Secretary," he said slowly, "I resent the insult to you, and through you to our country, which you represent, but if I thought that by complying with the unjust demands which the Emperor of Germany has seen fit to make I could prevent war between the United States and his country, I naturally would comply. When I see, however, that the Emperor of Germany refuses to respect the rights of an American citizen in the house of his Ambassador, I realize that the destruction of my film will not save the situation." He turned to the Emperor. "I regret that I cannot comply with your commands. The matter is now between our two Governments."

The Emperor laid his hand upon his sword and made a movement as though he intended to strike, at which every sword in the room flashed from its scabbard, save only that of old von Lichtenstein, who pressing forward laid a dissuasive hand on the Emperor's arm.

"Don't let him draw you on," he whispered to his master; "this may be some trick." Then to the rest he said in a contemptuous tone: "Don't make fools of yourselves and make Germany ridiculous."

The Emperor turned to the Secretary. "Sir," he said in a voice trembling with agitation, "you have heard the insult that has been offered to my Imperial person, and if you do not deliver this man over to my police, I shall at twelve o'clock tomorrow night declare war against the United States of America, and until that time"—threateningly—"I shall hold you personally responsible for him."

Edestone coolly took out his watch and noted that it was exactly twenty-five minutes past eleven o'clock, a proceeding which almost caused the Emperor to lose control of himself again, but he was once more held in check by General von Lichtenstein.

"I know now that this is a trick, Your Majesty," he declared.

The Acting Ambassador bowed slightly to the Emperor's last attack. "I shall report to my Government all that has passed," he replied, "and exactly what Your Majesty has just said, and I shall, as soon as I receive an answer, report to Your Imperial Majesty." He finished, and stood waiting as if to force the Emperor's immediate departure.

Then with scant formality, and showing by the unpardonable rudeness of their behaviour the contempt in which they held all Americans, the Emperor and his entire suite left the Embassy without taking the slightest further notice of Edestone.

CHAPTER XXVII
ALL CARDS ON THE TABLE

The royal party had scarcely gotten out of the house and Edestone and Jones were still standing in the middle of the reception room when the return of General von Lichtenstein was announced.

The old General came in as quietly as if nothing had happened. He greeted the Secretary cordially and smiled benignly at Edestone.

"Young man," he said, "you needed my old head on your young shoulders badly tonight. I have returned to have a talk with the Acting Ambassador, and I think that if he can prevail upon you to be reasonable I may be able to settle this little difficulty between you and His Imperial Majesty, the Emperor. If you will only lead us into some smaller room, Mr. Secretary, we can sit down and over our cigars discuss this matter quietly."

"I am sorry that my machine—" began Edestone, but he was quickly interrupted by the General.

"Tut, tut, that is nothing at all. That was simply two young men losing their tempers, and ought to be soon settled. One being an Emperor makes it a little more difficult, I will admit, but I have seen Emperors angry before and they are just like any of us. They cool off when they realize that they have," and he lowered his voice with a quizzical look, "been a little bit foolish."

When they were all comfortably seated around the table in the library of the Embassy, and the General and Edestone had lighted cigars, while Jones, who never smoked, looked on, the old General, statesman, philosopher, and writer opened the conversation.

"We have now come to the last hand in this game which we have been playing," he said, "and I think it would be just as well for all cards to be laid on the table."

Edestone looked at him in surprise, for instead of the simple, smiling old gentleman, with the soft gentle voice and fatherly manner, he saw a crafty, dangerous, and determined man of steel. His voice was cold and harsh, his winning smile had gone. He had come to fight and to fight desperately to the finish.

"In the first place," he continued, "we do not know exactly what is the relationship between you," looking at Edestone, "and the United States of America," with a wave of his hand toward Jones, "and as there can now be no reason for further concealment, since we are virtually on the verge of a declaration of war—a step which I am here to prevent if possible—I will say that it makes no difference to His Imperial Majesty's Government what that relationship may be, so long as Germany gets the use of Mr. Edestone's invention. But we will declare war upon the United States tomorrow night unless we get an assurance from you that we shall have the exclusive right to the one and only flying machine in which this invention has been installed."

At this Jones looked over at Edestone with a glance of inquiry.

"Yes," said Edestone in answer to this, "there is only one."

"Germany understands, of course," proceeded the General, "that the United States will construct others, but so will Germany. Germany is willing and prepared to pay well for this, although she knows that by holding Mr. Edestone she controls this machine and could have it without paying for it. We admit that we do not know where it is, but we are confident that Mr. Edestone does,"—he turned upon Edestone the look of a wild beast who has his prey and loves to torture it,—"and we intend that he shall communicate with the commander and see that this ship is sent to some place where we can take possession of it."

And then with a grim smile he leaned forward on the table, looking first at the Secretary and then at Edestone.

"You are both virtually prisoners in this Embassy," he said. "That is my hand."

"Then we are now at war," said the Secretary with a quiet smile.

"No," replied the General, "it has not come to that yet. And it does not necessarily have to come to that. We should be able to arrange this matter here tonight. As I have said, Germany will pay well. She is willing to start on even terms with the United States, who can build just as fast as we can. Germany will bring this war to an end within a week, and then she and the United States can come to an agreement as to how they will divide up the rest of the earth."

Edestone smiled and made no answer.

The Secretary said: "I can do nothing until I have communicated with my Government."

"I am sorry," said the General impatiently, "but we cannot wait until we get an answer from your very slow and inefficient State Department. We must have a reply before tomorrow night at 12 o'clock. Have you nothing to say, Mr. Edestone? You are perhaps personally the most deeply interested, because I tell you," he grinned cruelly, "we will get your secret if we have to put you on the rack and go back five centuries in the eyes of the rest of the world, should it be necessary to do that in order to give it the blessings that can only be gotten under German rule. I ask you again, have you nothing to say?"

"Nothing, General," replied Edestone.

He was slowly blowing rings of smoke, seeming almost to fascinate the General, who would often stop speaking to follow them with his eyes until they broke or were lost in the darkness in the corners of the room. This was an old trick of his to divert the attention of his adversary, therein improving on Bismarck who always used his cigar to gain time when driven to a corner.

"That is your final answer?" said the General.

"My final answer," Edestone bowed.

"And you, Mr. Secretary?"

"I am but the mouthpiece of my Government, and she has not spoken yet."

"Well, gentlemen," said the General rising, "I think we understand each other."

"I think so," replied Edestone. "Good-night, sir."

The Secretary accompanied the visitor out into the hall, leaving Edestone, who as soon as he was alone rang for a servant and sent for Lawrence. In the meantime he just had opportunity to glance at the note which General von Lichtenstein had given him. It was a mere scrap of writing asking him to come to the Princess Wilhelmina immediately after the departure of His Imperial Majesty.

When Lawrence came in he hastily slipped this into his pocket.

"Lawrence," he said, "I want you to send a message for me as soon as Jones has given his consent. I will ask him in regard to it as soon as he returns, so you had better wait and hear what he has to say."

A moment later the Secretary came into the room with a very worried expression on his face. "Edestone," he said impressively, "this undoubtedly means war."

"And if so," rejoined Edestone, "we will win."

He then explained to Jones how he was in daily communication with "Specs" and was now only waiting for the Secretary's consent to send for him and he could have him over Berlin in seven hours. He also explained to him about the instrument that was in the penthouse on the roof of the Embassy.

"But what do you propose to do, Jack?" frowned the Secretary. "Do you intend to fight these people single-handed and thereby drag your country into a cruel and disastrous war? That seems to me to be unnecessary."

"No, I propose to save you and the members of the Embassy from a very disagreeable experience and from what may develop into a very dangerous situation; for I am convinced that these Germans will not hesitate to fire upon the Embassy if you do not deliver me up to them. The only hope of stopping war without loss of life is through me and my invention. I therefore ask your permission to send the following message," and he handed the Secretary a scrap of paper upon which he had written:

"Be exactly over American Embassy Berlin tomorrow night at nine o'clock. Take station at 5000 feet and there await instructions.

"E."

The Secretary took the paper and read it through twice very slowly.

"I fear," he said with a sigh, "that is the only way."

CHAPTER XXVIII
WHERE IS IT?

The Secretary left the room after practically turning the entire matter over to Edestone. He feared that the time had come to show force. The Germans, in what they felt might be a desperate strait, had thrown to the wind caution, tradition, and the usages of civilized warfare. They were preparing some desperate move which he felt that he was powerless to stop. Diplomacy with them now was as useless as pure logic on a charging elephant.

How they expected to stand against Edestone and his diabolical mystery of the air, he could not comprehend, but he had lived long enough with this nation to know them. Simple, kind, and lovable in their ordinary lives, they were nevertheless, on the subject of war, individually and collectively mad and they were ready to die fighting.

Whereas any sane man could see that their fight with Edestone was hopeless, they with their absolute confidence and conceit were preparing to pit themselves against him and some unknown secret of nature. While he, with his discovery, was apparently in a position to let loose upon their defenceless city an engine of destruction too terrible to think of. Edestone, like the pilot who has come aboard the ocean liner, had now taken entire charge.

The first thing was to get off this message, so he sat down to work out the cipher known only to himself and "Specs." He said to Lawrence:

"My initials J. F. E. are the call which must be repeated three times, then twice, and then finally once. This must all be repeated with one minute intervals until answered by the single letter 'E,' which will be repeated eight times, once for every letter in my name, and after an interval of five minutes, once again only.

"After you have satisfied yourself that you are in touch with Mr. Page, my head man, 'Specs,' I call him, send him this." He handed Lawrence one word of twenty-two letters, or rather twenty-two letters which he had apparently taken indiscriminately from a small pocket dictionary. "Have him repeat, and see that there is no mistake," and continuing, he said: "We are certainly being watched by the German servants; the condition of my trunks shows that, so the first thing to do is to get them out of the way. Call them all down into the ballroom, and say that I wish to speak to them. See that everyone is there, and if there is a single one missing, search the house from garret to cellar until you find them all. I will give them a little talk which will give you and Black time to get off this message. I will, incidentally, show them that I propose to put up with no nonsense whatever."

As Lawrence was leaving the room he said to him with a jolly laugh: "Oh, by the way, how does it feel to be rich again? I have been so occupied with other things that I have not had time to thank and congratulate you on your splendid work. What a fine story it will make when we get back to New York, which will be very soon, I hope."

When the servants came in he first gave them a little insight into the real state of affairs from a standpoint that they had never known. He then explained to them that the Embassy was practically in a state of siege, and that he was in command, and that if he heard of any one of them having any communication whatever with anyone on the outside, he would treat them in the way that he had treated the people in the pictures which he had shown them, only he would put them out of the window and they would keep going up and up and never come down again. So when Lawrence returned and signalled that he might let them go, a more thoroughly scared set of domestics never waited on the word of "Ivan the Terrible."

"Well, Bo," said Lawrence as he threw himself into a comfortable chair, after slopping whisky and water all over the tablecloth and dropping a large piece of ice on the floor which he kicked violently at the retreating servant at whom he had bellowed, giving a perfect imitation of a Prussian officer in a public restaurant when American ladies are present, "this has certainly been 'some day.' Will you please be so kind as to put me wise on a few of your dates?

"In the first place, who was the 'wise guy' who rushed out from nowhere and swallowed up my J. F. E. like an old trout from under a bank who had never seen a Silver Doctor before? Where is he? How is he to get here, and what is he going to do when he does?"

Edestone quietly finished the lighting of his cigar, and after he was thoroughly satisfied that this was perfectly done and it was going to draw to his entire satisfaction, he said:

"Well, now that you are to be my fellow-partner in crime, and Jones is our associate, I will tell you. Do you remember the summer way back in the 90's that you and I spent in Switzerland mountain climbing?"

"Yes, perfectly," said Lawrence, "but that was a long time ago. We were nothing but kids then."

"Do you remember that you, kid-like, insisted upon going over a very flimsy-looking snow bridge, simply because the old guide told us that he had never seen that crevasse bridged before, and that the tradition down in Chamonix was that it had only been bridged once or twice in the memory of man?

"And do you remember," went on Edestone, "that at first he refused to go, saying that if it broke after we got over, there was no possible way of our getting back?"

"Yes," acknowledged Lawrence, "the old 'chump,' and I remember that we went over and got back all right, and those guides are talking about it yet."

"Well, do you remember," continued Edestone, "that when we scrambled up over the next rock ridge we looked into a regular bowl-shaped valley that had the appearance of a crater of an extinct volcano?"

"Yes," said Lawrence.

"Well, 'Specs' is there in that valley, where perhaps no human being has ever been before. I sent him there for that reason. He has been there for the last two months and a half, unknown to anyone on the face of the earth and thoroughly protected from the storms that sweep over that portion of the French Alps."

"Well, I'll be damned," said Lawrence. "Is 'Specs' the skipper of that pretty little toy you were showing on the screen?"

"No, Captain Lee is the skipper," laughed Edestone. "Dear old 'Specs' is my boss. He is the Admiral."

"Well, for the love of Mike," exploded Lawrence. "What a swell chance those mortars out there with their long distance telephone attachments will have with that Queen of the Milky Way. You don't mean to say that he is coming over here with his forty thousand tons and float around up there five thousand feet above the Embassy?" he exclaimed as he looked up at the ceiling with a look of alarm, as if he expected to see it come crushing down on him at any moment. And jumping out of his chair he ran about the room, making the most ridiculous gestures, crying: "Air, I want air!" while Edestone laughed until the tears rolled down his cheeks.

"But say, Bo," said Lawrence, "there is nothing to it. What do you suppose those crazy Dutchmen are thinking about? Why I thought that sky pirate belonged to the United States, and was now probably tied to a dock in some mud flat, with a crew of two brass polishers and a Sunday School teacher, while the Virginia creeper and the North Carolina milkweed twined about it to make nests for the Dove of Peace."

"No," said Edestone, "it is what you have just called it, a Sky Pirate, and I am the buccaneer."

"Did the Emperor know that when he got so gay with you tonight?" asked Lawrence.

"No, he does not know that, but he knows everything else."

"Well, what is his game?"

"Well," said Edestone, after thinking for a while, "as far as I can make it out it is this: They do not want to kill me; they are using me to bait the trap with which they hope to catch the 'Queen of the Milky Way,' as you call her. They will take her dead, now that they cannot get her alive, and they hope to be able to put new life into her after they have taken all life out with the 'long distance telephone attachments,' as you call them."

"Why is he so certain that you will not drop bombs on his city?" asked Lawrence.

"I do not know," replied Edestone, "unless he knows that I am more of a gentleman than he is. Or perhaps he thinks that I will not allow any damage to be done until I am safely on board, which may or may not be perfectly true."

"*Tu as raison, mon vieux,*" shrugged Lawrence.

"They will do nothing to me until they are certain that they are going to lose me. They want me alive, but would rather have me dead than in the hands of the other fellow. Now do you understand?"

"Not exactly," replied Lawrence, pretending to look very wise. "What do you mean about taking her dead if they can't get her alive, and what have those wires got to do with it?"

"I mean by taking her alive," said Edestone, "buying her from whoever she belongs to, and keeping me here to show them how to run her. And when I spoke of taking her dead, I had forgotten that you had not heard what I said tonight while showing the pictures. I will explain this to you sometime when we get on board and we have more time, but you will understand enough when I tell you this."

Lawrence listened attentively as Edestone continued.

"They know that she floats by virtue of an instrument that I have; they know that she will not float if brought in contact with the earth or if connected with it by means of some electrical conductor. They propose to establish an electrical connexion between her and the ground by throwing those wires over her with mortars, just as the life-saving men throw a life-line to a ship in distress."

"Oh, that was why they were so carefully connected with the water main," interrupted Lawrence.

"Yes," replied Edestone, "and when they get her down they will expect me with my instrument to float her off again."

"Well, what do you think of their chances of pulling this off?" asked Lawrence.

"I think," said Edestone thoughtfully, "their chances are small, but you can never tell what these very resourceful people may do. They are buoyed up by a hopefulness that is almost uncanny and they can't all be crazy!"

CHAPTER XXIX
THE DIFFERENCE OF THEIR STATIONS

Edestone and Lawrence sat quietly for a few minutes, Lawrence watching him with a merry twinkle in his eye while Edestone was unconsciously fingering the note that General von Lichtenstein had given him. Finally he said:

"Well, I'm off for bed. I have a hard day before me tomorrow."

"Yes, you are, you old fox!" said his companion. "I'm on to you. There is something up, and you can't hide it from me. You have been sitting there fingering that note from—well, I guess I can pretty well call you, because your lady friends in Berlin are limited—with the silliest expression I have ever seen on your face. Now, out with it! You had better get it off your chest by telling your troubles to papa."

Edestone put the note quickly into his pocket, and was about to force through his bluff when Lawrence stopped him by saying:

"You can trust me, old man; now out with it."

"Well," said Edestone in an embarrassed tone, "General von Lichtenstein did give me a note from Princess Wilhelmina," showing it to Lawrence.

"My dear fellow," Lawrence said, "what do you propose to do? If you are going to take a chance for the pleasure of seeing a beautiful woman, I am with you heart and soul; but if you are taking a chance because you believe she is sincerely in distress and calling on you, an American here in Berlin, when she's got all of those becorseted Johnnies around her, you had better allow me to advise you."

"I am perfectly willing to take a chance," cried Edestone in an angry tone, "if you choose to call it that, because I have absolute confidence in her."

"Say, Jack, I think you are beginning to get a little bit soft on the Princess. You may be all right when it comes to straight electricity, but I think you will admit that I have had more experience in this kind of animal magnetism than you. She is certainly a snappy little induction coil."

"Lawrence, please don't," said Edestone.

"Well, you don't know perfectly well, Jack, that General von Lichtenstein would not have delivered that note from a Princess of the house of Windthorst to you, a low-born American plebeian, unless it was part of their scheme. Why it's as much as his life is worth, if it is as you believe it to be," and he gave Edestone a knowing look.

"Now, cut that out, Lawrence," said Edestone in a decided tone. "Do not think for one moment that I have any illusions as far as that young lady is concerned. She is evidently in trouble of some kind, and the fact that she is so young offsets that of her being a Princess."

Lawrence shrugged his shoulders, and occupied himself smoking while Edestone continued:

"I think that General von Lichtenstein thinks she is working for them, but I am just fool enough to think that she is not. In fact, I know she is not, but even if she were, I would like to show those people that I will not allow them to sacrifice her dignity and compromise herself in her own eyes even for them, so I am going, if for no other reason than to keep her from doing something which she may some day deeply regret. I'm off. If you want some excitement, why you might drop into some of the clubs and feel out the officers."

"Ah," said Lawrence, "that is a good idea. I will be just about as popular as a baby rabbit in a litter of foxes."

"And you can enjoy watching them as they sit around, licking their chops," interjected Edestone, "as they think of the dainty morsel you will make when they eat you alive tomorrow. Be careful. We want no false steps, and there are some pretty skittish ponies in the Emperor's stable. He can hold in check his plough horses, but these young thoroughbreds are getting nervous at the post."

"Well," said Lawrence, "I never was very strong for these Prussians, but they made a hit with me tonight in the way in which they started for you. They were a pretty fine looking lot of handsome young chaps," and curling an imaginary moustache, he continued: "Almost as good as our eleven of 1903," and they both stood and toasted grand old Harvard, and he was leaving the room singing, "Here's to dear old Harvard, drink her down!" when Edestone called him back and said:

"Lawrence, get one of the Embassy automobiles and I will drop you on the way."

Edestone, whereas he knew that his movements were being watched and that this meeting had been arranged, if not by the German General Staff, by some of its female lieutenants, was determined to show them that he did not intend to compromise this little Princess by calling upon her at that hour of the night in a secretive manner.

All was perfectly quiet in the streets, and the automobile was allowed to pass without interruption. When he arrived at the Palace he imagined that the coast had been cleared for him, for on entering he discovered that there was some sort of an entertainment going on, which would have necessitated the presence of waiting automobiles on the outside, which were conspicuous by their absence.

He was evidently expected, and was immediately conducted to a small room. He could hear music and laughter in another part of the Palace, but saw no one except the flunkeys in the hall.

The room into which he was shown was evidently one of those used by the family in their home life, as was shown by the papers, books, and fancy work lying about.

The situation would ordinarily have been most amusing to him, and had he not been so occupied with such serious matters, and had there been less of a difference in their ages and social positions, he would have enjoyed the excitement of a mysterious rendezvous with this extremely charming and attractive young woman.

He was thoroughly conscious of her attractions, and though he might have denied the necessity of this, in thinking of her he always kept before his mind the fable of the fox and the sour grapes.

He was kept waiting for about fifteen minutes, and he began to wonder if the whole thing had not been arranged, and would not have been surprised if when the door quietly opened he had seen von Lichtenstein or even the Emperor himself instead of a very much frightened little woman.

She was apparently supported by sheer will power and the pride of the Princess, which she had inherited from her long line of ancestors, extending back into the unwritten pages of history.

She was dressed so simply that the lines of her most graceful little figure were perfectly revealed, but with such modesty that though she followed the dictates of the modern fashions, which leave little to the imagination, the effect upon Edestone was that of reverence in the presence of such youth and innocence.

To him she seemed to be draped in some soft silky material, and though her neck and arms were bare, they were enveloped in a shimmer of tulle, which she held about her as if for protection. Her hair, parted in the middle, was flatly dressed, and held close to her small head by a little band of jewels which encircled it and crossed her low white brow.

She was perfectly calm, dignified, and had herself well in hand. There was an expression upon her face of resolution, and as if to help, she assumed a more royal and dignified bearing than he had ever supposed she was capable of.

She had evidently been crying, but her voice was steady and rather haughty in its tone as she said, giving him her hand:

"I am glad that you have come."

Edestone took it gently in his own, and bowing, scarcely touched it with his lips, but when he felt its icy touch, and caught the faint perfume, he felt a thrill, and for a moment he forgot that he was in the presence of a Royal Princess, who looked upon him as something a little bit better than a servant, and not as good as the most miserable Count that ever wore a paper collar or passed a fraudulent check at the Newport Reading Room.

Recovering himself quickly, however, he dropped her hand and stood in an attitude of deep respect, but not until she had caught the look that he had given her.

Not daring to look up at her for fear of her indignation at his presumption, he busied himself arranging the cushions in a seat for her.

Raising her hand to her throat, which had moved convulsively, she watched him with a quiet little smile, as if waiting to finish the deadly work which she, young as she was, knew that she had started. Like a great ring general, she did not intend to allow her adversary time to recover before she administered the *coup de grace*.

When he recovered sufficiently to allow himself to look at her, although he resolved to keep strictly to the object of their meeting, he was so struck with her great charm that he could not resist saying:

"I sincerely hope, Princess, that you will pardon me if I take the great liberty of saying to you that you are looking extremely beautiful tonight."

She answered with a smile.

And then in a light and frivolous tone, and looking at her in a manner which she could not misunderstand, with the deepest respect he added:

"If I were a Prince and a few years younger, I would humbly kneel and worship at your shrine, Princess."

A cloud passed over her face, but recovering, with a look which if Edestone had been younger and less sensible would have finished him:

"Well, Mr. Edestone," she smiled coquettishly, "I understand that you were tonight a match for an Emperor; and I am feeling very old myself."

With a smile acknowledging her condescension in allowing this slight exchange of repartee, he assumed a fatherly air, and said, having recovered himself entirely:

"Now, my dear and very sweet little Princess, your very old and most humble servant awaits your orders. The only reward that he expects is that he be allowed to see you one or two times before he dies of old age, or you are seated on a throne."

With an impatient gesture, and an almost imperceptible stamp of her little foot, she said:

"Please don't talk that way. I hate being a Princess, and the way you say it makes me hate myself," and with a quick glance and a tone of great seriousness: "I don't think you are so old as all that.

"I have sent for you," changing her voice, "to warn you again. It was absolutely necessary in order to arrange this meeting to lead them to believe that I was willing to do that which you must hate me for—use my power as a woman to persuade you to give up the position which you have taken, and though I hate them all for it, in order to save you from certain death I have compromised myself in my own eyes, and have done that which will cause you to hate me."

"That I could never do," said Edestone, which brought a faint smile to her lips. "Princess, I appreciate more deeply than I can say your great kindness, and if there is anything that I can do which will save you from these people when they find that you have failed in your undertaking, you can command me. Your warning, however, comes as no surprise to me; but I appreciate it none the less."

"Could I not hold out to them," she anticipated, "that you had agreed to reveal this secret to me, and in that way gain time, and you might be able to get out of Berlin?"

"But what would become of you when they discovered that you had played them false?" asked Edestone. And then, as if hesitating to refer to the delicacy of her position, an English Princess in Berlin, he added: "They are relentless, and they might suspect you of playing into the hands of England.

No, Princess, there is but one thing for you to do, and that is to say that I declined absolutely and entirely to consider any proposition of any kind.

"If you were in any way associated with me in what I have already done and what I propose to do, I should not be willing to leave you in Berlin, and though I know you are absolutely sincere in your intentions to assist me in my work, there is no possible way for me to protect you other than by taking you with me, which is absolutely out of the question. You would not be safe even in the American Embassy."

She thought for a while, and then, as if an idea had struck her, she said blushingly:

"My mother, like myself, is perfectly loyal to England, and if as I understand it is the intention of the American Government to come out on the side of the Allies, would there be any impropriety in my going with her to the Embassy and taking my chances with the Secretary's family?"

"That would be impossible," said Edestone. "They have taken you into their confidence, and would not allow you to leave the country. I think mine is the only plan. Say to them that I would listen to no proposition, and allow me to go and take my chances."

He could not trust himself, and he knew his only hope of keeping her esteem was in getting out before she discovered his real secret, and rising in a most dignified manner he kissed her hand, and then allowing himself to press it gently to his cheek for a moment, left the room abruptly, while she sank into a seat and covered her face with her hands.

CHAPTER XXX
THEY CALL FOR ASSISTANCE

The next morning everything was perfectly quiet on the outside of the Embassy. The soldiers had apparently settled down for a siege. They contented themselves with singing hymns and drinking songs, and with mock reverence rendering the "Star Spangled Banner," closely followed by the "Marseillaise," and "It's a Long Way to Tipperary."

But there was mutiny within the walls. Mrs. Jones had flatly refused to leave the Embassy. She said that she had not the slightest idea of going up in Jack's foolish flying machine, to be shot at by the soldiers or dropped into the middle of the ocean; that for her part she intended to stay exactly where she was. The Secretary might go if he wished to risk his life in a balloon or if it was his duty, but she thought she was safer in the Embassy. She was perfectly sure that the Germans would not dare to shoot at it while the United States flag was flying over it, and there were women inside.

The Secretary seemed to agree with her, and said: "It was only on your account, my dear, that I was going. As long as the flag flies above this roof, my duty is here, and I sincerely hope that you are right."

"But we are now at war with these people," said Edestone, "and they may take it into their heads to shoot that flag away, and they have plainly shown that they will kill and burn women and children if in their judgment one single point, however small, can be gained in their national game of war. It is a ruling passion with them, and they think that all of the nicer feelings of honour, humanity, and even religion must be crushed, and that these sentiments are foolish and are for women and weaklings only."

At which Mrs. Jones seemed worried. She preferred, however, she said, to stay and take a chance rather than go to certain death with Edestone.

"I think," said he, "that if we were dealing with any of the other civilized nations, the Embassy would be perfectly safe, even if war had been declared or forced upon us without any formal declaration, but with the Germans in their present state of nerves, it is quite different. They have a strange method of retaliation, not for an injury to themselves, but for the failure on their part to inflict one upon others, which can only be accounted for by their savage passion for revenge. The real danger, however, will be before this while they are trying to prevent my escape."

The Secretary was anxious to remain at his post as long as possible, so he was glad to side with Mrs. Jones. Lawrence begged for and obtained permission to go with Edestone.

"You can take absolutely nothing in the way of luggage," said Edestone. "I can fit you out when we get on board. I have just told Black, Stanton, and James the same thing, and I suppose your boy would like to go with you also."

"Certainly," said Lawrence.

With no preparations to make, there was nothing to do but wait. Lawrence was the only one who was willing to go out on the streets and stand the ugly looks that were given by all those who in some way or another knew that they were Americans.

On his return he reported that the papers were silent on the subject of the Kaiser's call at the Embassy the night before. One of the afternoon papers, he said, did report that a very large Zeppelin had been seen flying over Berne at 9 o'clock in the morning, at about 5000 feet, judging by her size. At first it was thought that she was on fire from the clouds of smoke that she was emitting, but she continued on her way in the direction of Berlin at about fifty miles an hour. She was up too high, the papers stated, to be identified, but as the Swiss Government knew that none of the Allies had Zeppelins, it was suggested that a protest would soon come from Switzerland for a violation of her neutrality.

Lawrence said that evidently the German General Staff had received some information, for he found no officers at the Club, and troops with anti-aircraft guns and mortars with their two-wheeled trailers were moving in all directions.

The general public, however, as usual, seemed to have no information, and were going about their duties in their usual stolid manner.

The troops around the Embassy had been reinforced and were showing great activity. He thought that the Kaiser was making a personal inspection judging by the number of high officers he saw going and coming.

The soldiers were most insulting in their manner and kept him moving, and would not allow him to go anywhere near the mortars which were stripped for action. The covers over the two-wheeled drums were unstrapped so that they could be thrown off at a moment's notice.

"You are right," said Edestone, as he and Lawrence stood looking out of one of the windows of the Embassy at about 5 o'clock in the afternoon. "They have heard something. I am surprised that we have heard nothing from them today. You can depend upon it, they will try to get me without an actual fight. They know that they can bamboozle our Government, but fear the temper of our people will not stand for any killing, which they certainly intend to do if necessary. I do wish Mrs. Jones was not here.

"If 'Specs' was over Berne at 9 o'clock," he went on, "and he wanted to, he could have been here hours ago. He is evidently jogging along slowly. He cannot now be more than fifty miles away; he is perhaps just about at Leipsic. I think we had better speak to him and tell him to go higher up and not to come over Berlin before dark. You know he does not know what is going on here. I am afraid to warn him about the wires, for if by chance they should intercept our message they would know that they had struck a very good answer to my 'Little Peace Maker.'"

"You don't mean to say," cried Lawrence, "that there is any chance of their pulling you down with those wires?"

"It all depends," replied Edestone. "It would take me some time to calculate the amount of metal it would require to take the current that would wreck us, but if they do get that amount in contact with us and the earth at the same time we will come down."

"My God!" said Lawrence.

"Well, that is the reason that I do not want to take any chance by mentioning wires at all. They don't know now that one wire will not do the trick, and if they get the idea that it is a question of the largest possible number, they will double up on us. As it is, they have sixteen, and we have a fighting chance. At any rate, I will speak to 'Specs' and tell him not to come over the Embassy until after dark."

"Won't he have some difficulty in finding the Embassy?" asked Lawrence.

Edestone laughed. "You do not know old 'Specs.' In the first place he studied for six years in Berlin and knows it from end to end. Besides, he has all of the cities of Europe plotted, and he can get his bearings from a dozen different points. He will feel very badly unless Capt. Lee puts him within a few inches of where his calculations tell him he should be. Why, you should see him calculating! He used a 6 H pencil, and he can cover a large sheet of paper with microscopic figures before you have even sharpened yours! It will be just like 'Specs,' if it is a still night, to drop a plumb line and check himself. When you see him coming down slowly, you can be sure that he is going to drop his ladder at exactly the right spot.

"You see to it that the servants are all out of the way. If necessary, lock them all down in the basement. I will work out the message."

When Lawrence returned and stated that everything was clear, Edestone said to him: "Send this. It says:

"*Stand by at 50, up 10,000. After dark follow orders. If called come quickly.'*"

They then took the elevator and went together to the roof, where with powerful glasses they searched the south-western sky. On all sides they could see Taubes, which like great birds were circling in all directions.

Edestone was startled by seeing something that looked like the "Little Peace Maker," but it turned out to be one of the largest German Zeppelins.

"Why, my boy," laughed Lawrence, "Captain Lee could make that fellow look like an *ante bellum* picnic in a thunderstorm, all hoop skirts and bombazine, before Count Zeppelin could get it under the shelter tent.

"It is circling now," he exclaimed; "he must have his eye on a Belgium baby, the old buzzard!"

After Edestone had gotten Lawrence to his wireless instrument by first running the car down until the top was at the level of the roof, and after Lawrence had stepped on running it up to the top of the penthouse, he then dropped the car down and came out on the roof again.

He looked about with his glasses; and was not surprised to see soldiers on the roofs of the other buildings where they had stationed powerful anti-aircraft guns and searchlights.

"I am rather glad Mrs. Jones is not coming with us," he thought. "It is going to be pretty hot here for a little while. We shall be under fire for about ten feet; Captain Lee will not dare come down any closer."

When Lawrence came down, he said: "I got him and he answered me. I am sure someone was trying to cut in. I could not tell whether he could get us or not, but he was trying to mix us up."

Edestone worked with his little book for a few minutes, and then read aloud:

"*Passed over Leipsic up 5000. Have been seen. Will stand by at 30, up 10,000.*"

"That means that he is about over Dessau, and could get here in fifteen minutes easily if called. So far so good. But those machine guns are worrying me. I did not want to make any show of force, but self protection may drive me to it.

"Run the elevator down, Lawrence, and come back by the stairs. We can walk down. I want to look over my ground and plan my campaign."

"How foolish," he thought, "not to have remembered the machine guns on the roofs. The only protection we have on the Embassy are the chimneys and the penthouse, and they will protect only halfway up the landing ladder. There is always that ten feet in which we will be exposed on all sides to a fire under which nothing could live for half a minute."

He then examined the door to the bulkhead at the head of the stairs. It was strong, but there was no way to fasten it on the outside. There was another door at the bottom of the stairs that could be locked, but it was an ordinary door and could easily be broken down. He found only one place on the entire roof where there was what might be called a zone of safety, and that was by no means perfectly safe.

He carefully worked out the plan of defence, giving to his enemy the part to play which he thought they would naturally take.

When Lawrence came up he explained his plan to him. He said: "When they see that we are attempting to escape by the roof, they will rush us by coming up those stairs. I do not intend to allow my men to fire unless it is absolutely necessary."

"Oh, just shoot me one little one," begged Lawrence.

Edestone frowned disapprovingly. "When they have broken through the lower door, we can stand here between the penthouse and the chimneys, and by keeping down below the parapet be comparatively safe. I will then tell them that I have a machine gun trained on the bulkhead door, and that it will be certain death for them to attempt to come out that way. If they fire on the Embassy, I will order my large guns to silence every gun that bears on it."

As they went downstairs the sun was just setting.

CHAPTER XXXI
"SIT DOWN, YOU DOG!"

As Edestone and Lawrence were coming down the stairs they were met by one of the German servants, who told them in a rather excited manner that the Secretary wished to see them both in his library.

Hastening down they were surprised as they arrived in the main hall to see through the iron and glass grille a squad of German soldiers standing at the front door.

"This is their last card," said Edestone in an undertone, "and if it fails there is nothing left for them to do but kill me. They have received word from Leipsic and they know that there is no time to lose, so we can look out now for anything. You had better get our party together, Lawrence, and see that every man has a pistol. There are two automatics in my room. When you get back, if you find me standing, or if I rise, or if I light a cigar, make some excuse and get up to the roof as quickly as you can and send your S. O. S. call to 'Specs.' He can be here in fifteen minutes after he receives it. Then, lock that grille and station someone there you can trust."

"I wonder what they'll charge me with?" he thought as alone he entered the room where the Secretary was sitting calmly, although Edestone could see that he was making a great effort not to show his indignation to the German officer who was standing in front of him.

Edestone knew him so well that when he saw his mouth fixed as though he was whistling quietly to himself, the forefinger of his right hand at his lips as if to assist him in his musical efforts,—he who could not turn a tune,—he knew that Jones had himself well in hand. In his left hand the Secretary held a formal-looking paper with which he was quietly tapping the table in front of him as though keeping time to his soundless and imaginary ditty. With his chin well down, he was looking from under his heavy eyebrows with eyes that were dangerously cold.

The officer who had delivered these papers was apparently waiting for his answer and stood very erect, looking straight ahead of him. He did not change his position or notice Edestone as he entered the room.

"Good-morning, Count von Hemelstein," said Edestone on seeing who it was, and the soldier then condescended to acknowledge the greeting with a slight bow.

The Secretary leaned forward, and putting both hands flat on the table while looking straight at Count von Hemelstein, said in a rather judicial tone, as though delivering an opinion from the bench:

"Mr. Edestone, Count von Hemelstein has just delivered to me an order for your arrest on the charge of giving assistance to the enemies of Germany. He also charges Lawrence Stuyvesant with insulting the Emperor's uniform and his dignity by impersonating a Prince of the Royal Blood and rendering that Prince ridiculous. He states, however, in your case that the Emperor will accept your explanation if you will accompany Count von Hemelstein quietly and make it to His Imperial Majesty in person. In the case of Lawrence Stuyvesant, he demands an apology and has paroled him in my custody until this is received, and as in the first case he makes a further condition, which is that the Emperor will accept an apology made by Lawrence Stuyvesant to the Prince himself, provided only that you agree to accompany Count von Hemelstein quietly and at once."

Then turning as if addressing a prisoner on trial before him he said, in that soft and quiet voice always assumed by a judge in speaking to a criminal, even though he knows that the culprit has just boiled his mother:

"In the case against you, Mr. Edestone, in your absence I have flatly denied the charge. In the case against Lawrence Stuyvesant I deny all knowledge of, and decline to express an opinion until I have had an opportunity of looking into, the circumstances of the alleged offence."

Edestone who had stood during this went over and took a seat at the Secretary's side of the table. "It is just as you said it would be," he observed to the Count with a mocking laugh as he passed him. "You Germans are so thorough."

The Count made no reply, only stiffening up, if it were possible to give any more of that quality of German militarism to a ramrod in human form.

He stood as if expecting the Secretary to continue, or to hear further from Edestone, but both men sat perfectly still looking at him. The Secretary, as if having delivered his ruling, he was waiting for the case to go on, settled back into his chair, while Edestone, with the look of a lawyer who is perfectly satisfied with the ruling of the court, was grinning at his opponent, toying with both hands with a small bronze paper-weight made in the shape of a ploughshare, recently received from Washington with the compliments of the Secretary of State.

As neither man seemed to have the slightest intention of breaking the silence, after a moment which seemed an age, Count von Hemelstein brought his hand with a snap to a salute.

"My orders are to bring Mr. Edestone with me," he said, "and if you decline to deliver him to me, Mr. Secretary, I must use force."

"That I have no power to prevent you from doing," said Jones. "You are now in the Embassy of a friendly nation, on soil dedicated by His Imperial Majesty to the use of the representative of that nation, whose safety and that of those he may see fit to protect are guaranteed by the most solemn promise that it is possible for one nation to make to another. If His Imperial Majesty intends to break his solemn word, I am as powerless as the lowest peasant in his domain. As to my word of honour as to the safe-keeping of Mr. Lawrence Stuyvesant, you have by your act reduced me to the rank of a simple American citizen, and as such, and not as representing the Ambassador at the Court of Berlin—for after this there can be none—I tell you that I will not give my word to those who do not keep theirs. As to Mr. Edestone, I can simply, for his own sake, advise him to go with you, but not before I tell him that his country will resist with all its power the indignity which His Majesty has seen fit to offer it."

Lawrence, who had come in during this speech, was standing looking in amazement from one to the other.

Then Edestone rose. "Mr. Secretary," he said, "I regret to have been the cause of putting you in this most trying position, and before I decide to accompany this officer or detective I must think, so with your permission I will light a cigar." He walked over to a table and very slowly selected one from a box that was there.

Lawrence, as if he had forgotten something, left the room hurriedly.

Edestone very deliberately took his cigar and very slowly lighted it. He then as slowly walked back to his seat and sat blowing ring after ring, holding all the time the box of matches in his right hand.

In the meantime Lawrence had walked to the front door, as if looking out to see why the soldiers were there, and turned the key of the grille so noiselessly that it failed to attract any attention from the men on the outside. Then turning to Fred, the Bowery boy, who was waiting for him, he spoke in an undertone.

"Don't let any of the servants open that door or even go near it," he said, and, satisfied that his order would be obeyed, stepped inside the elevator and closed the door with a bang.

Edestone, who had meanwhile been doing anything simply to kill time, heard this. He knew that Lawrence would work quickly, and had had ample time to carry out the first part of his instructions. As if about to drop into his pocket the box of matches he was holding, he drew with a quick motion a .38 automatic, and leaning across the table covered the Count with it.

"Hold up your hands!" he said without raising his voice. "It is safer."

There was on his face that unmistakable look of the man who intends to kill. The other man saw it and understood, and reluctantly raised his hands above his head after making a half-gesture as if to draw his own pistol from his belt but thinking better of it.

"This is very foolish, Mr. Edestone," he said with a disdainful sneer. "Will you fight single-handed six million men?"

Jones, who when a young man had spent a good many years in a frontier town, was too accustomed to this method of punctuating one's remarks and calling the undivided attention of one's listener to them, to be much surprised. At any rate, he showed none, and besides he knew Edestone to be a perfectly cool man whose trigger finger would not twitch from nervousness.

"Be careful, Jack," he contented himself with saying very quietly; "I suppose you know what you are about." Then he settled back to wait for Edestone to explain what he would do next.

"Yes, William," said Edestone, "I know exactly what I am doing, and in order to relieve you and your Government from any responsibility, I here, in the presence of the Emperor's representative, renounce my allegiance to the United States of America and to all other countries, and I now become a law unto myself, accountable to no one but myself—in other words, an outlaw, a pirate." He turned then to the emissary of the Kaiser.

"Count von Hemelstein, as I intend to keep you in that position for some little time unless you will allow me to remove your arms—not your sword," he explained quickly on seeing the look of horror that came over the Prussian's face. "I will allow you to keep that barbaric relic of the Middle Ages and modern Japan, to which you and the Knights k of the Orient attach so much importance. But that very nice automatic I must have. I beg that you will allow me to take it without any unnecessary fuss." He walked around the table and, gently pulling the pistol out of its holster, put it into his own pocket, keeping the Count carefully covered all the while.

"Now you can take down your hands. I know that you can hide nothing more dangerous in that tight-fitting uniform of yours than a long cigarette holder and a very pretty box. I am delighted that you have been so quiet, as no one could come to your assistance. Your soldiers are locked outside of the iron grille and would have some difficulty in breaking it down, even if they could hear you; so sit down. I wish to explain a few things to you.

"It is now exactly a quarter before eight o'clock. By eight the Little Peace Maker will be over the Embassy, and you with your boastful knowledge of other people's business must realize what that means. You have heard what I just said to the Secretary representing the United States at the Court of Berlin, and my object in making that statement before you was to relieve him and the United States of America of the responsibility of any of my acts. The Little Peace Maker is my own personal property, and before she fires a gun or drops a bomb I shall haul down the flag of the United States and run up my own private signal, which on my yacht, the *Storm Queen*, is well known in all yachting circles. In short, from now on I declare myself an outlaw.

"If your Emperor will allow me and my men to go abroad peaceably, I will do so and all may be well, but at the very first act of violence I will take the necessary steps to protect them. I intend to keep you here until I am notified that the airship has arrived, and when I leave this room, my advice to you is not to follow me, but go at once and notify your superior officer and thereby save the great loss of life that will otherwise ensue.

"Now, Count, as we will have about ten minutes longer together, I am quite sure that the Secretary will not object to your joining me with one of the Ambassador's extremely good cigars," and he winked at his friend Jones.

He walked over to the table as if to get the box, but the moment his back was turned the Count jumped and started for the door like a flash. With a quick side step, however, Edestone threw himself between him and the only exit from the room, and giving the fugitive a good poke in the stomach with the muzzle of his gun, said:

"I allowed you to do that to show you that you are absolutely in my power. Sit down, Count von Hemelstein, and if you will give me your word of honour that you will not move I shall not tie you. Do you accept these terms?"

The Count nodded his head and sat down, and the Secretary, who all this time had been sitting perfectly quiet, said with a very little bit of a smile on about one-half of his mouth:

"Count von Hemelstein, if I were you I should sit still. You must see that you are powerless to do anything, and whereas I know that Mr. Edestone does not intend to kill you unless it is absolutely necessary, I am equally certain that he intends to if it is. In fact, I do not know that he might not kill me if I stood in his way. He has just declared himself to be an outlaw, and it is my duty to turn him over to the authorities, but I should hate to have to try to do it now that he seems so bent on leaving us."

Edestone, who quickly caught the idea that the Secretary was trying to convey to him, turned on his friend.

"If you, my friend, whom I have known for years, desert me now," he declared in a loud and apparently much excited tone, "or attempt to deliver me over to these wild people to kill, I will kill you, if it is the last act of my life." He faced about so that one eye was hidden from the flabbergasted German and gave another significant wink. Then turning back to the Count he resumed: "I will kill any man who prevents me from going on board the Little Peace Maker tonight. Now let us talk about more pleasant things for the few remaining minutes that we are to have in each other's company."

But the Count was in no mood for conversation. He sat staring at the floor, while Edestone with his watch in his hand waited for word from Lawrence. It was now eight o'clock and still no response. Could there be some mistake? Had the Germans been able to prevent his message from going through? Or was Lawrence waiting to be sure that the airship was coming before leaving the roof to notify him?

On the outside all was quiet, and as long as the soldiers did not suspect, everything would be all right. But suppose that the Emperor should grow impatient and send another messenger? He was just congratulating himself that the Count did not know what time it was or that the Little Peace Maker was now overdue, when a clock somewhere struck eight.

The Count straightened up and his look of k interest changed to hope, and finally a smile broke over his face as the minutes slipped by.

"Well, Mr. Edestone, your little dream will soon be over," he taunted, after sitting for about five minutes longer.

Even the Secretary was growing fidgety. He knew that something would have to happen soon or the German General Staff, with its usual thoroughness, would ask the reason why, and this question would be put in their usual forcible manner.

It was now ten minutes after eight, and Edestone expected every minute to hear a ring at the front door. Besides, the dusk was coming on and the servants would soon be in to light the lights. He had decided that if they did he would retreat to the roof, forcing the Count to accompany him, and there make a last stand. He formed a mental resolution never to leave that roof alive except on board of the Little Peace Maker. He had always said that he had rather be dead than a failure. He did not want to live to see his life's work, his beautiful ship, which must finally come down, used for war, death, and destruction, his dream of universal peace gone forever; or by his own discovery remove still farther from the grasp of the long-suffering world that relief which it was vainly reaching out for in its present desperate plight.

Was this the end? If so, he would meet it calmly, but not until he had made a fight. Then he would meet Fate with a smile, for she had been good to him. Perhaps an all-wise Providence had decreed that man must fight on to the bitter end, and to punish him for his presumption in attempting to alter an unalterable law had led him on only to destroy him just as he, with his petty little mind, thought he had reached the goal.

The Count was now laughing and explaining to Jones what was going to happen to him, to the United States, and especially to Edestone, and Jones was beginning to look as if he thought there might be some truth in what he was saying.

It was nearly half-past eight when the long-expected ring at the front door came. The Count laughed out loud in triumph.

"Mr. Edestone," he said, "don't you think that it is just about time to ask for terms? It is not too late even now. You are a game man, and I hate to see you go to destruction when it is not necessary."

The ring was followed by another longer than the first.

Edestone was leaning well over the table and looking at the Count with a light in his eyes like that in those of a tiger about to spring.

"I return the compliment," he said.

There was now heard on the outside much noise and confusion. The bell was rung again and the sound of someone violently shaking the front door was followed by the breaking of the glass in the iron grille. Above this din, which was really not so great as it seemed to the overwrought nerves of the three men who had sat looking at each other for the last forty minutes, there came the unmistakable rattle of machine-guns, which at first was distant and light in volume, but with incredible rapidity increased until it was a roar that seemed like a great wave rolling up from the southern part of the city.

Edestone, who knew that this meant that the Little Peace Maker must have been sighted by the German look-outs on the roofs, ran to the window.

The Count hesitated for just one moment, as if there were two forces within him fighting for mastery, and then with a quick movement he made a jump for the door.

"Sit down, you dog!" cried Edestone turning just in time to see him, and he sent a bullet crashing through the door just above the Count's hand where it rested on the knob.

Count von Hemelstein stopped, and turning braced himself to receive the ball that he thought must certainly follow.

"Come back and sit down, you poor thing. If you cannot keep your word without help, I will help you next time."

But the soldiers on the outside, on hearing the shot, redoubled their efforts to get in, and now could be heard running around the house and trying the other doors. In the midst of all this uproar, Lawrence came down, and in imitation of one of his favourite characters, the sailor who announced to Captain Sigsbee the sinking of the *Maine*, said:

"Sir, I have the honour to report that the Little Peace Maker has been sighted on our starboard bow." Then throwing off his assumed character he added: "Get a move on you, they will be in at the front door in a minute!

"And what are you going to do with this?" he asked on seeing the Count. "Don't you think we had better wing it before we leave? Ish ka bibble."

"No." Edestone pushed him ahead of him out of the room. And to Jones: "Good-bye, William," he called over his shoulder. "I am sorry to have given you so much trouble."

When he had closed the door they both ran into the elevator and started for the roof.

"Where are all of those who are going with us?" asked Edestone.

"They are all on the roof. No, by Jove!" Lawrence interrupted himself, "Fred is still down in the front hall."

"We must go for him," said Edestone, halting the car and starting it down.

"Why not leave him? Mr. Jones can take care of him."

"No, they won't stop at anything." Edestone shook his head.

By this time the car had arrived at the main-floor level, and as Edestone flung open the door the Count was seen just coming out of the library, while Fred, who had seen Edestone and Lawrence take the lift, was running up the stairs. In the dim light the Count saw him, and cried to the soldiers who had their guns through the grille:

"Shoot that man!"

There was the report of several rifles in quick succession, and the Bowery boy, who was now at the top of the great monumental stairs, fell dead. His body rolled to the bottom and lay there perfectly still.

CHAPTER XXXII
L. P. M.

Almost beside himself, Lawrence resisted all of Edestone's efforts to get him back into the elevator.

"You damn' dirty Dutchman, I'll pay you for this!" he yelled over his shoulder, as he struggled to break loose from the firm grip which held him, and get at the Count.

It was not a time to permit of argument. Overpowering him with his great strength, Edestone simply dragged him back, and flung him into a corner of the car, where he sat crying like a baby with uncontrollable rage.

After he had started the lift, however, Edestone went over and patted him soothingly on the shoulder.

"I am sorry, old man," he said regretfully, "awfully sorry! He thought it was I, and I almost wish it had been."

This brought Lawrence back to himself. He knew that Edestone meant every word he said and, jumping to his feet, he threw his arms around his friend's neck.

"Bo!" he exclaimed, half-laughing, half-sobbing, "you are a king among men!" little dreaming of the amount of truth there was in what he said.

A moment later he dropped back into the vernacular, where he was more at home.

"You are the best sport I ever knew," he said, "and I am nothing but a rotten squealer! Forgive me, and I will try to be good. But, Bo! that did hurt!" The tears came to his eyes once more. "He was such a nervy little chap!"

By this time they had gotten to the roof, where they found Black, Stanton, and James eagerly awaiting them.

"Where is Fred?" asked Black, noting his absence as the other two stepped out to join them.

"Dead by God!" Lawrence started again to become hysterical. "That devil, Count von Hemelstein, killed him!"

"Shut up, Lawrence!" broke in Edestone sharply. "Cut out that swearing and get to work. We have no time to lose."

In the same quick, authoritative tone, he issued his orders to the others, as they stood staring at the news, each in his different way showing his breeding. Black was commencing to whine; Stanton with a scowl of rage was in sympathy with Lawrence; while James, demonstrating his years of training, stood statue-like with hand behind his back, leaning forward as if to catch his master's next order, and carry it out with perfect decorum.

"Have you locked the door at the foot of the stairs? Ah! That is good!" he exclaimed, as he saw that they had barricaded the door of the bulkhead by putting a piece of timber between it and the coping around one of the skylights.

It had grown quite dark in the interval, but in the glare of the great searchlights which were playing upon her he could plainly see above him the Little Peace Maker which had swung into a position directly over the Embassy, and was now slowly descending.

She was not over a thousand feet above the roof as she hung there, three of her great searchlights bearing steadily on three different points in the city, and giving to her the aspect of an enormous spyglass standing on its gigantic tripod, and by its own weight forcing the feet of the tripod into the soft earth, as the ship slowly settled.

Shrapnel shells were exploding all about her, and at times she was almost entirely enveloped in smoke. Between the reports of the heavier artillery could be heard the staccato spatter of bullets on her iron sides as the machine-guns sprayed her from end to end. Now and then one of the gunners would reach one of her searchlights, and as the ray was extinguished, one almost expected to see her topple in the direction of her broken support, but in each case it was quickly replaced by another, and she continued to drop nearer and nearer to the earth.

Excepting for the searchlights there was no sign of life on board. Silently and without response of any kind, she came. But as she approached nearer, and the angle of the German guns was still further reduced, although they must already have been doing frightful damage in all parts of the city, the shrapnel and small bullets could be heard screaming over the heads of the little party on the roof.

"It is getting pretty hot here, and we had better lie down," Edestone said. But the words were hardly out of his mouth before Stanton fell with a bullet in his head, and James sat down, probably more abruptly than he had ever done anything before in all his life.

"I beg pardon, sir," he observed with a little gasp, "but I think, sir, as how they have got me in the leg, sir."

They all dropped down. Stanton was dead, and James was bleeding badly from the flesh-wound in his leg.

"That was the fellow in that tower over there." Lawrence made a reconnoissance. "He is now shooting straight at us."

"This has got to stop." Edestone frowned. "Lawrence send this message. No cipher; I would rather have them catch this.

"Tell 'Specs' first to haul down the U. S. flag and run up my private signal. Then he is to silence every gun he can find that is bearing on us, and train a machine-gun on the door of the bulk-head, ready to fire when I give the signal by throwing up my hat.

"Take Lawrence up to the instrument, Mr. Black," he directed, turning to Black who was giving "first aid" to the unfortunate valet. "I will do what I can for James."

When the elevator with Lawrence and the electrician had gone up above the level of the roof, leaving the shaft open down into the house, he could distinctly hear the soldiers running up the stairs. At any moment now they might be hammering on the door at the foot of the stairway leading to the roof.

He hated the idea of killing those innocent Germans, mere machines, as they were, in the hands of a Master, who with his entire entourage had become sick with a mania which took the form of militarism, imperialism, and pan-Germanism. But after the death of his two fellow-countrymen—for at heart he was still true to the land of his birth, although to save her he had just renounced the flag—he felt that he was justified in what he was about to do.

With a silent prayer for the peasant mothers who were soon to lose their dear ones, he commended their souls to God, and not as these mothers, poor benighted creatures, had done, to their Emperor.

He was startled from these sorrowful reflections by the white glow of a searchlight from the Little Peace Maker sweeping across the roof, and playing hither and thither. Evidently, "Specs" had received his order, and was now feeling about for the bulkhead door.

A moment later he located it. Immediately the night was made hideous with the roar of the guns from the airship, as they sowed bursting shells in all directions, and carried death and destruction to the heart of this great and wonderful city, built up stone by stone, and standing as a living monument to one of the greatest people on the face of the earth—a people that science teaches are the very last expression of God's greatness shown in His wonderful evolution of matter into His own image. And for what? That one family might maintain the position given to one of their ancestors in the remote, dark, and grovelling ages of the past for prowess of which a modern prizefighter might be proud, but for acts to which he with a higher standard might not stoop.

The telling response of the Little Peace Maker soon put an end to the storm of shrapnel and bullets which had been singing, whistling, buzzing, and screaming about them, and Edestone might have been able to stand up, but for the pertinacity of the snipers, those serpents of modern warfare, who were searching every dark corner of the roof.

Matters were fast coming to a climax, however. By the time that Lawrence and Black had returned from sending the wireless message, and had crawled over to where Edestone lay, the soldiers had broken down the lower door, and were pounding at the upper, which "Specs" was holding as with a rapier point at the heart of a fallen foe, ready to strike at the slightest movement.

Crawling over to the elevator shaft, Edestone called down a warning in a loud voice to those below:

"I have a machine-gun trained on the top of the stairs! If you order your men to break that door down, I will order my guns to fire, and will kill them faster than you can drive them up!"

For a moment the only response to his challenge was silence. Then a voice rang out which he had heard before, arrogant and commanding:

"As God has ordained that I and none other should rule the earth, with Him alone, I shall. By my Imperial order, and with His assistance, bring that man to me, dead or alive!"

A brief pause ensued. Edestone could hear the officers urging on their men. Suddenly pistol-shots rang out, and with a mad rush they came on. The door swayed and shivered under the impact. It split and shattered. Finally it fell.

"May God have mercy on his soul!" murmured Edestone, and he tossed his hat high in the air.

"Specs" from his look-out caught the signal; and instantly the doorway became a writhing, shrieking mass of wounded humanity. Like vaseline squeezed out of a tube, it was forced out of the opening by the pressure of those behind and spread in wider and wider circles across the roof, until the aperture itself was choked and stopped with bodies.

But Edestone and his companions were spared the full measure of this sickening sight, as the rapid manoeuvres of the Little Peace Maker compelled them to devote their attention to her.

As the great ship descended to within about ten feet of the chimney-tops, men appeared on her lower bridge and dropped over the insulated ladder which extended almost to where the refugees lay.

Picking James up and putting him on his back where he clung like a baby, Edestone ran for the ladder, quickly followed by Lawrence and Black. He reached the bridge just in time to turn James over to one of the crew, and extend his assistance to Lawrence, who had received a shot in one hand, and was rather dizzily holding on to the ladder with the other. Eventually, though, they all gained the bridge, and with their rescuers already there raced up the gangway under a perfect hail of bullets for the open doorway at the top. But before the last man had passed through, two of the sailors had been shot, and had fallen to their death on the roof.

As they entered the ship, they were met by "Specs," Captain Lee, Dr. Brown, and other officers in uniforms which at the first glance might have been taken for those of the New York Yacht Club, except for the insignia on their caps which was a combination of Edestone's private signal and the letters L. P. M. Edestone, however, interrupted their attempt to salute him.

"Please waive all ceremony," he said. "We have wounded men here that must be attended to."

At this, Dr. Brown immediately came forward, and after ordering Lawrence and James to the hospital gave a start as his glance fell upon Edestone.

"You did not tell me that you yourself were wounded, sir," he exclaimed; and then for the first time Edestone discovered that his face, hands, and clothing were covered with blood which was streaming from a wound above his temple.

He was about to permit himself also to be examined, when there was heard from below the detonation of one of the Kaiser's big mortars; and pulling away from the Doctor, he called an excited order to "Specs":

"Throw on your full charge, and lift her as fast as you can!"

He ran to the gangway in time to see the wire carried up to a great height by the ball from the mortar settling down across the Little Peace Maker about midships. It was falling now, and would soon come in contact with the ship.

When it did, there was a slight jar perceptible, but no such result as the enemy had hoped. The wire was so quickly fused, accompanying an explosion giving out an intense light, that it seemed to shoot to the earth like a streak of lightning, setting fire to or knocking down everything that lay in its path.

Another and another mortar shot followed until the sky seemed to be filled with falling wires which were swinging, twisting, and snapping above him. The Little Peace Maker was the centre of an electrical storm, and was sending back by every wire messages of death to those who were striving to bring her down.

The ship was rising very rapidly now, however, and almost before Edestone had time to sing out, "Steady now, as you are," she was 3000 feet above the German capital, and out of range of the wire-throwers.

CHAPTER XXXIII
YACHTING IN THE AIR

While Lawrence's hand was being dressed by one of the assistant surgeons, he had an opportunity of observing how perfect were the appointments of the operating room to which he had been taken. The orderlies and nurses moving about were all dressed in spotless white gowns and caps. The doctor and those assisting him in cleaning and dressing the slight flesh-wound which had been inflicted looked at their patient through holes in a cap that completely covered their heads and faces. Every appliance was provided for perfect cleanliness and sanitation, and the apparatus was on hand to permit of any operation of modern surgery, no matter how complicated.

From where he sat, he could see into another room exactly similar where James was having the injury to his leg attended to with the same scrupulous care; and he had passed, as he was brought in, a long room which he was told was one of the surgical wards, and where he had seen several men on hospital cots. The surgical wards, he was further informed, were on the starboard side of the ship, and not connected in any way with the sick bay which lay over on the port side.

With his great love for ships and machinery, Lawrence was impatient to get away and make a tour of inspection of this strange craft upon which he had embarked; but while he was waiting he occupied himself in his usual fashion by giving vent to his high spirits and making a joke out of everything.

"Well, Doc," he remarked to the surgeon, "you certainly have got one nifty little butcher shop, but I want to tell you, before one of those Ku-Klux throw me down and slap the gas bag in my face, that I have no adenoids, and that my appendix was cut out by an Arabian doctor who threw a handful of sand into me to stop the bleeding. If you would like to study German sausages, though, there is a pile of it down there on the roof." And even he shuddered as he recalled that awful carnage.

A bright-looking chap, dressed in the smart uniform of a steward on a gentleman's yacht, appeared at the door, but was not allowed to come in by Lawrence's aseptic guardians. He had been sent down by Edestone to inquire as to the condition of the wounded, and to announce to Lawrence that if he felt well enough to join him, dinner would be ready as soon as he was. He begged, the messenger said, that Mr. Stuyvesant would go directly to his room and dress, and allow him to have the pleasure of showing him over the ship after dinner. If he would let the quarter-master's department have his measure, he would be fitted out.

Wild horses could not have restrained Lawrence from such an invitation, much less a little scratch on the hand; and his injury having been dressed by this time, he was about to set out with the messenger, when James appealed to him from the next room, begging to be allowed to look after his master's clothes.

"Beg pardon, sir," he urged, showing his embarrassment at not being able to stand, "but I am the only one who knows how Mr. Edestone likes his dinner clothes laid out, and his whole evening will be spoiled without me, sir. I only ask to be allowed to break in the new man, sir, as starting right in laying out a gentleman's clothes is half the battle, sir."

"Don't you think, you have had enough of a battle for one day, you dear old fighting fossil?" asked Lawrence in a tone of real affection, for there is nothing which draws men together, regardless of rank, more quickly than to fight on the same side, and he could not help but admire the cool manner in which the valet had borne himself under fire.

"Thank you, sir, but mightn't I be allowed to see to his bath, sir? A drop of hot water in it turns his stomach for a week. Just let me do that, and I will come straight back to these very kind persons." He glanced about at the men of science with the condescending manner of the English upper servant in dealing with the shopkeeper class.

But Lawrence shook his head. "I'm sorry, James, but—" he bowed low to the grinning circle of doctors and nurses, and assumed his most grandiloquent air—"you are now in the hands of the only acknowledged ruling class of the twentieth century, who hold you with a grip of steel, but whose touch is as gentle as a mother's kiss. So get out your knitting, Old Socks; you are doomed."

He turned with a laugh and a new impersonation to the surgeon as he left the room.

"Thank you, Doc. You've cert'nly been kind to me, a poor working girl. Just send the bill to Mr. Edestone. He is my greatest gentleman friend."

In his room, which was reached by an elevator, he found the ship's tailor waiting for him; but after this functionary had taken his measure and gone, he had an opportunity to look around.

He was in a room, he found, a parlour or sitting-room, about fifteen by twenty, neatly but handsomely furnished, and suggesting to him in its general appearance the owner's apartments on the largest and most perfectly equipped yachts. There was this difference, however, that nothing about it indicated that it was ever off an even keel. There were no racks or other contrivances to suggest that it was prepared to turn in any direction at an angle of forty-five degrees, and which to the land-lubber causes qualms even while the ship is still tied to the dock.

It might indeed have been a handsome living-room in a bachelor's apartment, but for the windows, which at the first glance seemed to be of the ordinary French casement form, running down to the floor, and looking as if they might open out onto a balcony; but to his surprise, he found, when he pulled aside the heavy curtains, that they looked into a perfectly blank white wall about two inches from the glass.

Adjoining the living-room was a bedroom furnished in similar style with the same sort of windows, and beyond, Lawrence found as attractive a bath-room as ever welcomed an American millionaire after a hot day in his office, or a game of polo.

After a boiling tub and a freezing shower, in the pink of condition—and nothing else—he went back into the bedroom.

"Now what," he had wondered, "will the Fairy Godmother have for me in the way of a union suit, and a pair of jumpers?"

But he had not wondered very hard. He found, as he knew he would, for he had yachted with Edestone before, a complete outfit, not forgetting the cocktail, which was standing on the table as quietly and innocently as if it had always been there, although in reality it had just been placed there by a man who, with years of experience in listening to the sounds that come from a gentleman's bathroom, had timed its arrival to the second.

Nor was it one of those cocktails that are poured from a bottle, and served hot out of a silver-snouted shaker on a sloppy waiter, but a masterpiece from the hands of an artist, who took pride in his handiwork.

With the modesty of a chorus girl with a good figure on a "first night," he toasted the valet with much ceremony.

Soon he was dressed in the mess jacket of a petty officer, and putting a yachting cap jauntily on his head, he went out to seek his friend. The valet told him he would find Mr. Edestone in the breakfast room, and he was shown thither by an officer who was waiting for him.

As he passed along, he could not divest himself of the idea that he was on board Edestone's yacht, the *Storm Queen* again, only that everything here was on a larger scale. The breakfast room, he discovered, was on the same deck but farther forward, and was reached by passing through a large room furnished as a general living-room.

Edestone came forward to greet him with a rather melancholy expression on his face. He was dressed in a yachtsman's dinner jacket which fitted him perfectly, and with his bandaged head, he looked more than ever the sea lord. His rank of Captain was shown by the stripes on his arm.

The room was, as one would expect Edestone to have in his New York or country house, simple but handsome.

He had just been giving some orders about the windows which were of the same form and size as those Lawrence had remarked in his own room, and like them opened against a wall; but at Lawrence's appearance, he interrupted these instructions.

"I am glad to see you aboard." He presented his hand, which Lawrence took with his left. "I had looked forward to your first trip with me with so much pleasure. But how different it is from the way I had pictured it. I cannot get Fred, Stanton, or my two sailors out of my mind."

Lawrence's own face saddened, but for Edestone's sake he endeavoured to speak philosophically.

"The fortunes of war, old man. Why grieve? You certainly were not to blame."

For a moment there was silence between them; then Edestone, as if attempting to shake off his gloomy reflections, struck a lighter note.

"How do you like being a pirate, Lawrence?" he smiled.

"Great! The dream of my life, with you for a captain!"

So they sat down to dinner. The men attending to their wants moved about unheard and almost unseen in the shadow outside the circle of soft light which fell only on the table. The room was filled with an indescribable aroma of comfort and good cheer. A newly-lighted fire crackled on the hearth, for it had suddenly become quite cold. Indeed, it was with difficulty Lawrence could realize that but a few hours before they had been in the midst of battle and sudden death, and that, as they sat, down there five times the height of the Eiffel Tower below them was the Embassy from which they were still removing the dead, or aiding the dying.

As he looked at Edestone with his sad, brooding eyes, he felt all at once as if his friend had been taken away from him, and had been lifted to a place so exalted, that for the life of him, he could not have taken the liberty of speaking until he was first addressed.

The dinner went on, and though the food was delightful and the wines perfect, both men merely toyed with what was on their plates, while Lawrence gulped his champagne as if he were trying to get its effect quickly in order to throw off this strange new diffidence and restraint which he now felt in the presence of his oldest and dearest friend.

He tried to imagine that they two were cruising alone on the *Storm Queen*, as they had so often done, and that this was just one of many evenings that they had spent in this way together; but

> *Where was the lap of the water at her side,*
> *Or the pounding of the launch as she rode at her boom?*
> *The groan of the anchor as she swung with the tide,*
> *Or the blowing off steam, which demanded more room?*

All was perfectly quiet. If there were storage batteries on board, they had been charged. There was no shovelling of coal; no shrieking and banging of doors in the boiler room, nor banking of fires. The only thing that remained true to tradition was the ship's bell. It had just sounded out five bells.

The silence was at last broken by Edestone; but, although he spoke, it was more as if he were merely letting his pensive thoughts run on.

"How different this has been from the way I had planned it. How different, too, has been your home-coming, old man—for the *Storm Queen* was like home to you in the old days."

But Lawrence by this time was beginning to feel the effects of champagne, and was certain that unless he very soon did something to lift the pall that had fallen on them, he himself would be dissolved in tears.

"I don't know what your plan was," he said; "but don't you worry about my home-coming. The thing that ought to worry you is my leave-taking. The L. P. M. has got the *Storm Queen* beat a mile, and I am booked for life. And, by the way, what is my rank on this ship? My old position of room clerk on the *Storm Queen* won't go here, as I don't suppose you intend to have any 'cuties' on board, not even for the New London week."

"No." Edestone consented at last to smile. "I am afraid, Lawrence, those days are all over for me. My little house of cards has fallen about me, and I have serious work before me, if I wish to build it up again. I have been thinking, and thinking very hard. From the moment that I saw poor Fred roll down the stairs of the Embassy, I knew that my first plan had failed. When Germany discovers that the United States is not back of me, she will apologize, and you know how quickly our present Administration will accept the apology, and how quickly they will disclaim any responsibility for my acts, if it means a fight?"

Lawrence nodded.

"Germany," went on Edestone, "will then call on all the neutral nations to join her in bringing me, an outlaw, to earth. This will give her a common cause with them, and she will hope in that way to strengthen her position relative to the Allies. She does not know my relationship with England, but she will undoubtedly declare that I am one of the means England is using to subjugate the world."

"And is there nothing you can do?" asked Lawrence.

"My last and only hope is that tomorrow, after they have realized the uselessness of opposing me, they will listen to a proposition of peace—without honour, from their old standard; but with great honour, from the standard that I intend to establish. I propose to send what is practically an ultimatum; and that is, that if they do not immediately open negotiations looking toward peace, I will sink every German battleship that floats, and destroy every factory in which guns, explosives, or any of the munitions of war are manufactured."

"Me for the junk business," exclaimed Lawrence with an inspiration. "Oh, you Krupps!"

But Edestone paid no heed to the frivolous interruption. "It is my intention," he continued, "to give sufficient notice, so that if they are willing to admit my supremacy, there need be no loss of life."

He halted, as an officer had just come in, and was standing after saluting, waiting for Edestone to stop speaking.

"The look-outs report, sir, that there are several Taubes climbing up toward us. What are your orders, sir?"

"Close everything down, except one of these." Edestone pointed to a window. "Expose no lights."

After the man had retired, he said to one of the servants in the room: "Put out the lights, and bring us two cloaks."

When the lights had been put out, Lawrence saw for the first time that during dinner the solid cubes of steel, the size of the windows, had noiselessly rolled back, leaving a square aperture or passage-way through the six-foot thickness of the armour-plate, and forming a sort of *loggia* into which they stepped. It was a beautiful night, and through the clear, rarefied atmosphere the stars seemed to Lawrence brighter than he had ever seen them before, while down below them he could just see the lights of Berlin.

The explosions of the motors of the Taubes could be plainly heard, but as yet nothing could be seen of them.

"What do you suppose those mosquitoes expect to do against us with their pop-guns and tomato cans?" asked Lawrence.

"I do not know." Edestone shook his head. "Perhaps they are just coming up to look us over. They will keep out of sight, and as they may not know that we are protected on top, will perhaps try to drop one of their tomato cans on us. That is, if they can get close enough. I hardly think that they will risk a miss, and drop bombs on their own capital, so long as the Only One Who Seems To Count In Germany is in the midst of his beloved people."

The Taubes could be heard on all sides, as if they were climbing in great circles around the Little Peace Maker. There seemed to be at least a dozen of them, although owing to the confusion of sounds as they crossed and re-crossed, it was impossible to count them.

At last, though, when judging by the noise they were about on the same level as the ship, Edestone turned to an officer who was standing by him.

"Tell Commander Anderson to load all of the big guns with a full charge of black powder only, and fire them all off at the same time.

"And, Lawrence," he advised his friend, "when you hear a bell ringing, stand on your toes, open your mouth, stick your fingers in your ears, and if you've never been in Hell before, prepare yourself for a shock."

Hardly had he gotten the words out of his mouth, when bells began ringing all over the ship. In just exactly one minute, Lawrence thought he had been blown into bits, as he was lifted and thrown from side to side against the steel walls of the passage. The noise was so great that his ears seemed unable to record it, and it was made known to him by the air pressure which seemed to be crushing him to death. The rush of air down his throat was choking him, while his very insides seemed to be turning over and over in their effort to escape. A dizziness and nausea followed, and he had to lean against his friend, trying to catch his breath in the thick, black smoke with which they were enveloped.

"This is Hell all right," he managed to gasp.

"That is the worst you will ever get," said Edestone. "It was noise that I was after, and black powder makes it. Your experience would not have been half so bad had the guns been loaded or had I used smokeless."

The ship which had trembled from stem to stern under the tremendous concussion was floating now as quietly as a toy balloon, while the wind was rolling up and pushing before it a great cloud of smoke which obscured the sky. On all sides there was perfect stillness, broken only now and again by the last explosion of gas caught in the cylinders of the Taubes by the sudden stoppage of the engines. The airmen were volplaning to earth as fast and as silently as they could.

"Well, that ought to hold them for a while," commented Lawrence in a tone which showed that he was almost himself again.

"And make them a little bit more amenable to reason in the morning," added Edestone, and he laughed, for action with him always drove away the blue devils.

"With that settled, too, we will just have time before turning in, to inspect my quarters," he continued. "Tomorrow I will introduce you to 'Specs' and Captain Lee, and you can go with them at eleven o'clock on their tour of official inspection. They will show you the fire drill, the life-balloon drill, the gun drill, the kitchen, and the cows. But now I want you to see a different side of the ship. We will look at my quarters, then at my guest rooms, and finally at my royal suite or state apartments as I call them."

He then took Lawrence through room after room, which were arranged in the form of a horseshoe, starting on the port side with his breakfast room, and working around to the starboard side with its opening toward the stern of the ship.

On the port side were Edestone's apartments—living-room, library, or den, bedroom, dressing-room, bath-room, and gymnasium. On the starboard were a number of guest rooms arranged in suites of parlour, bedroom, and bath, while at the crown of the arch was a large dining-room in which fifty persons could sit down to dinner comfortably.

The centre of the horseshoe was the large room through which he had passed, and like the general meeting room of a large country house was filled with all known kinds of games—instruments and devices to amuse that most unfortunate class of human beings who have no resources within themselves, and must play some foolish game, or do some foolish puzzle in order to get through the life which seems to hang so heavily on their hands.

From this they passed to a lower deck about amidships, to a room about eighty feet by one hundred and twenty feet, which extended the full width of the ship and up three decks. At one end of this large and handsome room was a raised platform arranged like the Speaker's desk in the House of Representatives at Washington with the desks at lower levels for stenographers, clerks, and attendants, while around the room in concentric circles were large comfortable seats and desks, also like a Senate Chamber, only more luxurious in appointments, as though it were to receive a more distinguished body of men than the Senate of the United States, if that were possible.

"This," said Edestone, "is where I intend to hold my Peace Conference, and when you see the names of the distinguished men who are to sit here, and the apartments that I have arranged for them and their suites, you will perhaps be glad to take your old position of room clerk."

Then after showing his companion through these magnificent "royal suites," as he called them, all furnished and equipped in the most sumptuous fashion, he suggested that they had better turn in.

"We will hope and pray for the best in the morning," he said, as he bade Lawrence good-night.

CHAPTER XXXIV
THE ULTIMATUM

The sun was streaming through the windows when Lawrence awoke the next morning. The valet had come in shortly before to throw back the curtains with a slam, and by moving about the room, slapping up shades and dropping boots, make the usual noises of a well-trained valet at that time of the morning.

"Mr. Edestone is already up, sir," he said when he saw that he had succeeded in waking Lawrence, "and is having his breakfast in his own apartments. Will you have yours here or will you go to the breakfast room?"

"Breakfast room," elected Lawrence sleepily. "What time is it?"

"Eight o'clock, sir. What will you have for breakfast, sir?"

"Anything and eggs," said Lawrence, and was about to turn over and go to sleep again when he realized where he was, and leaping out of bed to the window in one bound stepped out into the *loggia*.

The Little Peace Maker had dropped down and was now only about a thousand feet up; and when he looked down from his balcony, he could see that she had changed her position so as to float exactly over the Palace. It almost seemed to him as if he could step off and onto the roof of this great pile of masonry. The airship, too, must have just moved into this position, as was shown by the excited way in which the little people below him were running away in every direction.

He had his bath, and hurriedly dressing went into the breakfast room, where he found Edestone, who had finished his breakfast and was waiting for him, while reading from a lot of slips of paper which he was turning over in his hand. The master of the ship was dressed all in white and looked refreshed after a good night's rest.

"Good-morning, Lawrence," he greeted him. "Did you sleep well?"

"Like a top."

"And how is your hand?"

"I had almost forgotten it, only I did get the dressings wet while taking my bath, but that will give me an excuse for passing the time of day with the doctors. How is your head?"

"Oh, that does not amount to anything," said Edestone. "It will be well in a week. Have you seen the morning papers?" With a smile he handed him a sheet on which was printed all the news of the day which the wireless man had picked up during the night.

"The United States has not been heard from," he commented as he glanced it over. "I wonder what the Southern Baptist Union School Children will think of me now? You know the Secretary of State thought I was a Baptist. And as for him, why he will leave the State Department and stay away until it gets too hot in Florida, or the lecturing season is all over, while the President will write a most scholarly note to all of the Powers telling them how much he loves them, and what a glorious thing it is to be an American. He will then give an unqualified invitation to all of the dark-skinned downtrodden criminals of Europe to come over and be sprinkled with the holy water of citizenship, after they have made their mark to their naturalization papers which have been read to them by their interpreter.

"London reports that the news from Germany has filled the entire country with new confidence," he went on, "and that the Londoners have given themselves over to the most un-English and thoroughly Latin demonstrations by parading the streets and singing songs and indulging in another Mafeking. I see, too, that Lord Rockstone is reported to have said that he thought now the war would not last as long as he had expected. The King has called a special meeting of the Cabinet for today at 4 o'clock.

"Reports come from Rome that Italy will enter the war immediately, and the papers point out the fact that now since her friend America has joined the Allies it is high time that Italy should take her position.

"Petrograd reports that they have lost 100,000 men but have captured 250,000 Austrians.

"Constantinople," he went on reading, "declares that the Dardanelles are impregnable and that the city is perfectly quiet, but the Sultan and half of his harem have moved to his summer residence."

He laid down the printed sheet. "I have had no communication yet from down there," he said as he pointed down in the direction of the Palace. "My international law department is drawing up a proclamation which I will send as soon as it is finished. It will be along the lines that I spoke of to you last night, but framed in more diplomatic language. These are the latest bulletins I was just reading over when you came in."

Then while Lawrence sat eating his breakfast, Edestone continued to read now and then bits of the different press notices.

"Listen to this," he said with a laugh. "'The twenty Taubes sent up to make a night attack on the American airship inflicted great injury. After using up all their ammunition and bombs they were forced to retire before the large guns of the enemy. They all reached the ground in safety. The tremendous explosion that was heard in the city is thought to have been caused by the exploding of one of the large magazines.'"

"What's that from?" Lawrence glanced up from his "anything and eggs." "*Die Fliegende Blatter?*"

But Edestone did not smile, he was glancing at another of the slips.

"Ah," he said in a sad voice, "I seem to have killed about one thousand people last night."

"Still," argued Lawrence, "that was not as large a percentage of the German Empire as they killed of your little kingdom."

"No," granted Edestone; "and as long as they insist upon treating me as an outlaw I will be one so far as they are concerned. I will now go and see if my ultimatum is prepared. I am undecided as to whether I will send it by wireless or by a messenger."

Lawrence finished his breakfast and while he sat in the *loggia* smoking his cigar and looking down over the city, he decided to ask permission to carry the message to the Emperor himself. The idea delighted him, and he pictured exactly how he would walk and speak his lines like the prince in the story book. He only regretted that he was not to be dressed up in spangles, like the heralds of old, and have the triumphal march from *Aïda* played by trumpeters from the Metropolitan Opera House who would precede him in their brand-new Cammeyer sandals and badly fitting tights but he decided that if said trumpeters were obliged to read sheet music he would not allow them to wear glasses. He was just making up his mind what he would say to the Emperor when Wilhelm fell on his knees and begged him to intercede for him, as Edestone came in, and blasted all these glowing dreams with a word.

"Well, it is done," he said, "and I have given them until one o'clock to answer."

Lawrence was then formally introduced to "Specs" under his title of Admiral Page, to Captain Lee, and the officers, and he spent one of the most delightful days of his life, so much interested in what he saw that he entirely forgot that he was a pirate, waiting to destroy a peaceable city if it did not do his bidding.

Edestone had settled himself down for a quiet day of waiting, and Lawrence amused himself by inspecting every part of the ship and talking with all on board from the oil men to the Admiral.

"Admiral Page," he inquired, "where do you keep the Deionizer?"

At which "Specs" peeped at him with a suspicious glance through his thick glasses. "Has Mr. Edestone spoken to you of that?" he asked.

"Yes," replied Lawrence, "but he did not explain to me its working."

"Specs" hesitated to take even Lawrence into the holy of holies until he had obtained permission from Edestone to do so. Having by telephone communicated with him, and receiving his permission, he conducted Lawrence up into the bow of the ship. After passing through several heavy doors, which "Specs" unlocked, saluting the sentries at each, they came to a great iron grille and he motioned to Lawrence to look through, saying, "This is as far as I can take you."

Lawrence looked through, and he saw what appeared to be the door of an enormous safe-deposit k vault. "That," nodded "Specs," "is the door to the safe in which the Deionizer is kept. No one on earth excepting Mr. Edestone knows the combination that will open those doors. That is run by a one hundred H. P. motor in the engine room, and from it run the deionizing cables which run down the port and starboard sides of the vessel."

"Do you mean to say," said Lawrence, "that I have no weight?" as he felt his large biceps with an expression of pride.

This caused "Specs" to laugh, and in response to the numberless questions put to him by the young man, he explained the different mechanisms by which the weight of the ship and its contents was kept at the weight of the amount of air displaced by it.

"So," said Lawrence, "we are floating not by virtue of gas bags filled with gas lighter than air, but by the amount of air displaced by all metallic substances on this vessel, which for all practical purposes are rendered lighter than air?"

"Yes," replied "Specs," with a look of pity for the other man's ignorance, "I suppose that is the way you would express it. If you really want to understand, and are willing to give the time to it, come to my quarters, and I will give you the scientific explanation."

"No, thank you," said Lawrence; "I'll take your word for it, but I am glad to know that when I get back to earth I'm not liable at any time to be blown away like a thistledown."

At lunch Edestone appeared very thoughtful and seemed to feel great anxiety about the outcome of his note. They had observed that soon after the message had been sent automobiles were coming and going from the Palace in great numbers, and gathered that the Emperor apparently was holding a council of war. They had also seen with powerful glasses that, in certain parts of the city there was great activity of some kind, but they were unable to ascertain exactly what it was.

"I cannot understand," frowned Edestone, "how they can possibly decline a proposition *pour parler*. I asked them to agree to nothing. I assured them that I would use my influence in favour of a just settlement of all the claims arising out of the war and of the incidents leading up to it. I appealed to their humanity, and guaranteed as far as lay within my power to protect the lives and property of Germans all over the world if they would only stop all actual fighting until I could make an exactly similar appeal to the other Governments that are involved."

Just then an officer came in and handed Edestone a wireless message which had just been received.

Edestone read it hurriedly, but as he glanced up it was easy to see from the expression on his face that he was pleased.

"Well," he exclaimed elatedly, "these Germans are not so bad after all, and if they will only give up the idea that they are the only people on the face of the earth, the sooner will they get what they want. That is, if they are telling the truth when they state they are fighting only to bring religion, science, and culture to the entire world. They do sincerely and honestly believe, I think, that this can be obtained only under the German form of government, and many of the other nations would be willing to admit this in part were they absolutely convinced of their sincerity and did not suspect them of greed on the part of the merchant class and ambition on the part of the war party.

"They have apparently received my note in the spirit in which it was sent," he explained, "and have agreed to consider carefully the proposition which I have made. They only ask to be given until five o'clock this afternoon to draw up in proper form their reply to me and their message to the other countries. I am expecting every minute now to see a white flag displayed somewhere on or around the Palace, which was the signal agreed upon and is to be acknowledged by a similar flag displayed by me. This is not to be considered as an indication of any weakness on their part, or any surrendering of their rights or the acknowledgment of my power, but as a truce which will last only until five o'clock, or until such earlier time as I shall answer them. They stipulate that I, as an indication of good faith, withdraw to some point outside of the city, where it will be well out of range of my largest guns, and in order to fix some location which will be perfectly satisfactory they have suggested that I lie over the Gotzen See and have established my exact position by the ruins of an old castle on its north-eastern bank. There I am to remain until I receive their answer, which if not satisfactory terminates the truce. They have indicated very justly that they do not think they should be called upon to open negotiations for an amicable settlement with me while the Little Peace Maker is lying so close to the Emperor's Palace and threatening it with instant destruction."

As it was impossible for them from where they were to see the Palace, Edestone suggested that they go up on the upper deck.

"I hope that by the time we arrive on deck," Edestone said as they hurried along, "the white flag will be flying, and I sincerely hope that this will mark the beginning of the end of this cruel war and the realization of my hopes, the accomplishment of my life's work.

"Ah," he exclaimed as they arrived and looked down, "there she is! You can see it on the large flagpole out in front of the Palace, while the Imperial standard is still floating over His Majesty's residence." He called an officer to him and gave him his orders:

"Dip my colours and then run them up to the peak again. Display a white flag. Tell Captain Lee to call all hands, and get under way at once. Drop to within four hundred feet, man the rail, and circle the Palace. Haul down my colours and run up the German Imperial Ensign and fire a national salute of twenty-one guns, and then run at top speed and take a position over the Gotzen See at a point which I shall indicate."

The ceremony was executed faultlessly, as he directed, and when the Little Peace Maker, just skirting the tops of the buildings, cast the shadow of its nine hundred feet of steel as it came between the sun and the Imperial city, its big guns booming the national salute, the people of Berlin must have been impressed, for when she circled at about four knots they cheered. But when she changed her speed, and at one hundred and eighty knots disappeared from sight, they must have been relieved.

At such speed it was only a few minutes before they were hovering quietly over the old ruin on the banks of the lake, and they settled down to spend the afternoon as they would have, had they been anchored in Frenchman's Bay off of Bar Harbour in the month of August on board the *Storm Queen*.

It was a beautiful and quiet summer scene, and like a big trout in a limpid pool the Little Peace Maker lay perfectly still basking in the warm sunshine. Most of the ports were open and the men were lying around enjoying the relaxation of the first dog-watch.

Although it was with difficulty that Edestone could keep Lawrence still long enough, he forced him to join in a game of chess, which was Edestone's favourite form of relaxation. Lawrence, however, kept continually breaking in with the suggestion that they go below and take a walk among the ruins of the home of one of the ancient Barons of Prussia.

From time to time, while waiting for Lawrence to move, Edestone would consult his watch, and as the fatal hour of five approached, although perfectly calm he was anxious.

With the finish of the game, Lawrence, who had chafed under the confinement, insisted upon going on deck and talking with the officers and men.

When next he saw his friend, Edestone was walking up and down the general living-room with an expression of great anxiety on his face. It was half-past five o'clock, and although Lawrence had entirely forgotten it, he suddenly thought of the ultimatum.

"Well what did they answer?" he asked.

"Nothing," said Edestone.

"And what are you going to do?"

"I am going to Kiel to sink one of their largest battleships, and see if that will wake them up. We shall be under way in ten minutes and should be there by eight-thirty o'clock. I have ordered 'Specs' to get under way as soon as possible."

Lawrence was delighted; this was the best yachting that he had ever had, and he wanted to be in so many places at the same time that he ran about like a boy on his first ocean trip. He was just going up the companionway to the pilot house, where he knew he would find Edestone, when he was almost knocked off his feet by the impact of something against the side of the ship which felt as if it would tear out every rivet and buckle every beam. At the same instant there was an explosion which was worse than the black-powder explosion of the night before, and he was just thinking how unkind it was of Edestone not to have warned him before indulging in another one of his pyrotechnical demonstrations, when it was followed by another and another.

He had managed by this time to get into the pilot house, where he saw Edestone with an expression of rage on his face giving sharp peremptory orders while the life was being pounded out of the Little Peace Maker. In response to these orders, the ship suddenly shot up with such rapidity that it seemed to Lawrence as if his legs would be driven through the floor.

He was suffering great pain in his head and his nose was bleeding. He could scarcely hear what Edestone was saying to him, but finally he caught these words:

"So that is their answer, the liars! They have taken advantage of my willingness to remain here quietly, and with their thoroughness in all matters and their usual method of working in the dark, they have placed me where they have carefully worked out the range of their forty-two-centimetre guns. They hoped to be able to capture us, but seeing our smoke, and realizing that I was going to move, they took this unspeakable method of putting an end to the Little Peace Maker."

CHAPTER XXXV
A LYING KING MAKES A NATION OF LIARS

It seemed for a time as if Edestone had completely lost control of himself. Lawrence, "Specs," and Captain Lee, who had all known him for years, stood back staring at him in blank amazement. He was perfectly livid. Out of his face had gone every semblance of the man that they had known, loved, honoured, and respected for his kind, big, and forgiving nature, willing to stand an insult rather than use his great power where a smaller character would have demanded the last ounce of flesh. In its place was an expression of rage which would have been frightful to see on the face of a weaker man, but on his, with all the power and determination of his strong character behind it, it was appalling. It made them feel that they were held helpless by a powerful demon who would destroy and kill any who might stand in his way. Pushing everyone aside in a manner that was entirely foreign to him, he sprang to the wheel and taking it rang for full speed ahead. He swung the ship around so quickly that she banked and turned over at an angle of thirty degrees.

She was then at an altitude of from 7000 to 8000 feet and he put her head down as if he intended to drive her steel-pointed bow into the very heart of the city of Berlin. But when he had gotten her at about 400 feet he straightened her out and sent her at 150 knots. Without taking his eyes off his goal, which seemed to be the Palace of the Kaiser, he said in a cold and emotionless voice: "See what damage has been done and report to me quickly, and as there is a God in Heaven if a single one of my men has been killed I will hang the Kaiser after I have destroyed his city!"

While the different officers were busily telephoning to every part of the ship carrying out this order, Lawrence stood paralysed waiting for the answers. He sincerely hoped that none of the men had been killed, but as one officer after another reported all well in his department, and as the number of departments yet to be heard from grew less and less, he could not control a distinct feeling of disappointment, for he had silently said "Amen!" to Edestone's last sentiment. When all had been heard from, and it was found that none had been killed, and that the injuries to the ship were, so slight that they could be repaired within a week, Edestone said to the officer of the deck:

"Take the wheel. When you are over the city and have made the Palace, circle it at eight knots. I wish them all to see me. After you have rounded the Palace, run at full speed for Kiel."

And without a word to Lawrence he turned and left the bridge. On his face was a look that showed that the demon within him was under perfect control, but he had no desire to hide the fact that it was still with him. Lawrence would no more have thought of following him than he would have thought of following a wounded Manchurian tiger into its cave.

"I would have hated to hear that any one of our fine fellows had been killed," he said with a nervous laugh, "but my, what a swell little afternoon hanging that would have been! Nathan Hale with the original cast wouldn't have had a speculator in front of his doors. His front-row seats would be selling at box-office prices, while we would have sold out the house at ten thousand times the cost of the production before the first-nighters had even seen a press notice. There would not have been a piece of paper in the house except the Press and the Princes. By the sacred substance of John D. Rockefeller's hair-tonic, I hate to think of the money we would have made with the movies! The Crown Prince giving the Papa Wilhelm kiss, while the trap man plays on the melodeon 'It's the Wrong Way to Tickle Mary,' and the Ghost of the Hohenzollern, who ate up her two babies when she found they disturbed her gentleman friend, hovering over the scene like Schumann-Heink in the *Rheingold*,—I would not release that reel for less than a billion dollars down!

"But why talk about pleasant things when we have such serious matters on our hands."

"Mr. Edestone looked as if he meant serious business all right," said one of the officers. "Listen! I hear the wireless sending a message now."

Lawrence listened, and repeated as he heard: "The Little Peace Maker is now running for Kiel, where she will arrive at 8:30. At 8:45 I will begin to drop tons of lyddite and dynamite on the decks of all German ships of war, and in order that there may be no unnecessary loss of life I give this notice."

The instrument stopped, but Lawrence continued, as if still catching and translating the message:

"And realizing the extreme supersensitiveness of the German sailors, we are sending ahead by Parcel Post baskets for the cats and cages for the canaries. The women and babies, being contraband, must go down with the ships."

They were now slowly swinging around the Palace, and as the people of Berlin knew nothing, they took the accepted German position, which was that Edestone was afraid of the Kaiser's wrath, and they therefore came flocking out into the streets to see him dip his flag to that of the all-powerful German Empire.

Lawrence noted that the Imperial standard was no longer flying over the Palace. "It looks," said he, "as if we would have to put in an under-study for the leading man."

And then as if some sudden idea had struck him, he rushed from the bridge, and while the Little Peace Maker was slowly passing over the plaza in front of the Palace, the men on the bridge saw with a mingled feeling of horror and delight a large black object, which resembled a submarine mine, dropping from the port side of the ship, and they stood in breathless expectation of seeing the hideous Renaissance monument, erected by Schluter, blown to atoms. When the sinister-looking cylinder struck the pavement it exploded, but instead of death and destruction the flaggings were strewn with egg-shells, coffee-grounds, and garbage.

"I always did like that French chef," said Lawrence when he returned to the bridge, gasping for breath.

"I am sorry," he added, "that we didn't have our little lynching bee this afternoon, but the sinking of a billion dollars' worth of battleships must be almost as much fun as hanging a 'kink.'"

They were now going at top speed, and after waiting about for some time and finding that Edestone did not return to the bridge, he went to his room and dressed for dinner.

At dinner Edestone appeared, but he was very quiet.

"Lawrence," he said, "you must forgive me, but I really am not myself. I cannot recall at any time in my entire life when I was ever so angry as I was this afternoon. I think they call it 'seeing red.'"

"You were 'seeing red' all right," said Lawrence, "and you certainly got my goat."

"If one of the men on this ship had been killed, after that pledge had been given for their safety, I do not know what I would have done."

"Exactly what do you propose to do?"

"I intend to wreck and destroy everything in this country that will be of the slightest use to them for military purposes. Today it is Kiel with its ships, shipyards, and dry-docks; tomorrow, Krupps; and so on until they will have to stop fighting for the lack of munitions of war. I shall endeavour as far as possible to avoid loss of life, but," with an ironical smile, "if these people wish to indulge in a fanatical display of heroism and patriotism, I shall allow them the privilege of sinking with their ships, or dying with their pet inventions."

With everything closed down tight they were fast approaching Kiel, and going up into the conning tower Edestone and Lawrence were able to see the entire German fleet. His message had evidently been received, but the commanders, instead of accepting his warning, had steam up, were stripped for action, and with flags flying were making for the open sea.

Edestone, as quietly as if he were standing on the bridge of the *Storm Queen* giving instructions for the next day's cruise, turned to "Specs."

"Go out and circle them," he said, "meet the leading ship, and then with every gun, aerial torpedo, and bomb dropper destroy them."

The air was soon filled with the most frightful conflict that had ever taken place in the heavens above, on the earth beneath, or in the waters under the earth. Every ship in the fleet was, as far as possible, training all of her guns on them, while they, moving at the rate of thirty knots, were sailing around and around, dropping bombs on those under them, bombarding with their great 16-inch guns the distant ships, while the smaller guns rendered the middle distance untenable to any ship yet built by man.

In the course of an hour not one of the German ships could be seen above the water, and Edestone, with none of his usual kindness of heart and sympathy for others, leaving to their fate the dead and dying that filled the sea beneath them, gave the orders to destroy the shipyards and dry-docks before it was too dark.

For a week this rain of destruction was continued day after day until his prophecy had been fulfilled, and Germany, driven to her knees, was suing for peace.

CHAPTER XXXVI
THINK OF IT! WHY NOT?

Edestone, in the meantime, through Sir Egbert Graves, had communicated with the King of England, politely calling His Majesty's attention to what he was doing, and begging that he would call upon his Allies to stop all hostilities, and intimating that the same treatment would be meted out to any who declined to comply with His Majesty's request.

He also suggested that it was his sincere hope that His Majesty would call to a conference the representatives of the nations of Europe to discuss the settling of all questions that had caused the war, or had grown out of it, as well as the possible methods of securing for the world perpetual peace.

He stated that he would put at His Majesty's disposal the Little Peace Maker if it were necessary in order to accomplish this.

He intimated that, if it were perpetual peace that was sought, much time and many lives would be saved if all would, of their own accord, each for himself, do what he was doing for Germany as fast as possible, namely, destroy all ships and implements of war.

This raised a storm of protest, and international notes burned the ether of space as they flashed back and forth. Even the United States entered the controversy, seeming to have at last found something sufficiently threatening to her interests and insulting to her dignity to cause her to take her place with the other nations of the world.

Edestone was inundated with communications from the different nations, drawn in the most bombastic manner; for although they must have by this time realized that they were absolutely in his power, they were unable to set aside the boastful method of addressing their fellow-men which they had inherited from their savage ancestors, who, standing half-naked around the council fire, tried by this method to throw terror into the hearts of their listeners.

To all this he made but one reply, which was that nations which came together for the purpose of sincerely discussing universal peace must come absolutely unarmed, and those who refused so to do should be disarmed by force. When these protests finally took the form of an approaching coalition of the nations of the earth for the purpose of his destruction, his answer was to take possession quietly of two or three of the largest plants in Europe, which he forced to run to replenish the Little Peace Maker with munitions of war.

After a diplomatic correspondence had gone on, extending over several weeks, and Edestone had punctuated his demands with an occasional sinking of a battleship or destruction of a powder plant belonging to the nations who stood out against him, after he had visited all of the principal capitals, and representatives of the Governments had come on board to discuss with him, his terms were finally agreed upon, and the date for this great meeting was fixed. He declined to negotiate with any, other than the absolute heads of the respective Governments, and after much discussion all precedent was set aside, and it was agreed that the conference should be held on board of the Little Peace Maker. Franz Josef I., Emperor of Austria; Wilhelm II., Emperor of Germany; George V., King of England; Nicholas II., Czar of Russia; the President of the French Republic; Mr. Cockadoo of the United States of America, together with a company of lesser lights, all with suites in keeping with their rank, were there received and entertained by him.

Lawrence, accepting the position of Room Clerk, took great pride and pleasure in seeing that everyone was properly installed. This was not, however, his official position, as Edestone had turned over to him the task of answering the great volume of communications that he had received from amateurs, fanatics, ladies, and criminals, and it devolved upon him to answer these and also to provide for the entertainment of the representatives of the Anarchists, Socialists, Organized Labour, and Suffragettes.

To the Anarchists, in answer to their inquiries as to where they were now to obtain their explosives with which to continue their campaigns in the future, and without the use of which they could secure for their arguments no attention, he made no reply.

To the Socialists, he said that the best that he could do for them was to provide an overflow meeting at the foot of the stairs; the Emperor of Germany had refused to sit down with the traitors, as he called them, and for once Edestone agreed with the Imperial contention. There, Lawrence assured them, their point of view would be given serious consideration; in fact, he himself expected to have the great honour of addressing them and the Prohibitionists, the Anti-Vivisectionists, the Cubists, the Futurists, the Post-Impressionists, and the Reds.

To Organized Labour, Edestone wrote that he would represent their cause. Descended as he was from a long line of honest labouring men, who had succeeded without the assistance of an organization of lazy and inefficient ones combined under dishonest leaders, he assured them that he would insist upon their rights, and that under the new regime, honesty, efficiency, and sense of responsibility to those who employed them would be recognized and rewarded in a manner beyond their wildest dreams. This could not, however, be accomplished, he said, except by forcing the dishonest, lazy, and inefficient into their rightful position, that of a worthless by-product in this great world of recognition of true merit.

To the Suffragettes, Lawrence extended a most cordial invitation, but stipulated that no representative would be received who had not borne and raised twelve children, or were willing to appear at the meeting without their hats, with hair cropped close to the head.

The date selected by Edestone was the Fourth day of July; the place, in order to offend no one, was the beautiful valley of St. Nicholas in the neutral country of the Swiss, and the Little Peace Maker, painted and polished, was floating about twenty-five feet from the ground. About one-quarter of her length from her stern, leading from an opening in her bottom, ran a great flight of stairs which rested on a platform at their foot. This was constructed in a manner similar to the cradle upon which she was seen to rest by the King of England and his Cabinet. In this manner she was connected with the earth but absolutely insulated.

To reach this platform one had to walk up four or five steps, which were made of hard rubber, over which was laid a thick red velvet carpet, which continued across the platform and up this most impressive flight of stairs and disappeared into the opening in the Little Peace Maker. Bands were playing, children were laughing, but not one soldier was to be seen.

The Royalties, as they arrived, were received at the foot of the stairs by Edestone and conducted to their apartments where, surrounded by their secretaries and servants, they might live entirely alone, or could, if they desired to do so, mingle with the rest of the distinguished company.

When the great day arrived, and these Royal Potentates were seated in their places, which had been arranged with great consideration for their extreme sensitiveness on the subject of precedent, an exact science, Edestone, dressed in his simple yachting costume, walked slowly up through the aisle, on either side of which were seated Royalties, each in his favourite uniform of ceremony, soon to become as old-fashioned as the tattooing on a savage's face. With perfect composure and self-possession he took his place as Chairman of the Board and called the meeting to order.

Then in a perfectly businesslike manner he explained the object of the meeting, which he did with the greatest consideration for his distinguished listeners, but there was in his voice a ring of confidence, which they all knew was due to the fact that the suggestions that he made would certainly be put into effect, and whereas they came to discuss, they remained to agree.

He first briefly outlined the Utopian condition of the world as it would be after his first suggestion had been carried into effect, and all arms, ammunition, ships of war, and all destructive agencies had been destroyed.

He then laid down some new principles and relegated some of the old to the scrap-heap.

He scoffed at the theory of majority rule, equality of man, and perpetual peace through brotherly love.

Why should the majority rule, if the minority were more intelligent?

Why should all men be considered equal in intelligence, if not in weight and height?

Why should dried-up old women be able to do something that young men, in their full health and strength, had been unable to accomplish?

He then established a very limited ruling class, which he called, for the lack of a better name, the Aristocracy of Intelligence, over which he placed a head with absolute power, backed with sufficient force to see that its wishes were carried out.

He then finally laid before them the plan of administration which he proposed, which was that the entire world should be run by a Board of Directors, of which, for the present, he sincerely hoped that they would allow him to hold the humbler position of Chairman, while the President and glorious head should be selected from some of the distinguished monarchs within the sound of his voice.

He then very diplomatically explained that the form of government would be based upon the administration of the great corporations of America, which was his extremely polite method of informing them that the Chairman of the Board was the power, and the President was but the icing on the cake.

He stated that history taught them that all wars had come about on account of three things: Race, Religion, and Riches.

He suggested that the Race problem might be entirely solved by segregating the races of the world, and giving over to them a portion of the earth sufficiently large to support them in comfort in the climate and surroundings to which they were accustomed, in which section they should speak their own language, and were entitled to indulge in their own forms of religion, customs, and superstitions, and there and there alone they were supreme, and then only on matters of the administration of their own allotment of the earth, but were subject absolutely and entirely to the ruling of the Board of Directors as to their international policies.

The title of the portion of the world allotted to them was based not upon the claims of any barbarian of antiquity, fanatic of the Middle Ages, or the war lords of modern times, but upon the decision of the Board of Directors, which would annul all previous titles and be final and irrevocable.

If at any time any one or group of these left the portion of the earth to which they had been restricted, they lost all of their rights as citizens of the world, and while visiting the other sections must bow absolutely to the will of those whose hospitality they were accepting.

In the case of those nations who had no home, and who had been parasites on the nations of the earth for thousands of years, it was proposed that they purchase from the country now holding the cradle of their birth a home sufficiently large to accommodate their ever-increasing numbers under the hygienic and healthful condition of the countries which they swarmed.

Religion, he said, which had for so many years been the cause of wars and tumults, numbered by actual count up into the thousands, were in his opinion sufficient in number to satisfy all who were not wishing for personal aggrandizement or accumulation of wealth to create others. Therefore, he stated, that all religions which had been established up to the beginning of the nineteenth century might be allowed to continue, but all others, being drawn on rather too scientific and financial lines, were to be eliminated.

Coming to the last, and, as he expressed it, the cause of the present war, namely, Riches, he showed that in the new form of government competition would be eliminated, the interest of the whole being controlled by one head with power to police, and greater profits to all would accrue by the elimination of waste of time and money and by the efficiency of a single administration.

He then suggested that a grand and international festival be held, at which the combined fleets of the entire world be gathered together in the middle of the Atlantic Ocean, and there, as a bond of good faith of all, in the midst of universal rejoicing, they should be consigned to the bottomless depths of absolute and eternal darkness.

In the meantime, Lawrence was addressing an assemblage of Reds, I. W. W.'s, Prohibitionists, and other thoughtful members of society. To these he was serving grape juice and patent medicines. The percentage of alcohol in these beverages quieted the nerves of most, but rendered the Prohibitionists quite hilarious. They listened with much attention and applauded violently the scheme which he outlined before them.

"You should be allowed," he said, "to settle in the middle of the Desert of Sahara, where you could all live in beautiful glass houses, and where the soil produces no stones of a throwable size. There will be no saloons there, clubs or dinner parties, but drugstores with their alluring lights will decorate every corner. There with your palates parching with pain your motto should be 'Speak Easy' for the sake of the Cause. The lives of the inhabitants will be regulated by priestesses and preachers, and to them will be submitted the most intimate affairs of the family. Yours will be a maternal government; to each member of every family the Government will daily, after taking the temperature, issue canton flannel underclothes of the proper weight to be worn during the day. Alarm clocks set by the Government will be issued to all. Your food, your cooking, and your babies—if you have any, and God grant that you may not in such a dry place!—will all be according to the canons of your religion. Should you at any time find that the inhabitants are drying up and blowing away, you can recruit from the malcontents of other portions of the globe."

With the Anti-Vivisectionists he was most sympathetic. "Ladies and cranks," he said. "I, too, am very fond of dogs, but as it is absolutely necessary for the progress of science to make experiments upon living subjects, I call upon you to volunteer for this work for all portions of the body except the brain; for that portion I am creditably informed that the doctors would prefer to use wood pulp."

This was received with violent protestations of disapproval by the Cubists, the Futurists, and the Post-Impressionists, who claimed that this was entirely unnecessary, as they were able in their pictures to reveal the most secret workings of the brain, and that upon their canvases they laid bare for the study of the scientific world all that it was necessary for it to know.

To the representatives of the Allied A.M.L.Q. American Architects, he expressed his most sincere thanks for the kind expression of their approval and offer of assistance, and in recognition of their co-operation, he gave them entire charge of the competition for the laying out and decorating, with befitting whirlwind monuments, hot air fountains, and castles in the air, the great Edestone aerial highway which was to encircle the globe.

Aloft Edestone, on the other hand, was having more trouble with his audience, for his speech when finished was received with loud protestations of disapproval, rendered in the most kingly and imperial manner by this group of cousins, first cousins, double first cousins, and half-brothers. Fortunately, however, for the welfare of the great mass of the people of the world, they were well represented by the strong, serious, and intelligent-looking men who sat at the elbow of this consanguineous group, some of whom had by a process of intermarrying degenerated into mere effigies of the strong men from whom they were descended. These powers behind the tottering thrones of Europe realized and bowed before the inevitable.